MAXWELL'S HOUSE

A thrilling murder mystery with plenty of twists

M.J. TROW

A Schoolmaster Murder Mystery Book 1

JOFFE BOOKS

Revised edition 2024
Joffe Books, London
www.joffebooks.com

First published in Great Britain in 1994

This paperback edition was first published
in Great Britain in 2024

Cover art by Imogen Buchanan

ISBN: 978-1-83526-428-7

A NOTE TO THE READER

Please note these books were published in the 1990s, when social attitudes were different.

CHAPTER 1

The kids called it the Red House; exactly why, none of them could tell you. But then, none of them was asked until that summer. The summer they found her there.

It was only in winter that it was visible, when the oaks were naked and the bracken lay brown and dead at its feet.

It was always a house of secrets. There was a swing there once, under the boughs of the cedar. Someone let the jungle in. The tennis court has gone now; it was down there, where the broken wall lies derelict and forgotten. And in the orchard was the summer house where the young ones flirted in the evening glow and the fireflies flashed. A different world. So long, long ago.

It was always a house of shadows; spiders spinning in the cracks, woodlice crawling through the fallen plaster. The window frames hang black and creaking precariously on long-rusted hinges they cannot trust. All that graces these walls now are the green and black mottlings of mildew and the silver wanderings of the snails. Shutters hanging at tragic angles. The dark grey sludge of a carpet for too long open to the rain and the merciless sky. Pipes and plumbing that bang and rattle when the wind is from the west.

It was summer when they found her. She'd been murdered. But then, this was always a house of death.

* * *

Chief Inspector Henry Hall was a copper of the new school. One of those elitist, grammar school educated oiks who had somehow survived the great leveller that was comprehensive education by living in a backward county that refused to abandon the Eleven Plus. His friends had all become chartered accountants or civil engineers or PR men. Funny how he'd lost touch with them all now he'd joined the force. At first there'd been the usual jokes about the pointed head and the flat feet and the planted evidence and the fabricated statement. That was because they never expected him to survive Hendon. When he did, they took bets on how long he'd survive his first beat. Some said the two and a half mile an hour pace would wear him out. Others that he'd be called upon to deliver a baby and would die of embarrassment. When they put him on the cars, they said he'd wrap himself round a bollard, drive the wrong way around the M25. But he found the pace all right. He wasn't asked to deliver a baby, ever. And he was driving in one direction only — to the top.

As he got out of the car on that wet, blustery evening, he was staring his fortieth birthday in the face. That day he had doubted would ever come. It was a time of frailty. Of doubt. Of second guessing the ego trip that was youth. But now was no time to reflect. Now was all blue flashing lights and cordons fluttering in the wind and lads in uniform with chequered caps keeping sightseers away. Where do they come from, these ghouls? Do they smell blood? Do they rise, primeval, from the swamp? They always look, always sound, always smell the same.

'Who is it?'

'Somethin's up.'

'Is it an accident?'

'Is anybody dead?'

All in good time, thought Hall. But there was never much of that, was there? And for the girl upstairs, time had run out.

Faces peered at him through the rain, features hard, inquisitive, wrapped in hoods and cagoules. Where had this bloody weather come from? They jostled as close to the cordon as they could, until the long arm of a motor-cycle policeman stopped them and shepherded them back. Who was he, they were wondering. The bloke in the sharp suit and the gold-rimmed specs. Must be the coroner. Isn't that what they called them on Quincy? Bit of a kid, though. He ought to be older.

Hall heard his own feet crunch on the gravel of the drive. Jim Astley's estate lay at a rakish angle near the steps. He noticed the fishing rods in the back. Oh dear. That didn't bode well. Some uniformed lad on the door saluted. He nodded back. Scenes of crime had brought arc lamps in and the old house glowed with a fierce light it had never known until now, the shadows of men huge and sharp on its walls.

'Up here, Chief Inspector.' Hall recognised the voice of DI Johnson on the landing. 'Watch your step. It's like a bloody swamp in here.'

Somebody flashed a torch on the stairs and he picked his way up through the debris of bird droppings into the room to his left. It struck him for a second that he had stumbled into that overrated stable in Bethlehem. A posed group crouched around a floodlit something in the middle of the floor, some on one knee, some on two. 'Joseph' had a straggly, grey-streaked beard and a tweed cap, a Barbour flung back to give himself space — Dr James Astley, the police surgeon, doubly pissed off because they'd called him from his beloved river bank and because he was staring at the body of a young girl. 'Mary' looked up at him, her mouth open, her eyes blinking. DS Jacquie Carpenter, out of ciggies, out of her depth. Hall looked back at her, his eyes blanked in the reflection of his glasses by the arc light.

'Jacquie,' he said softly and threw her a packet of cigarettes from his pocket. She caught it and was grateful for the excuse to move away.

'Somewhere else,' 'Joseph' growled as she fumbled the packet into trembling hands. 'Light that somewhere else.' Hall jerked his head to the door.

'I'm all right, sir.' Her voice was steady.

'I know you are,' Hall told her, 'but there's a crowd of well-wishers below. I want their names and addresses before we move them on.'

She suddenly felt like crying, bit down hard on her lip and lurched past the 'three kings' who looked, in the eerie light, suspiciously like DI Johnson. Hall saw him grin, chuckle, shake his head. Like most of the force, Johnson raised misogyny to a fine art. A tough, tight-lipped career policeman, he'd been too close for too long. And no one could see it, least of all himself.

He joined the Magi at the shrine of death. No boy-child in a manger, in swaddling wrapped, but a girl aged seventeen, staring at the half-ceiling through sightless eyes. Funny, with the rain falling on her like that, that she didn't blink. Funny, in the arc light, how pale she looked. She was frowning a little, as though she didn't understand what she was doing here, what all the fuss was about.

'Jim,' Hall said softly.

'No,' the doctor muttered, knowing what the Chief Inspector would say, 'it doesn't matter. They weren't biting anyway. Too damned wet on the river. I heard a vague rumour this was supposed to be summer. How's Helen?'

'Fine.'

'Kids?'

'Three — when I counted last.'

'Ah, it'll be what they give you in the staff canteen. Do you know who she is?'

'Oh, yes,' Hall nodded, 'I know exactly who she is. She's Jennifer Antonia Hyde. She was seventeen on 8th March. There'll be an old scar on her left forearm, where she fell off her trike just after her fourth birthday.'

The doctor lifted up the unoffending limb. Though it was streaked with grime, the scar was clearly visible. 'A few stitches in that, I shouldn't wonder,' he said.

‘How’s Marjorie?’ Hall said. ‘I forgot to ask.’

‘So did I,’ Astley snorted. He looked at his watch. ‘On to her sixth gin by now, but thanks for asking. Sweet of you.’

‘Ready for the photographs yet?’

‘Why not?’ Astley grunted as he got to his feet. ‘I wish these people would die at waist-height. All this clambering about does my sciatica no good at all.’

Hall’s mouth was already open when Astley’s raised hand stopped him. ‘Yes, it looks sexual,’ he said.

It did. Jennifer Antonia Hyde lay on her back, both arms thrown back above her head, her long dark hair splayed out over them. Her school blouse was ripped open and the front catch of her bra had separated to reveal small breasts and dark nipples. Her skirt was rucked up, wet and heavy at her hips, and her legs were spread.

‘Pink underwear,’ Astley said. ‘Is that standard at . . . where was she at school?’

‘Leighford,’ Hall muttered, ‘Leighford High.’

* * *

Leighford High was one of those brave new world buildings some idiot envisaged in the ’60s. The Labour Party occasionally threw up a government or two in those days and among their most levelling concepts was that of the comprehensive ethos. It was known earlier as ‘Jack’s As Good As His Master’ and later as the politics of envy. So milkmen’s sons rubbed shoulders and other things with the daughters of chartered accountants in that great adventure that was adolescence. And to make sure that the pipe dream came true, that scores of Waynes and Shanes went on to read Greats at Balliol, they built schools like Leighford in the image of Harold Wilson. A central tower block, all leaking panels and filthy glass, where the classrooms blazed in the summer and froze in winter, where the central heating was endlessly conking out. To the west lay the squatter wing of the Languages Department, their rooms gutted and regutted as language laboratories and carrels had gone in and out of fashion. To the east, the Science labs, smelling vaguely of gas and rubber tubing and formalin, where unspeakable things floated in liquid as they might have done in Mengele's study or the cabinet of Dr Caligari. To the south, the newest addition — the Technology block, smelling of new carpets and government money and promising a return to the concept of the Workshop of the World. Except they couldn't decide, to the south, where exactly they were at. At first there had been woodwork and metalwork where a boy could drive in a nail or use his granny's tooth till the cows came home. Then they'd changed the rules and the terminology and the initials were born — CDT, Craft, Design and Technology. And the craft disappeared and vacuous design was all and creation was in the cursor of a computer screen. Everybody was doing a Blue Peter, making Blenheim Palace out of toilet rolls. Then, the government had stopped it all, like a latter-day Frankenstein realising its creation had run amok and had shattered the fetters that bound it. There was nothing so confused as a CDT teacher in the '90s.

It was to the north that the policemen travelled, rolling gently over their namesakes sleeping beside the bike sheds.

'There was a bike at the old house,' Johnson said, peering through the raindrops. 'At the Red House. A bike.'

'Was there?' Hall asked.

'I've got it here.' Johnson flicked open his notebook. 'A Mr Arnold was walking his dog night before last and he passed the place. Said there was a push-bike leaning up against the wall.'

'Did he see anybody?'

'With the bike, not a soul. It was a man's bike, though. Crossbar.'

A single car was parked between fading white lines. An Orion. Not exactly state of the art. There was a mobile library van beyond that, straddling the lines, and a contractor's vehicle or cowboy wagon, ignoring the lines entirely and blasting out, through its open door, the inanities of Steve Wright in the Afternoon — 'Easy Life'.

Hall and Johnson climbed the low, broad concrete steps, gazing at the glass doors ahead.

'Six weeks' bloody holiday,' Johnson grunted. 'Bloody teachers. We went into the wrong job.'

Hall liked to see dedication in his men. It kept them loyal, unswerving, professional. The loyal, unswerving, professional Inspector held open the door for his Chief. Ahead of them a handwritten sign told them that the caretaker was in the A Block and a shaky arrow pointed to the right. A more expensive — and permanent — brown and white job showed where reception was. Johnson's knuckles hit the door first. Nothing. Never one to stand on ceremony, he shoulder-barged his way in.

Here was an inner sanctum, clinical, cold for all it was late July. In the corner, an overfed spider plant threatened to engulf the room, and between its arachnid fingers, a faded, framed certificate boasted that the school had won some Department of Education and Science initiative back in the '80s, when they still handed out cash, almost without strings. A glass partition slid back and a mousy little woman peered out at them, like something out of *The Tailor of Gloucester*.

'Good morning,' she said. 'Can I help you, gentlemen?'

'Chief Inspector Hall and Detective Inspector Johnson to see the Headmaster.'

The mousy eyelids flickered for a moment. It wasn't often detectives arrived at Leighford High. Constable Bob Grenvill, yes, but he was the School Liaison Officer, six foot three of bark, but no bite at all. And anyway, he wore a uniform and the kids raised two fingers at him behind his back. These two were altogether more sinister. The way they just stood there; their eyes boring into you; their lips strangers to smiles.

'Er . . . yes, of course. Mr Diamond is expecting you. Will you walk this way?'

She led them back into the foyer where the fuzzy felt of the industrial duty carpet was black with the passage of countless feet, and on down a corridor, darkening as they walked. Old sports notices flapped from the walls, reminding faceless kids that cricket practice was at twelve thirty and that girls' netball was postponed because of the theatre trip. She turned sharp right into a brighter passageway where artistic creations lined the walls under expensive perspex. Here, Christ dangled on the wire and a rambler's boot lay incongruously on an upturned packet of Rice Krispies, all in the name of A level Art.

The sign on the door, in regulation county brown and cream, read 'Mr James Diamond, Headteacher'. All very arty-farty, Johnson thought. His headmaster's door had had a brass knocker on it and a trio of lights that signalled if he was busy or otherwise. There wasn't a surname, let alone a Christian name. Johnson had only been there once. To receive the cane. He hadn't been back.

'Mr Diamond?' Hall asked. It was almost like looking into a mirror. Diamond was a shade broader than Hall, a shade older, but the grey suit and the gold-rimmed specs could have been straight off the same rack at Rent-an-Ambition.

'That's right,' he said. 'Chief Inspector Hall?'

They shook hands in the corridor.

'This is Detective Inspector Johnson.'

They nodded at each other, the Headmaster and the Inspector. Neither liked the moment. It was suspicion at first sight.

'Margaret, coffee please. And no calls. Gentlemen?' Diamond ushered them into his office. Hardly palatial, but at least it didn't have photographs of a dead girl plastered over its walls. There was another spider plant in the corner. Hall noticed it, and wondered if John Wyndham had been an old boy of the school, long ago. Johnson saw it too, but he didn't wonder at all.

The policemen sat side by side on an over-soft, over-new L-shaped sofa, the sort that compilers of educational office furniture catalogues still imagined were in vogue twenty years after industry had considered them obsolete. Johnson found himself wondering why the Head still wore his suit on the first day of his summer holidays. The thought did not occur to Hall.

'Thank you for seeing us,' the Chief Inspector said.

The Head had reached his swivel chair and waved the comment aside.

'Least I could do,' he said, 'I've been teaching fifteen years and I've never known anything like this. I don't know how the school will react next term. In a way, it's a blessing it's the holidays. Gives us a chance to mend, perhaps.'

'Mend?' It was a curious choice of word to a man like Johnson. The sneer on his lips said it all.

Diamond looked at the man over the rim of his glasses, a professional air he had carefully cultivated ever since his Head of Sixth Form had called him 'Sonny' in an unguarded moment at the summer fete. 'A school, Inspector, is like a hothouse flower. It has its moods, its depressions, its joys, its very heart. You can bruise it, break it. With the wrong treatment, you can kill it.'

'Somebody killed Jennifer Hyde,' Hall said quietly. 'We'd like your help to discover who.'

'Yes.' Diamond cleared his throat, embarrassed that his rhetoric had been flattened by the one irrefutable reality that was going to dog the summer. 'Yes, of course.' He rummaged in the out-tray on his desk and produced a shabby orange folder. 'This is her file. My secretary dug it out for me from Mr Maxwell's filing cabinet.'

'Maxwell?' Hall raised an eyebrow.

'Peter Maxwell, our Head of Sixth. Or, more properly, Years 12 and 13 now, I suppose.'

'May I?' Hall leaned forward and took the thing. Inside was a thin sheaf of papers. Flimsy carbonised report forms that told the Hyde parents that Jennifer was a highly able girl, but that the recent exam results had been disappointing. Yellowing pages that gave her next of kin, her GP, her tetanus injection and her date of birth. Another, in the dead girl's own hand writing, with its curious flower designs on the dots of the 'i's spoke of her hobbies at the age of eleven. She adored her pony, she played netball and tennis. She had grade three piano and a cup for elocution. When she grew up she wanted to be an air hostess. Hall's eyes rested on the update of that. In her GCSE year, the writing was finer, the spelling improved. There was no mention of the pony or the netball, although she was a member of the tennis club. She had persevered, with what resentment was unknown, with the piano and had reached grade five. But the mile-high club had been replaced by academe; she wanted to be a marine biologist.

'UCAS?' Johnson was reading over his boss's shoulder, just one of his irritating habits.

'Er . . . the new university entrance syndicate,' Diamond explained. 'It's officially opening in September. An amalgamation of UCCA and PCAS.'

The Inspector looked blank. They had initials run riot in the police force, but nothing like this.

'Jennifer was applying to university?' Hall checked.

'I believe so. You'd have to ask Maxwell.'

'Not much here.' Hall closed the file. His own on the dead girl was already four times as thick.

'No,' Diamond agreed. 'No, perhaps not. It's difficult, you see. With nearly eleven hundred pupils, it's difficult for my staff to compile a vast amount. Anyway, we don't usually need it. . . I mean . . . well . . .'

'What sort of a girl was she, Mr Diamond?' Hall asked, his fingers pressed to his expressionless lips.

'Oh, bright,' he said quickly, confidently, 'very bright. Yes, she'd have been good red brick. Not Oxbridge, I don't think, although I understand she intended to try for it; but red brick, certainly.'

'Popular?'

'Very. Very. I was about to make her a prefect next year. Perhaps even Head Girl, if it weren't for Heather Robotham.'

'Heather . . .' Johnson was writing things down in a little black book.

'Robotham,' Diamond repeated. 'Father's a doctor. Practice down on the front.' The policemen nodded.

'Jenny was a good girl, though. Able. Co-operative. She was something-or-other in Godspell last year.'

'Boys?' Hall let his fingers drop.

Diamond frowned at him. 'I've really no idea,' he smiled. 'You'd . . .'

'. . . have to ask Maxwell,' Johnson chimed in. 'Yes, well, where do we find him?'

'Margaret will let you have his address, although . . .'

'Yes?' Hall said.

'Well, I don't think he's here. I mean, he's gone away.'

'For how long?'

'Quite a while, I believe. But don't worry, he'll be back by 19th August.'

'How do you know that?' Johnson asked.

Diamond leaned back in his chair, patting his waistcoat complacently. 'A level results,' he beamed. 'Peter Maxwell hasn't missed those in twenty years. Ah,' he reacted to the knock on the door. 'Come in.'

The mousy woman came in carrying a tray and assorted mugs, one of which proclaimed the marriage made in heaven of the Prince and Princess of Wales.

'Thank you, Margaret. Sugar, gentlemen?'

They shook their heads. Johnson knew he was sweet enough as he was. Hall had flipped open the file again. And was looking at the toothy grin of a little girl whose hair was lighter in the years behind. Whose eyes were bright. Whose hope was gone.

* * *

They couldn't find Peter Maxwell. His house, yes. And the old girl who fed his cat. They even saw a glimpse of his white bike parked in his back passage. But for the rest . . . silence. They'd have to wait until 19th August. He'd keep until then. And in the meantime, there was a murder enquiry under way.

* * *

The jangling, fierce signature tune gave way to flashing blue lights and screaming vehicles. Then it was the studio with slightly embarrassed-looking men and women sitting by phones and VDUs. The camera panned back to the friendly, comfortable face of Nick Ross.

He was only half listening to the special edition of *Crimewatch* they'd put on in the holiday month of August and, in that endless struggle with nature in which most men wrestled with needle and thread, he wasn't watching the screen at all. Just darning his walking socks. It came to him as though in a dream. A series of names. Images. Coincidences. Then he looked up and could not look away. The socks were a tangled heap on the floor.

'It was 23rd July,' Ross was saying from the television screen, 'the last day of the school term. A tramp found Jennifer's body here, in this old house at the end of Kissing Tree Lane. She had been strangled.'

He watched Ross cross the studio floor and a different camera took him up. 'Jenny was a bright, clever girl, in the first year of her sixth form at Leighford High School.'

A rather flattering library picture of the school's frontage appeared on the screen. He fancied it had been taken when the school was the focus of all that industrial action back in '86. Or was it '87? Hard to remember now.

'Friends describe her as a friendly, outgoing girl. She was last seen alive at three thirty that afternoon. School had broken up at two o'clock and Jenny had gone with her boyfriend to a cafe in the town. At two forty-five he left her here, at the corner of Grassington Street and Rodwell Avenue. Did you see where she went after that?'

A lookalike was on the screen now, crossing Rodwell Avenue, plodding on towards the golf course.

He shook his head. 'Too heavy,' he said. 'That's all wrong.'

But Ross couldn't hear him. 'Jenny was wearing her school uniform. Black skirt. White blouse. Black shoes. She was carrying a school bag, like this one . . .' He paused by a table and held up a grey Samsonite. 'Her own has not yet been found. At about three thirty, a woman on her way home from work saw a girl who may have been Jenny talking to a young man here, on the edge of the Dam, an area well known by courting couples. She remembers they seemed to be arguing and she heard her say "No" several times.'

The lookalike and a tall bit-player duly went through the motions, then she turned and followed the line of the old railway towards Moorfields and the sea.

'It's not known what Jenny did for the next half an hour, but at just after eight o'clock this man, David Arnold, was walking his dog along Kissing Tree Lane. After a fine day, it had started raining and Mr Arnold put his anorak hood up. His dog wouldn't come when he called and Mr Arnold had to enter the grounds of a ruined house, known locally as the Red House, in search of him.'

The Red House filled the screen, the room, his mind. Mr Arnold was suddenly sitting in an indescribably awful living-room, reminiscing. He had thick, bottle-bottom glasses and a shapeless cardigan. The wayward dog sat at his feet, its tongue lolling under the studio lights.

'I remember seeing a bike, like,' Arnold told his viewers, 'sort of leaning up against the Red House. I thought to myself, that's unusual. Because it was. Oh, the Red House used to be a place for courting couples. You know, just kids. But I'd seen no one there for months on account of it was so derelict, you know. Anyhow, old Shep here, he'd gone inside and he wouldn't come down, so I went in after him. It was then I saw the tramp.'

'Dan Guthrie,' Ross was in command again, taking the story on, 'was a well-known figure in the neighbourhood. He'd been sleeping rough throughout most of July — remember the weather had been good until that last week — and he'd gone into the Red House about eight o'clock, hoping to find shelter.'

'Jesus,' he whispered, 'Jesus.'

'Chief Inspector Henry Hall.' Ross sat beside a tight-lipped detective in immaculate gold-rimmed glasses. 'You're in charge of the case. Is there any message you have for our viewers tonight?'

'Yes.' Hall seemed at ease with the radio mike clipped to his tie. 'The dead girl was just seventeen years old . . .'

'Seventeen years and four months,' he argued with the television.

'She had her whole life before her. Someone out there knows why she died and who killed her. 23rd July. A Thursday. Did someone you know come home later than usual that night? Was he behaving strangely? Has he been behaving strangely since?'

'Presumably, you want to interview that man seen talking to Jenny at the Dam? Let's just have a description again.'

A bad drawing filled the screen of a scruffy lad of twenty or so, with dead, pencilled eyes and an attempt at stubble.

'He was eighteen to twenty-five years old.' Ross padded it out. 'Wearing denim jeans and a white or cream shirt. He was well-spoken.'

'We need him to come forward,' Hall said, as the camera swung back, 'to eliminate him from our enquiries.'

'A particularly senseless killing,' Ross commented. 'There is an incident room set up at Tottingleigh and you call it on 0391 421638 or the studio here on 0500 600 600; that's 0500 600 600, where a team of detectives is waiting for your call. Remember, if you'd like to speak to a BBC researcher instead, your call will be treated with the utmost confidentiality.'

Ross turned to a third camera, outstaring every villain in the land. 'Jenny Hyde was only seventeen. She hadn't an enemy in the world. But it's possible that the killer may strike again. It's up to you to make sure he doesn't.'

Then the mood was lifted, the silence gone, and the smiling face of Sue Cook filled the screen. 'Were you in the centre of Birmingham on 14th May?' she asked.

He stood up, crossed the room and switched off the set. 'I wouldn't be seen dead in the centre of Birmingham,' he said. He looked down at the blackened screen, lifeless, blank. 'And don't tell me not to have nightmares, Nick. Because they're already here.'

CHAPTER 2

There was only one topic of conversation really. Jenny Hyde.

'I taught her French in Year 9.'

'Wasn't she in Godspell?'

'It's come to something, hasn't it, when you can't let your kids out after dark?'

'The death penalty. That's the answer.'

'I blame the '60s, of course. All that peace and beads bollocks. It's left us with no morals. No norms. We've lost our way.'

Ever been in a staff room? It's more or less like hell must be. Or purgatory. John Milton would have been a comprehensive schoolteacher, if only he hadn't been born three hundred years too soon. 'The awful sound of hissing in the hall.' They sat, clutching assorted mugs and whispering. In the Special Needs corner, the Nappy Brigade, Joan Wilson's needles clacked together like those of Madame de Farge as something shapeless for the latest grandchild grew inexorably. Next to her, Sally Greenhow was shaking her head, smoking frantically and muttering about how society had gone to the dogs.

Under the window, the 1981 Committee, all track suits and cynicism, lounged amidst their piles of comics and collected memorabilia of all the school-generated gaffes of the last thirteen years. The clannish Modern Languages

Department, separated from their fellows by a European understanding, a devotion to Maastricht and the smoking of Gauloises, attempted to make small-talk with the extraordinarily homely French *l'assistante* who had just got off the garlic train and wondered what she had come to.

Then the suits walked in. James Diamond, forty something. A bright young creature of the '80s, he had not moved on and up, as everyone predicted he would. Instead, he got older and greyer, but no wiser, as the government and governors and parents threw things at him from all directions at once. He stayed inscrutable behind his gold-rimmed specs. Roger Garrett was a year or two younger; still forty something, but less forty something than his boss. When you're First Deputy, they shit on you from two directions — above and below. He was responsible for the curriculum, and his waking nightmare was the timetable, that all-destructive juggernaut in which people were sacrificed to mathematical equations; in which humanity sank without trace in a morass of options and coloured pegs on an office wall. And whom did he blame, when all about him were losing their heads and blaming it on him? SIMS, of course. The computer system that was to revolutionise administration but which never quite did what you wanted it to. How many kids were in Year 7 doing Geography? The computer knew, but it wasn't telling. Some days it was down. Some days it was out. Down and out in Leighford High. Then there was the third triumvir — Lepidus to Diamond's Caesar and Garrett's Mark Antony — Bernard Ryan. What, you may ask, is a Pastoral Deputy? Not Bernard Ryan, certainly. When you're still wearing nappies and your knees aren't brown yet, how can you pretend to cope with the social hell of the underprivileged, the children of the flower children? Young Bernard was discipline's last resort. Many was the wayward urchin with the wedge haircut who was sent to his office for a damned good letting off.

Peter Maxwell sat in the corner he had made all his own and turned to his fellow Old Contemptible, Geoffrey Smith, the Head of English. 'Don't you just love being in control?'

Smith smirked. He was a bald, sparkly fifty-one, with a penchant for black and white films and Dylan Thomas. He'd scored a victory recently with his refusal to administer Key Stage 3 Standard Attainment Tests in English; the government's attempt to impose conformity on a system that was as individualistic as kids in a school. In an oblique way, John Patten, the Secretary of State for Education, and John Major, the First Lord of the Treasury, had shaken their fists at him and prophesied classroom chaos in the summer because of his intransigence. But the summer had gone and no one had noticed. And not many of them could spell intransigence anyway.

'Can we make a start, please, ladies and gentlemen?' Diamond begged.

The hubbub around the room barely subsided. He went on anyway.

'Ever seen *Seduction of a Nation*, Geoff, me ol' mucker?' Maxwell asked.

'Don't know,' the Head of English said. 'What is it?'

'A documentary on Hitler. The most marvellous footage of the former art student giving a speech. He's got ten thousand people in the palm of his hand, just waiting. He just stands there until they're quiet. Riveting.'

'Did he pass that on to you for your classroom control?'

'No,' said Maxwell, straight-faced, 'I passed it on to him.'

'A number of things . . .' Diamond was saying.

'Jenny,' Maxwell shouted. 'What about Jenny?'

The hubbub stopped. All eyes turned to the Headmaster. In the loneliness of command he stood there, his trousers oddly ill-fitting for a former whizz-kid.

'I don't think this is the time or place, Max,' he said quietly.

The eyes swivelled to the grizzled old man in the corner. Not a punch-up already? Not so soon in the term?

'Here we go.' Paul Moss was the Head of History and he muttered under his breath. Peter Maxwell was the worst maverick in his department, but he loved these moments. They were pure gold. He saw the man reach up slowly to take off his shapeless tweed hat — who the hell wore a hat in the '90s? He saw the barbed-wire hair spring free, the forehead furrow, the eyes focus. Maxwell was uncoiling, like a mamba. It wasn't going to be pretty.

'With respect, Headmaster,' he said slowly and you felt the gravel of his voice scrape you to the bone, 'Jenny Hyde was one of my sixth form; a member of this school. She's dead. If this isn't the time and place, I don't know what is.'

There were cries of 'Hear, hear,' around the room and the Headmaster knew what defeat was. He'd experienced it before. Every time he'd crossed swords with Maxwell, in fact.

'Now, come on, Max . . .' Ryan's high-pitched whine attempted to extricate his Head from a jam, but he got no further, because Maxwell's eyes burned into him and he sat back, the smile frozen on his lips.

'You know as much as I do,' Diamond said, perching now on the counter that ran the length of the staff room. 'The police are carrying out their own enquiries. I understand they have been talking to various people over the holidays. Friends of Jenny's and so on. I spoke to them myself the day after it had happened.'

There was a silence.

'And that's it?' Maxwell asked.

The hubbub began again. The Head raised a hand. 'Roger, would you like to go over the timetable changes, since July, I mean?'

And that was it. The Staff Development Day. Before the kids came back and made the place untidy again. But the weather knew. August had been wet and blustery. Ian McCaskill grinning, with no apology whatever, to tell a waiting world that tomorrow would be more of the same. Then, it was term time again and the Indian summer came — a cloudless blue sky and sharp shadows on the fields and across the quad.

Peter Maxwell carried his coffee across to the sixth form block. He wheezed his way up the two flights of stairs and down the corridor, gleaming now after the annual polish. He fumbled for his keys. Somebody had fixed the lock at last and the door swung wide. He threw his hat at the hook he had treated himself to at B&Q: one of those plastic, self-adhesive jobs that needed no screws. Put a screw into a wall or a door around here and the lot would come down.

It dawned on him as he opened his filing cabinet that he hadn't seen Alison this morning. Don't say she was starting already? Here was a woman, his Assistant, who took morning sickness to a fine art. This was her third pregnancy. How the hell could she claim to be a teacher at all? Still, her subject was Biology, so that must explain it. No doubt she'd stagger in later, palely loitering with the distaff section on the staff, talking endlessly about painful nipples and back-ache. What a cop-out, he thought. Then a memory hit him. Sharp. Painful. And he slammed the cabinet drawer shut.

'Mr Maxwell?' A voice made him turn.

A grey-suited man stood in his doorway, flanked by another.

'Yes?' he said, frowning. These two didn't look like prospective parents. And anyway, the new Year 12 wasn't due until the afternoon.

'I am Chief Inspector Henry Hall. This is Detective Inspector Johnson.'

'Ah,' Maxwell said, 'I've been expecting you, gentlemen.'

'Really?' Hall allowed himself to be ushered to one of the hard, upright seats. 'Why is that?'

Maxwell took his own seat across the desk from the policemen. 'I suppose because I'm the nearest thing to a father figure Jenny Hyde had, here at school, that is. How are the Hydes taking it?'

'How d'you think?' Johnson asked.

Hall flashed him a telling glance. 'As you might expect,' he said softly. 'Only child and so on. They're still distraught. I don't think it's something you can come to terms with easily.'

Maxwell nodded.

'What was your relationship with the dead girl, exactly?' Hall asked.

'I was her Year Head,' Maxwell said, 'and her History teacher.'

Hall exchanged another glance with his Number Two. 'You'll have to explain that,' he said. 'I don't remember having Year Heads when I was at school.'

'I am responsible for the academic and pastoral welfare of the sixth form,' Maxwell told him. 'Two hundred and eighteen sixteen- to nineteen-year-olds, with differing temperaments and from differing backgrounds. I'm a sort of cross between a Father Confessor and a policeman.' He beamed his gappy smile at Johnson. 'A nice policeman, of course.'

The Inspector scowled back.

'Did you know Jenny well?' Hall asked.

Maxwell looked at him. 'You've seen her file?' he asked.

Hall nodded.

'Then you know my sum knowledge of Jennifer Antonia Hyde,' he said. 'I predicted grade B at A level — Paul thought an A, but he's young.'

'Paul?'

'Paul Moss, the Head of History. I'm second in the History Department in addition to my pastoral duties. Let's see. She could construct a logical argument, read widely, had a mature, fluent style of writing.'

'Is this useful?' Johnson asked.

Maxwell looked at him. 'You asked me if I knew Jenny well,' he said. 'I'm giving you the full extent of my knowledge.'

'Forgive me,' Hall changed position, 'but if I remember right, Jenny wanted to be a marine biologist. Isn't it rather odd to be taking History A level?'

'Intellectually, no.' Maxwell leaned back in his chair. 'I won't bore you to death with the importance of History in the curriculum. Everything has a history, Chief Inspector. Even, I presume, marine biology. And certainly, the police force. As a discipline that teaches you to think on your feet, it's second to none.'

'Need to think on your feet a lot, do you, in your line of work?' Johnson sneered.

Maxwell smiled, and spoke to Hall. 'You're right,' he said. 'Vocationally speaking, it doesn't make a great deal of sense. It's an insuperable problem. Kids choose subjects because they enjoy them, because they do well in them, because their best friends are doing them, because they fancy Sir. It has no rationale, really. Then they discover a career — and what they're doing doesn't fit it. Anyway, these things come and go, like the wind. A few years ago, when the Herriot series was first on the telly, half the sixth form wanted to be vets. I did point out that there was surprisingly little glamour in shoving your arm up a cow's bum . . .'

'And is that why Jenny Hyde did History?' Johnson asked. 'Because she fancied Sir?'

Maxwell's eyes narrowed against the venom of the remark. 'I'm old enough to be her grandfather, Inspector,' he smiled.

'Yeah,' Johnson grunted. 'Exactly.'

'Did *Crimewatch* come up with anything?' Maxwell asked. 'I was on holiday at the time. It came as quite a shock, I can tell you. I almost dropped a stitch.'

'Enjoy needlework, do you?' Johnson asked.

Maxwell shrugged. 'It's either that or a hole in my sock,' he said.

'Are you married, Mr Maxwell?' Hall leaned forward.

Maxwell looked at them both, the one passionless, the other wishing that hanging was back in vogue. 'No,' he said slowly. 'Not at the moment.'

'The BBC were very helpful,' Hall said. 'We had a lot of calls.'

'The scruffy lad — the one Jenny was seen talking to . . .'

'Nothing useful on that,' Hall said. 'At least, nothing conclusive. Mr Maxwell . . .' Hall stood up. 'We've talked to all Jenny's friends. And frankly, we've got nowhere. You see them on a daily basis, in a working atmosphere. Would you do us a favour?'

'If I can,' Maxwell said.

'Keep your ears open, will you? And your eyes? Someone must know something. They're just not talking yet. We need a break, to be honest.'

Maxwell stood up too and nodded. 'I'll do what I can,' he said.

And they saw themselves out.

On the turn of the stair, Chief Inspector Hall glanced at Detective Inspector Johnson. 'What's the matter, Dave? You look as though you've just met the Krays.'

'Smug bastards,' Johnson said, shielding his eyes from the glare of the sun. 'Especially ones who wear pork pie hats — did you see it, hanging on his wall? And bow ties. What's a teacher in a third-rate comprehensive school doing wearing a bow tie?'

'I take it you didn't altogether like Mr Maxwell, then?' Hall grinned.

'Let's just say I think he's about as straight as Jeffrey Dahmer. And there's one other thing.'

'Oh?'

They reached the ground, where teachers stood talking in knots, carrying sheaves of papers, and a pale, pregnant woman scuttled past them.

'There were bicycle clips on his desk,' Johnson said. 'Our Mr Maxwell rides a bike.'

'We know he does. One of the constables we sent to his house reported seeing it in the holidays.'

Johnson nodded. 'I just like to have these things confirmed,' he said.

* * *

She'd had one of those things fitted, one of those fish-eye lenses in the door that make visitors look so horribly deformed. This visitor in particular looked more deformed than most, a bunch of chrysanths where his face ought to be.

She clicked back the safety chain and let him in.

'Well, y'all, Miss Martha,' he drawled in his best Kentucky. 'Ah declare, if'n you ain't the purdiest little thing Ah ever did see.'

'Thank you for these, Max,' she said, taking the flowers from him. 'I'd been meaning to cut them down myself. The wind plays havoc with my front.'

'Not from where I am.' Maxwell suddenly jack-knifed so that he was puffing an imaginary cigar, Groucho Marx style, at the level of her bosom. She tapped him playfully around the head so that his hat fell off.

'Loosen your cycle clips,' she chuckled. 'I'll find some water for these.'

He joined his hat on the settee. 'Any fear of a drink?' he asked.

He heard her clattering in the kitchen. 'Help yourself,' she called. He tugged off his clips and rolled on to his knees in front of the MFI cabinet. Pine, certainly. MFI nevertheless. Pernod. Vodka. Sherry. Ah, Southern Comfort.

'Can I get you one?' he shouted.

'Got one.' She was back in the lounge, a glass in her hand. 'How was your day?'

'"All Hell Day", Nursie,' he sighed. 'I write it in my diary every year. I interviewed sixty-three little shits today, one by one, all of them, for reasons I can only guess at, wanting to join the sixth form. All of them clutching in their grubby little hands their results of the Greatest Cock-up Since the Eleven Plus.'

'I saw that toe-rag Henderson,' she said, kicking off her shoes and stretching out on the settee. 'Oh, sorry, Max, I've pinched your seat.'

'Not often enough.' He winked at her. 'Yes, I didn't interview Henderson. Alison did. One of the eighteen she had time for.'

She caught his mood. 'Now, Max,' she scolded gently, 'Alison is having rather a hard time at the moment. I thought she looked awful this afternoon.'

'Yes,' he nodded, sipping his drink, 'you're right. She did. Not as awful as Henderson though, I'll wager.'

'I thought you said he'd be back in the sixth form over your dead body?'

Maxwell looked at his watch. 'There are four more hours of the day to go yet, Nurse Matthews. Who's to say by the time it's over I won't be twirling from your banisters?'

'I am,' she said, moving smartly into the kitchen at the sound of a hissing saucepan, 'because in a flat on the fourth floor you'd be hard put to it to find any banisters. Ratatouille.' She announced the menu as though she'd read his mind. 'OK?'

'Delicious,' he called back. 'And knowing your culinary expertise, Sylvia darling, it'll have just the right amount of rat. Talking of which, how is Roger Rabbit by the way?'

He counted silently to himself with a rather silly grin on his face. In three seconds, well, a little less actually, she was framed in the doorway, a rather vicious-looking ladle in her hand. 'If you are referring to the Deputy Headmaster,' she said, 'you know very well that was a ridiculous rumour put about by . . .' Then she saw his face and snorted, returning to her pots and pans.

'. . . me, I expect.' He joined her in the steam.

'There's only one man in my life,' she said, clattering again and straining things over the sink. Then she stopped, quite suddenly, and looked at him. 'And that didn't work out, did it?' She swept past him, busying herself hurriedly. 'Will you open the wine?'

'Oh, God!' He banged his head on the cupboard. 'I would, Sylv, but it's lying disconsolately in my fridge at home. What an arsehole. Oh, pardon my French.'

'Never mind,' she smiled. 'There's a bottle of something Australian in the rack. No. To your left. That's it.'

'I'm sorry,' he said.

'Sit down. The corkscrew's on the table. Oh, can you carry this through?'

He took the dish of steaming goodies and attacked the cork.

'Max.' She was suddenly serious as she sat opposite him, holding up her glass for him to fill.

'Hmm?' He poured for them both.

'Who killed her, Max? Who killed Jenny?'

He put the bottle down. Sylvia Matthews was still a striking-looking woman with a mass of auburn hair and bright eyes in which the candlelight danced. She'd been the Matron at Leighford High for nearly six years, at once Florence Nightingale and Claire Rayner, though she'd never been known to carry a lamp or call anyone lovey. 'It's been going through my mind,' he said, passing her the salt. 'How long have we been doing this, Sylv, you and I?'

'What? Having dinner on the day before the term starts?' She smiled at him. 'For ever.'

'For ever,' he smiled back. 'And in all that time, in all those for evers, have you ever known me unable to give you an answer?'

She shook her head. 'I don't think so,' she said.

'Well, this time, I can't.' He took his first mouthful. 'Nursie,' he moaned, closing his eyes, 'you've excelled yourself.'

'Did the police talk to you?' she asked. 1 heard they were at school.'

He nodded. 'Some Chief Inspector named after a '30s band-leader and a noxious sidekick like something out of *The Sweeney*.'

'What did they want to know?'

He looked at her, sipping his wine, biding his time. 'The same thing you do,' he said, 'except they were less direct. They asked me what my relationship was with Jenny.'

'Relationship?' she repeated. 'You didn't have one . . . did you?'

He leaned back in his chair. 'Good God, Sylvia, if I'd known your line of attack I'd have worn my body armour — or at least my mac and trousers cut off at the knee with nothing above them.'

'Oh, Max.' She tapped his knuckles with her fork. 'You were Jenny's Year Head, that's all. I know that.'

'That's right,' he nodded, suddenly distant, elsewhere. 'And that wasn't enough, was it?'

'You've nothing to reproach yourself for.' She tore into the baguette.

'Haven't I?' he asked her. 'A detective asked me today what I knew about a dead girl, a girl I've taught for three years, and I was stuck for an answer. She was my responsibility,

Sylv. I should have been there. What is it the Americans say — "for her". I wasn't there for her.'

'Oh,' she threw her napkin down and topped up their glasses, 'now you're being daft, Max. She was seventeen . . .'

'Seventeen and four months,' he reminded her.

'All right, then, seventeen and four months. She had a mind of her own, that one. And she had parents. Your responsibility only goes so far, you know.'

'In loco parentis, Sylv. That's the phrase. How's your Latin?'

'Non-existent,' she admitted. 'Except for bits of the body, but that one I do know. Teachers are, under the law, said to be in loco parentis — in place of parents. But that's during the day, surely? Nine to four?'

He looked at her, sure, steady as she was. 'I don't know,' he said. 'I only know she was one of mine and she's dead. And you know what?'

'No. What?' She smiled at him, recognising that certain light that shone from his eyes.

'I'm going to do something about it. Care to help?'

* * *

They sat as the mock coal glowed flickering orange on the ceiling. Maxwell had removed his shoes, his tie and as much of the front he wore for the world as he was ever likely to. Sylvia Matthews curled up at the feet of the Great Man — her Alexander to his Aristotle; except that she had no worlds to conquer and his philosophy was born at the chalk face — a quarter of a century of civilisation against the barbarian hordes.

'Shouldn't you be chewing a meerschaum by now?' she asked.

'Indeed, Watson.' He flared his nostrils much after the manner of Basil Rathbone by way of Arthur Wontner. 'A three-pipe problem and a seven and a half per cent solution.'

She frowned up at him. 'I'm sure that's clever, Max, but I haven't actually ever read any Conan Doyle.'

He patted her head. 'Nor I Gray's Anatomy,' he said. 'Of course, if this were the '50s, we'd be wearing trench coats and drinking tea and talking about "chummie" in terribly plummy voices.'

'Weren't you at Cambridge in the '50s?' she asked.

He swiped her round the head with his scarf end. ''60s, dear girl,' he said. 'Early '60s, I'll grant you, but '60s nonetheless. When you were screaming over the Fab Four, I was struggling with tripos complexities. And no, before you ask; I did not know Burgess and Maclean! How old do you think I am?'

She patted his knee. 'You're timeless, Max,' she said. 'So what do we know?'

'Jennifer Antonia Hyde.' Maxwell leaned back on the settee. 'Date of birth 16.3.76. God, I took a trip to the American Revolution Exhibition at Greenwich that year. Quite good. A bit expensive.'

'Max!' She brought him back to the present.

'Sorry. I digress. Eight GCSEs. Currently taking Biology, Chemistry and History to A level.'

'Form tutor?'

'Janet Foster, spinster of this parish and Head of Art.'

'Divorcee.'

'Just a figure of speech,' Maxwell said. 'A woman of discernment, vision, finesse. And I've just remembered the old besom owes me five quid.'

'When did Jenny . . . you know . . . When did it happen? Precisely?'

'Well, that's the bitch of it.' Maxwell got up and freshened their drinks. 'I was taking those three weeks in Cornwall and despite the assurances of the inventory they sent, the cottage telly was on the blink. I even missed the last *Taggart* episode as a result.'

'It was the hotelier,' she told him.

'Yes, of course.' He clicked his fingers. 'Had to be, really. Anyway, I pestered the owners who lived down the road and they got an engineer in. It was that night I saw *Crimewatch*.'

'Didn't you see a newspaper?'

'You know I don't read newspapers, Sylv,' he said. 'In the beginning God made newspapers for us British to wrap our fish and chips up in. Now that some Eurocrat has stopped all that, they have no function in society whatsoever. Anyway, you know I like to switch off entirely in the summer. Back to nature for a bit. You can reach out and touch the past. But you were here.'

'Yes, I was. I didn't get off till the following week.'

'Tell me, then.'

'Well, it was on the Saturday lunchtime news. I'd got it on for the weather forecast. I couldn't believe it. It was awful. The next day, of course, the Sundays were full of it. The *Mail* had a double-page spread. That school photo of Jenny and one of Diamond.'

'Ah, so Legs made the big time for a day, did he?'

'It was the parents I felt sorry for. You know how the media hound people. They were there on Monday. Giving a press conference. It was awful. Just awful. Some bastard actually asked Mr Hyde how he felt. Can you imagine that? He was younger than I expected, Mr Hyde. Have you met them?'

'Once, I think. I wasn't smitten. She was something of a cow, I thought.' He held his hand up. 'I know, you shouldn't speak ill of the parents of the dead. But life has to go on.'

'Is that why you're doing this?' she asked him.

'What?'

'Investigating her death?'

He chortled. 'I'm not investigating her death,' he said.

'Well, what else would you call it, then?'

'This?' he asked. 'Moving mountains, my dear girl, that's all.'

'I see.' She looked up at him. 'And tell me, Mr Maxwell, Mr I-Don't-Want-To-Get-Involved Maxwell, whose mountains are they? Somebody else's? Or yours?'

He looked down at her, at her eyes bright in the firelight. Then he nodded. 'They're mine,' he said. 'My mountains.'

She nodded. 'Yours. Where will you start?'

'That "you" has an appalling singularity about it, Sylvia darling. What happened to the "we" of earlier this evening, Kemo Sabe?'

She rested her chin on his knee. 'You can call round whenever you want to, Max,' she told him. 'I'll burn the midnight oil with you. I'll give you the benefit — for what it's worth — of my feminine intuition. But more than that . . . No. You see, I saw their faces, the Hydes. I saw what it's done to them. I'm not cut out for investigative journalism. Leave that to Fleet Street or wherever it is they keep journalists now. And the police. Leave it to the police.'

'Is that what you're telling me to do?' he asked. 'You just told me they're my mountains. Jenny Hyde was my girl. As much as she was the Hydes'. Nobody kills one of my girls and says, "Lump it." I'm not made that way.'

She was smiling at him, her eyes glistening. 'I know you're not,' she said, an iron-hard lump in her throat. Then she knelt up and kissed him hard on the lips. 'Take care of yourself, Peter Maxwell. Because . . . because I'm afraid.'

He smiled and held her face in his big, comfortable hands. 'Why?' he asked her. 'Why are you afraid?'

She shook her head. 'I don't know,' she said. 'But I'm afraid of the bogeyman I used to think lived in the folds of my curtains. And the gurgle of the plumbing when I pulled the chain as a kid. But most of all . . . most of all, I'm afraid of the Red House, Max. I'm afraid of the Red House.'

CHAPTER 3

It had been the *Clarion* once, at a time when newspapers were new and editors men of the people. Now it was the *Advertiser,* and the change of title reflected the way of the world. Maxwell had been to the front office before to look up old stories on the microfiche. That was an eternity ago when Leighford ran that ghastly Mode 3 CSE course on local history. It should have been a good one, but unfortunately, Mode 3 was synonymous with moron and the hapless Waynes and Traceys who were expected to tackle it couldn't cope with the present, never mind the past.

He asked at the desk in the palatial new offices. Whatever the depth of the recession, he noticed the media hadn't felt it. A middle-aged woman looked at him suspiciously, then with reluctance collected a bundle of blue gels and switched on the machine for him. It was quicker, she said, than ploughing through the paper itself. Anyway, it had been the lead story for three weeks and there was the letters page. Easier to find it quickly on the screen.

Maxwell forced himself to it. What had wood pulp done that the world so scorned it now? Why did an entire generation think it right to spend a fortune on computers and nothing on books? He shook his head as he twiddled the gadget.

Then, there was Jenny. Looking at him. It wasn't her school photo, the proof of which was clipped to her file. It must have come from home and it was out of date. Her hair was shorter, lighter. There seemed to be some tinsel behind her head. Christmas. She had been a pretty girl, if skinny. Not for her the blandishments of the tuck shop and school pizzas. She'd offered him a lunch time sandwich once. Wholemeal bread with something-good-for-you on it. He'd turned it down, on his way to the pub.

To be honest, there wasn't much in the story that helped. Not much he didn't know. There was a bad photo of Tim Grey, Jenny's boyfriend, an insipid, scrawny lad now entering Year 13 — unlucky for some — without any clear ambition at all. His parents were working-class people who couldn't decide if they wanted their Tim to go to university. If he did, he'd be the first Grey ever to do that. Maxwell didn't want to think of the odds against it. Chief Inspector Hall was quoted as saying something obvious and trite. There was a creepy photo of the Red House, suddenly made all the more sinister because you knew what had happened there. Except that Maxwell realised he didn't know what had happened there and the not knowing haunted him.

He checked the by-line — Tony Young.

'Tony? Anyone seen Tony?'

Upstairs in the palatial new office of the Advertiser was a bedlam of VDUs and coffee cups and bits of paper. There was no privacy here, no peace. Only the bustle of a local paper trying to make its name in the world. Someone had once told its managers that the Guardian had been a local paper once, so the precedent was there and the world had better look out.

A hawkish young man in jeans and T-shirt emerged from the shredding room.

'Hello,' he said, his face humourless and cold. 'I'm Tony Young.'

'Peter Maxwell,' Maxwell said and something told him not to extend a hand.

'Yes?' Clearly the name meant nothing to Young.

'I teach at Leighford High.'

'Well, we've all got our cross to bear,' Young told him. 'Look, I don't do school events. Brenda Somebody-or-other covers that. It's probably her coffee break now.'

'It's about Jenny Hyde,' Maxwell said.

The journalist's eyes narrowed. 'Is it now?' he said. 'Well, you'd better have a seat.'

He ushered Maxwell to a soft chair under the window. There was a low coffee table and a picture and a plant, to give an aura of a reception/interview area. It didn't really fool anyone. It was just part of the corridor.

'You covered the story of her murder,' Maxwell said.

'That's right,' Young nodded. 'Look, can I get you a coffee, Mr . . .'

'Maxwell. Peter Maxwell. No thanks. I just want some information.'

'Shouldn't I be asking the questions?' Young said.

'There's nothing I can tell you.' Maxwell shrugged. 'I'm buying, not selling.'

Young smirked. 'This isn't the fucking *Sun*, Mr Maxwell. I'm not authorised to carry a cheque book. If you've read my articles, you know what I do.'

Maxwell smiled. 'I doubt that, Mr Young,' he said. 1 know there are things you can't print. Theories you have.'

Young looked at him. 'Do you?' he asked. 'Like what?'

'Your article talked about sexual assault. Was she assaulted?'

Young hesitated, then he grabbed a jacket hanging on a chair-back and hauled a cassette-recorder out of the pocket. He clicked it on. 'You don't mind?' he said. 'Just for the record.'

Maxwell clicked it off. 'Yes I do,' he said. 'This meeting is off the record. You don't have to talk to me.'

Young grinned at him, with what contempt Maxwell could only guess. 'Don't worry, Mr Maxwell,' he said. 'As long as you don't call anybody a bastard over the air, you'll be all right.'

Maxwell leaned forward, invading the other man's space. 'I want to know who killed Jenny,' he said steadily. 'That's all.'

'We all do,' Young answered, just as levelly, 'but for me, it goes with the territory. She was killed on my patch, so to speak. I should imagine Chief Inspector Hall feels the same way. What's your interest?'

'She was one of my sixth form,' Maxwell said. 'My responsibility.'

Young leaned back. 'Do you mind me asking how old you are?' he said.

'I don't mind,' Maxwell answered. 'I'm fifty-two. Why?'

Young snorted. 'Well, well. Perhaps you are,' he said.

'Perhaps I are what?'

'Old enough to have that quaint old sense of vocation teachers apparently used to have.'

'Used to have?'

'Yes, you know. Before the industrial action. Before it became a battle of wits between you and the government, with kids bouncing around like tennis balls between you both.'

'Well, well,' Maxwell said, 'I wouldn't have thought you were old enough.'

'For what?' Young sensed the ground shifting beneath him.

'Old enough to have that quaint old sense of the quest for the truth journalists apparently used to have.'

Young stood up, a muscle in his jaw ridged and flexing. 'I'd like to help you, Mr Maxwell,' he said, 'but I'm a busy man. On the day after Jenny's body was found I tried to talk to your Head. He was singularly unhelpful.'

'Legs? Of course he was.' Maxwell shrugged. 'Unhelpful is his middle name.'

'I then tried County Hall.'

'Who?'

'Jenkins.'

'Ah, the Chief Education Officer himself. Now, there's a cautious man.'

'Cautious to the point of not giving interviews, in fact. Where were you when all this broke?'

'On holiday in Cornwall,' Maxwell told him. 'That's why I'm here this morning. I'm trying to put flesh on the bones.'

Young looked down at the greying, side-whiskered teacher. 'For that you'll need to go to the cemetery,' he said. 'Plot 841. There's no headstone yet.'

Then he turned on his heel and vanished into an inner office. First he typed something on to his computer screen. Then he faxed the incident room at Tottingleigh that was handling the Jenny Hyde case.

* * *

The pace had yet to slacken in the Tottingleigh incident room; the dogs had yet to be called off. Men in shirtsleeves sat in front of computers or hunched over phones. Cups of coffee sat with stewed contents on table corners and the air was heavy with cigarette smoke.

'Well, well, well.' DI Johnson paused in the middle of his takeaway pizza. 'A fax from our favourite newshound.'

Jacquie Carpenter stuck her head around the VDU. 'What's it about, sir?'

'Dave,' Johnson leered. 'We agreed. Dave.'

'What's it about?' she repeated, noncommittally.

'That weirdo Maxwell; that Head of Sixth Form or whatever he calls himself from Leighford High. He's been snooping around the Advertiser.'

'About Jenny?'

'Yeah.' Johnson put Young's fax on a pile in his in-tray. 'What do you make of that, Jacquie, darling?'

She looked at her superior with ill-disguised loathing. 'If he killed her, sir, he'd hardly be asking questions at the Advertiser, would he?'

'Of course he would.' Johnson spat pepperoni in all directions. 'He wants to know how much we know. To cover his back.'

'Perhaps you should tell the DCI then,' Jacquie suggested.

'Yeah,' Johnson grunted. 'Or maybe I should just break Maxwell's kneecaps while asking him a few questions?' And he threw his remaining pizza into a bin before dragging himself out of his chair. 'Must just point Percy at the porcelain,' he said and fondled the girl's shoulder through her blouse as he walked past.

'How can you stand it, Jacquie?' the WPC next to her asked.

Jacquie Carpenter picked up the fax. 'I just console myself with the daydream that one day I'll plug his bollocks into this computer and switch on.'

She read Young's blurb to herself. 'Peter Maxwell, Head of Sixth Form, Leighford High. Asking questions re Jenny Hyde. Thought you ought to know.'

* * *

The oldest graves were nearest the road. When the town had become respectable and upper middle class, and colonels from the hill stations of the Raj had decided to retire there, they'd expanded it to the south-west. Inevitably, in a seaside town, the navy was there too and fouled anchors green with verdigris lay at rakish angles on carefully rough-hewn cairns.

The last resting place of Jenny Hyde was far away from these, among the polished marble and green chippings that were the trappings of modern death. Most people were cremated nowadays, but Jenny's granddad had insisted, apparently, that she should be buried, his little girl and when they'd finished cutting her about in the post-mortem room, that's what they did.

It was just a little mound of earth and a simple plywood cross, smothered in flowers, some still in their cellophane wrappers. He read the cards — 'Goodbye, darling Jenny, Mum and Dad.' 'We miss you, Darling, Auntie Ethel and Uncle George.' 'For Jenny, with love from Tim.' Funny that, Maxwell noticed, as he knelt in the wet grass of the September evening; the card from Tim Grey was the only one that mentioned love. Then he stood up. He didn't like graveyards. They were empty places where you stared down at your own mortality. Look. Look around. There is a stillness in the cold wrought iron that is deadly. Maxwell found himself breathing loudly, just to prove that he could.

'Goodbye, Jenny,' he whispered.

No one could have called Peter Maxwell windy. When he'd been to see The Exorcist years ago, he was the only one still sitting upright in the cinema. Everybody else was hiding under their seats. Yet now, with the dead for company, he felt it: a chilling, creeping something that he couldn't place, didn't like. What was that line in that old biography he'd read — 'the scythesman at your elbow'? He turned sharply, half expecting to see him, cloak outspread, hourglass in hand and the sand drifting through. Instead, it was an old boy in a grubby anorak, leaning on a spade.

'I'm locking up,' he said through ill-fitting teeth. 'You goin' to be long?'

Maxwell smiled. The Bard of Avon would have recognised this old bugger and used him for comic relief. Perhaps some things were eternal, after all.

'Just going,' said Maxwell and made his way to the gate.

He didn't look back.

* * *

He wheeled his bike across Wellington Road, down Buckett Street and on towards the golf course. Three streets away, he knew, the Hydes lived. At Number Thirty-two. He should go to see them; offer his condolences. After all, he'd missed the funeral. And even if Diamond had gone or some county representative, it wasn't the same. He should have been there. But now, at the last moment, his nerve failed him. He was at the end of the road; could see the house with its clematis trellis, its bird bath on the front lawn, the green Rover in the drive. Then he swung his leg over the crossbar and pedalled White Surrey away into the rain.

* * *

It was like the siege of Troy the next morning. The rain had gone and left dark concrete patches under the drying sun. Arrayed in all their panoply along Hardens Lane, the gentlemen of the press stood in little knots, like so many Ajaxes and Achilles, probing the weak spots of the citadel that was Leighford High. In a brief and heated exchange, Diamond and Garrett had ordered them off County Council property. The staff weren't there to see it — they wouldn't have believed it if they had been. But there was no law to stop the paparazzi standing on the pavement, cameras at the ready, ciggies blowing smoke to the morning.

No law either that could stop them accosting each likely-looking kid who arrived for the first day of term. You could tell them, the different groups. The first year, all crisp shirts and ties and blouses, the girls in white ankle socks below summer-tanned legs. They said little to each other, each one in his or her own private anxiety — the first day of the rest of their lives. The older ones, battle-hardened, boisterous, barely conventional in what was left of their uniforms, pushing and laughing their way along the streets. The hardliner lads were instantly recognisable. They flouted regulation as brazenly as they dared. They wore trainers, scuffed and old, with the laces loose and the tongues protruding in defiance at the ankle. Ear-rings caught the sharp morning sun and the last of their ciggie smoke wafted away on the September air as they rounded the corner. Their faces said it all. They brooked no interference, no insult. They watched for the lingering look, the stare of disapproval or contempt. Their fingers were in the air instantly as they slouched past the Old People's Home where ancient citizens, barely human, despised them from behind fading nets. The older girls, their molls in an earlier generation, chewed gum and vied with each other in having the dangliest ear-rings. They already wore their winter uniform — the ubiquitous thick black tights under the ankle socks, snagged here and there by the over-rough approaches of the lads, whose long-nailed fingers were forever straying, in a pubescent way, up their skirts.

But none of these were the targets of the paparazzi. They were here to talk to anyone who might have known Jenny Hyde. And the sixth form weren't hard to spot. They wore no uniform. So, go for the older ones — the seventeen- and eighteen-year-olds. Two in particular the pressmen knew, because they'd talked to them before, way back in July when it happened. Anne Spencer, Jenny's best friend. And Tim Grey, the boy she was going out with. They'd set up a similar siege around the Spencer and Grey houses for three or four days. But no one was talking then. Mr Grey had come out and threatened to put one on them. That went with the territory.

What the paparazzi didn't know, however, was that most of the sixth form came in the back way, across the common from Andersleigh. That was where the sixth form block lay, jutting out to the south-west, beyond the Art block and the tennis courts. They should have known that, because at least two of the cameramen exchanging titbits with the national boys were former alumni of Leighford themselves. Still, show me a crowd of reporters and I'll show you a room temperature IQ.

So Maxwell missed the barrage of questions that morning, his ancient Raleigh wheeling over the still-dewy grass. His way in took him past all those memories of his childhood, a long, long time ago and many, many miles to the north. Something of the terror of a new academic year gripped him still, if he was honest about it. The mist in the morning, the jewelled cobwebs in the hedgerows as he rode. Then, when he was eleven, his bike was smaller and the stiff, new, detachable collar of his shirt rubbed his neck. The satchel bounced uncomfortably on his back and he could still smell its glorious leather and the saddle soap his dad had used on it.

Well, the bike was bigger now, fattier. The collar was soft and his satchel was the old, battered briefcase they'd given him when he'd left his second job, strapped behind his saddle. He looked at the world through different eyes now, but the little pangs were still there, even after all these years. The tightness in the chest, the tingle in the wrists. And this term, of all terms, wasn't just his thirtieth in the business. It was altogether different. Altogether sadder. Altogether more haunting.

'Well, I was here at eight,' Alison Miller told him, as though to justify all the times she hadn't been, 'and they were here then.'

'What did they want to know?' Maxwell hauled off the double-length scarf that told, in faded wool, the pedigree of his academic past.

'If I knew Jenny,' she said, watching his face, unsure of how he'd react. Like most Maxwell's younger colleagues, male and female, she was a little afraid of him.

'What did you say?'

'I thought "No comment" was best. Then they asked me if I knew you.'

'Me?' Maxwell plugged the kettle in. 'Why me?'

'I don't know,' she said, sorting out papers. 'They didn't say.'

'And what did you say to that?'

'"No comment",' she shrugged. It had got her out of a jam once. It could do it again.

He patted her cheek. 'Consistency,' he laughed. 'I like that in a woman.' Then he looked down at her bulge, quite increased since July, and was reminded of her frailty, the cop-out clause all women carried under their frocks. 'How are you?' He nodded in the direction of her stomach and immediately wished he hadn't bothered. The whole litany of morning sickness came pouring out.

'Of course, Keith's been great,' she smirked, as though somehow it was a special honour for her husband to behave well towards her.

'Oh.' Maxwell knew the man. And knew things about him that Alison didn't. Or claimed she didn't. What a good man, she had said, too often to be convincing, a moral man. So good, Maxwell knew, so moral that he'd knock off anything in a skirt, whether his wife was pregnant or not. You don't tell colleagues that sort of thing about their husbands. You just carry on drinking your coffee and you keep your thoughts to yourself.

There was a knock at the open door.

'Mr Maxwell.' The Head of Sixth Form recognised the whine without turning round.

'Miss Lacey,' he beamed.

'Have you got the master key for the lockers?'

'You know perfectly well I have, Madeleine.' He turned, continuing to smile at her like a basilisk. 'On account of how you borrowed it on average three times a week last term. What happened to our little chat? Remember? The one where you said you'd turn over a new leaf and organise yourself this term, what with A levels being a few months away and all.'

She grinned and let a giggle escape. Yes, that was it. The height of wit and repartee for Madeleine Lacey. Maxwell flicked open his lower drawer and threw her the key with the huge plastic tag that carried his name. 'Straight back to me,' he said, as he always did when he lent the thing out. 'I should start charging.'

In the corridor, the giggly girl all but collided with James Diamond, who looked at her disapprovingly and made a mental note to tackle Maxwell again on the appearance of his sixth form.

'Max,' he said, nodding at Alison and closing the door.

'Headmaster.' Maxwell gave his customary start-of-term bow. Its obeisance fooled no one. 'Are you assembling this morning?'

'In the library as usual. Ten minutes from now. Did you want a word?'

'With the sixth form. Yes please. What with all this going on . . .' He waved an exasperated hand to the cluster of people at the gate, where Roger Garrett was again attempting his King Cnut impression by stemming the overwhelming tide of modern journalism.

'Just like King Cnut.' Diamond must have read Maxwell's mind, but Maxwell wasn't at all sure he'd got the spelling right. 'What a mess. And then . . .' The Head turned the full focus of his gold-rimmed specs on his Head of Sixth Form. 'I'd like to see you in my office.'

'I am Inducting this morning, Headmaster.'

'Can't Alison do it?'

They both looked at Maxwell's Number Two, promoted above her level of incompetence because she happened to be in the right place at the right time. She thought of the prospect — ninety or so kids poised on the threshold of a dream, determined to ignore Maxwell's advice about not wasting the golden year that was the Lower Sixth. They had a common room — of sorts — for the first time and free periods and coffee machines. Bliss-on-a-stick. She needed all that like a hole in the head.

'I'll be all right,' she said limply as though they'd asked her to climb the north face of the Eiger.

'Good.' Diamond was utterly unaware of the short-comings of his staff. Just as he was unaware of his own.

All three of them made their way down to the library on the first floor. It wasn't bad as libraries went, Dewey classifications largely hidden by geraniums and other exotica brought in by Miss Ratcliffe, stereotype of stereotypes who stood behind her counter in the term that was minutes old, tapping her feet and hating her job all over again. She loved books, but hated the people who read them.

'Ravishing as always, Matilda.' Maxwell winked at her as he swanned in with clipboard and lists.

She scowled at him under her iron-grey thatch and twirled the rope of beads that secured her reading glasses in unguarded moments. Only Maxwell called her Matilda. No one else dared. To begin with, it wasn't actually her name. She had explained that to him once, when she'd first got the job; as he told people, on the day when Hitler invaded the Low Countries. But he thought she looked like a Matilda, so Matilda it was.

'How was Sittingbourne this year? Enervating as ever?' He didn't wait for a reply, but slammed down his clipboard and let rip with the stentorian roar for which he was famous. 'Right, you shower. Let's make a start, shall we?'

The tumult subsided. Faces new and old turned to him. They all knew him. Some of them hated him perhaps, many of them loved him. But they all knew him. To them, and to the generations before, he was identified with the characters of the film-world they knew he loved. Knew because his lessons were full of it. No one except Geoffrey Smith, the Head of English, ever called him Maxim, after Laurence Olivier's haunted character in Rebecca. That was because no one, not even Smith and Maxwell, was of that vintage any more. Maxwell had still been in nappies and his dad's take-home pay £3 0s. 6d. a week when David O. Selznik released the film. Even now, though, when he thought about it, there was something of the sinister, deranged Mrs Danvers about the school librarian, glaring at some hapless child out of her upstairs windows. And the generation of sixth-formers had long gone who called him the Blue Max and identified him with the rather unpleasant character played by George Peppard as the First World War ace obsessed with the rather tacky enamelled medal. But there had been no film to replace Maxwell's still current nickname among the sixth form. Although the dashing Mel Gibson had first hacked a bloody path through the bikeways of the future when the present lot were at playgroup, the epithet 'Mad Max' still clung to him in whispered common room conversations. He toned it down himself and on the last mufti-day they'd had, before the dead hand of Jim Diamond stopped those enchanting days when the school functioned as usual but everyone wore fancy dress, Maxwell had turned up in studs and leather with his hair standing on end and carrying a placard — 'Beyond the Hippodrome'. His own youth culture and theirs woven into one.

'Good morning.' Diamond attempted to capitalise on the silence Mad Max had created with the indefinable something that made him the last of the dinosaurs.

There was no reply. That was why Maxwell had never begun any address to kids like that. There never was a reply. Each one would talk to you individually; some chatty, some abrupt. Some might even bare their souls. But collectively? Never. All you got was a wall of silence. Except that Maxwell could get them laughing. Here was a man for all seasons who had lost his way in his own darkness and when he emerged, there was this unforgiving and inescapable rut.

'Many of you will have noticed,' Diamond said, with no attempt to project, 'that there are journalists outside school this morning. Obviously it's about poor . . . er . . . Jenny Hyde.'

Maxwell watched the Head's audience. In particular, his gaze fell on Tim Grey, a sallow, unprepossessing youth, who ought to have been spotty, but wasn't. The boy's eyes fell. One or two of his mates glanced in his direction, then looked away. Then Maxwell found the pale, hard face of Anne Spencer and it puzzled him. He'd expected tears perhaps, a downturn of the mouth certainly. Instead he saw a look that unnerved him, a coldness in the eyes. He didn't like it. But was fascinated by it and couldn't look away.

'It's a tragedy of course,' Diamond was mumbling, 'especially to those of you who were her friends. But it's also very delicate. The police enquiries are continuing. I know that some of you have talked to the police already. And I understand that they have more interviews to conduct. If these happen on school premises, I shall expect to be informed. You have a right to have your parents present at these interviews if you wish. On no account, however,' he lifted his voice now to be heard over the rising muttering, 'on no account,' and he flashed a dark stare at Maxwell, 'should you talk to the press. Certain journalists have a habit of twisting anything you say. It's far better to say nothing. If anybody pesters you for information, tell a member of staff if it's here in school time; or your parents if it's outside school. Now, a moment's silence, please, while we remember Jenny.'

Maxwell had not been ready for this. He looked at Alison, whose eyes widened. Behind Diamond, the form tutors shifted uneasily. Geoffrey Smith pulled his head out of the *Guardian* and Matilda Ratcliffe stopped stamping.

'How bloody fatuous,' Maxwell thought. The time for all that was at the girl's funeral. Now it seemed out of place, grotesque. Legs Diamond was not the sort of Headmaster to command silence, even for a minute. He was too new, too callow to take the bull by the traditional horns on Armistice Day and talk of the slow drawing-down of blinds. He didn't have the nerve for it and he didn't have the heart. Only Diamond stood with his head bowed and long before the moment was up, the sixth form, with a collective mind of its own, began shifting and whispering. One of them was dead. And they were all on alien ground.

CHAPTER 4

Six- or seven-year-old artwork still stood under glass in James Diamond's office. Maxwell remembered the artist well. A promising graphic designer described by the Head of Art as a natural with a distinctive feel for form, she now put all her artistic talent into serving up Zingers and other incomprehensible tasties in the local Kentucky. Well, it was the way of the world.

'You wanted a word, Headmaster?' Maxwell had never seen Diamond so tight-lipped.

'You talked to the press,' he said.

'Yes,' Maxwell nodded. 'Look, do you mind if I sit down? The old knee isn't what it was.'

Minutes earlier, he'd seen Roger Garrett and Bernard Ryan scuttle out of the Head's room to their respective offices. The triumvirate with their backs to the wall. They reminded Maxwell of a rather seedy version of Horatius and Co., although in this case the dauntless three weren't keeping the bridge too well, all things considered. Maxwell was a past master at outmanoeuvring his opponents. Now, in order not to loom over him, Diamond had to sit down too and he had to shift a pile of papers from the chair in order to do it.

'Why, Max?' Diamond was trying the old pals approach. 'Why did you do that? And to Tony Young of all people?'

Maxwell shrugged. 'He might split the odd infinitive,' he said, 'but we've all got to bend with the tide, Headmaster.'

'Don't get flippant with me, Maxwell,' Diamond warned.

The grey old plodder paused. Well, well, the worm had turned. All that Diamond had had going for him for some time was that he seemed a nice guy. Now, even that had gone. No more Mr Nice Guy.

'I'm terribly sorry, Headmaster,' Maxwell said, with the air of one who has never regretted anything in his life. 'I merely wanted to know what everyone else seems to know.'

'What are you talking about?'

Maxwell leaned back on the Head's uncomfortable new furniture. 'When Jenny Hyde died,' he said, 'I was away on holiday. I missed it all. The finding of her body. The immediate police enquiries. The funeral.'

'So?'

'Did you go to the funeral?'

'No.' Diamond couldn't outstare Mad Max for long and he glanced away. 'I believe Janet Foster went.'

Maxwell nodded. 'She's a good form tutor, Janet,' he said. 'I'm glad she was there.'

'But why Tony Young?' Diamond persisted.

'He covered the story for the Advertiser,' Maxwell told him.

'Why didn't you tackle the nationals? They were there too.'

'Aha,' Maxwell smiled, 'I tried that once. When I was doing some research into the war, for the new GCSE History course. Not only was it impossible to find anybody who knew what I was talking about, I was expected to pay an astronomical sum to use their articles. The Advertiser was free.'

Diamond got up, his face taut. He whipped a newspaper off his desk. 'I take it you haven't seen this?'

Maxwell hadn't. 'What is it?' he asked.

'It's Young's lead story for this week's Advertiser. He's networked it all over the place. That's why we've got those people out there. We might have got away with a quiet start to the term, Max, but you've made that impossible.'

Maxwell's face darkened as he read the proof. 'I don't like the tone of this,' he said.

'Do you think I do?' Diamond snapped. 'As soon as John Graham sees this, he's going to want some answers, I can tell you.'

Maxwell was unimpressed. John Graham was the Chairman of Governors, that group of ineffectuals the government had rocketed into a position of pre-eminence to keep an eye on the leftist teachers their paranoia led them to believe lurked in every classroom. He read on, frowning. 'This makes it sound as if I'm some kind of ghoul,' he muttered.

'Aren't you?'

Maxwell was suddenly on his feet, bad knee or not. 'You sanctimonious bastard!' he bellowed.

He saw Diamond turn white, standing as they were toe to toe.

'I beg your pardon?' was all the Head could manage.

'One of my sixth form is dead,' Maxwell said levelly.

'My sixth form too,' Diamond reminded him.

'Is that so?' Maxwell growled. 'Then join me, for God's sake.'

Diamond turned to his desk and sat down heavily behind it, distanced from the gauntlet that Maxwell had thrown down. 'What?' he asked. 'On some ludicrous quest?'

'Yes.' Maxwell leaned forward, gripping the desk with both hands, consciously invading Diamond's space. 'The Sangreal,' he said, then realized he was talking to a physicist and thought he'd better explain. 'The Holy Grail of truth, Headmaster. Out there,' he pointed to the world beyond the glass, 'is someone who put an end to a young life. Choked the breath out of a seventeen-year-old girl.'

Diamond looked up at his Head of Sixth Form and said softly, with a wisdom he didn't usually display, 'Let it go, Max. Leave it to the police.'

Maxwell straightened up, the fire dying in his eyes. 'I can't,' he said.

'They're the experts,' Diamond reminded him. 'They know what they're doing.'

'I don't dispute that,' Maxwell said.

'Well, then.'

Maxwell looked at him. What he was going to say would go over the Head's head, but he said it anyway. 'Do you know that poem by Mackintosh?' he asked. "In Memoriam".'

'Er . . . no.' Diamond had never been one for poetry. Maxwell knew that. It was because he had no soul.

'He wrote it for a Private David Sutherland of the Seaforth Highlanders who was killed in a German trench in May 1916. There's one verse that's oddly sharp in my memory at the moment:

'You were only David's father,
But I had fifty sons
When we went up in the evening
Under the arch of guns,
And we came back at twilight—
O God! I heard them call
To me for help and pity
That could not help at all.'

Diamond was confused. 'I don't see . . .'

'Mackintosh is making the point that he was closer to that dead boy than his own father, because he was there when he died. He was his officer.'

'What are you saying?'

Maxwell looked with contempt at the man behind the desk. 'I was Jenny's officer,' he said softly. 'Her Year Head.'

'But you hardly knew her, surely . . .'

'Hardly,' Maxwell nodded. 'But what if,' he was asking himself, really, 'what if on the night she died she called to me? To anyone? Called for help and pity? There was no one to listen, was there? Well, I owe her that much. I'm listening now,' he murmured, turning. 'I was her officer.'

'Mr Maxwell.' Diamond was at his firmest as the man reached the office door. He paused. 'You will not talk to the press again.'

Maxwell turned to him, smiling. 'I'll see myself out, Headmaster.'

Somebody — possibly a physics teacher, oddly enough — once analysed a teacher's working day. Only a tiny portion of it was contact time, actually in a classroom with the kids. The rest was paperwork. It wasn't only the police in the '90s who were strangled in red tape. The world of the teacher was bureaucracy run mad. It wouldn't be long before Roger Garrett would be pestering Maxwell for the necessary information for Form 7. How many girls under seventeen taking Maths and Science A level? How many boys? How many yellow socks? Who owned the zebra? Maxwell had long ago stopped asking why the Department of Education and Science should need all this stuff. And, come to think of it, why wasn't it called the Department of Education and History? It was becoming a mad, mad world where everybody wore white coats.

That morning, Maxwell got his contact time. The new intake, officially designated now Year 7, sat smiling in front of him, still crisp after two hours on the premises, bewildered, a little afraid. Eleven years old and already in the front line. He introduced himself, in the History room on the first floor that stood next to the library, and handed out small pieces of paper. Not for Mad Max the minutiae of the National Curriculum, that grey, flat concept in which each kid in the country would be doing the same lesson, from the same book, at the same pace.

'I want you all,' he said, 'to look very carefully at me.'

They giggled.

'This,' he turned to his left, 'is my best side.' Then to his right, 'This is not quite so good.' He turned his back on them. They were only first years, on their first day. He'd be all right. No knives in his back. He only got those in the staff room. 'But this,' he showed them the back of his barbed-wire head, 'is the best side of all.'

The giggles grew into laughter. That's it, Maxwell mused. Make 'em laugh, make 'em cry. Make 'em do History — especially when it came to option time and they had to choose between that and the waste of time that was Geography.

'Now,' he faced them again, 'I want you to write down on that bit of paper how old you think I am.'

There were guffaws.

'Do it properly.' He held up his hand. 'Look carefully. And try to get it right. I'm the only one who does the jokes here. No conferring.' He put on his best Bamber Gascoigne for them, although none of them had the remotest idea who Bamber Gascoigne was. Probably, in his heart of hearts, not even Bamber Gascoigne.

He wandered the lines of desks. Next lesson, he knew, Paul Moss, his Head of Department, would be in the room. He'd reorganise it, get the kids working in groups, playing with computers. Doing everything '90s educationalists expected. Until then, Maxwell would keep the desks in rows, where he could launch himself at each kid. And his computer was a blackboard, his cursor a piece of chalk. This year for the first time he'd had to buy his own. The school office had stopped providing it.

Some kids covered up their work with their arms. Others showed him what they'd done, grinning stupidly. This was the top set, supposedly. God help the rest, Maxwell thought to himself. Still, the names were right. Tamsins rubbed shoulders with Imogens and Williams and Harrys. Later in the day, when he met his Set 3, he'd find the Sharons and Traceys and Waynes and Shanes. Why, he found himself wondering again, had two entire generations forever ruined a classic Western by christening their moronic offspring Shane?

It was just as he was making his second circuit that he noticed them. Below the window. The boys in blue. Two uniformed constables, their diced headbands vivid under the painful glare of the September sky, threading their way through the bike sheds. There'd be smokers there in half an hour, the hardliners bent on lung cancer who'd cultivated that curious method of holding ciggies in the palms of their hands so the smoke didn't show. But it wasn't smokers the fuzz were after. They seemed to be checking bikes. Every now and again, one of them would stoop and say something to his colleague who'd write something down. Maxwell couldn't make out a pattern in their search. It seemed random. What were they looking for?

Then he was aware from the growing row that Set I's first task of their History careers was over and he told them to pass their papers forward so that no one could see what they'd written. When the little pile was high enough on his desk, he unfolded them one by one and read them out.

'A hundred,' he said and got a laugh. The figures actually read fifty-five, but that was too close to be funny and Maxwell a great believer in licence. 'Sixty-eight.' A titter. Thirty-four.'

A howl.

'Who put that?' he asked.

Slowly, furtively, a lad's hand climbed into the air.

'What's your name?' Maxwell demanded.

'Tom,' the lad said, still junior school enough to think that surnames names didn't matter.

'Tom what?' Maxwell asked.

'Wood,' the lad said.

'Well, Tom Wood,' Maxwell crossed to him, 'you are a fine judge of men and will make a first-class historian.' He held out his hand. 'Allow me to shake you by the hand. You've made an old man very happy.'

The others laughed. Then he read out their guesses. Four of them only were spot on. When he asked them, none of them knew why they'd carried out the exercise. Year by year, none of them ever did.

'Time,' Maxwell said. 'The most difficult idea you'll have to cope with in History. Most of you got my age wrong. You put me too old. There are two reasons for that. One, my hair is greying. Two, I'm a teacher. And all teachers are old, aren't they? Like mums and dads. Ancient. Teachers don't have lives of their own. They just climb into a cupboard at four o'clock and out again at nine. Somebody throws a switch and we start teaching. If I'd asked a class of five-year-olds how old I was, they'd have said two hundred, three hundred. Time is the most elusive thing to handle. It trickles through your fingers like sand on the beach. One casual misuse of it, one slip and it's gone for ever.'

The bell shattered the moment. No one moved. 'That's the signal for the end of the magic,' he told the eager, anxious faces, 'the breaking of the spell. You'll go on now to some irrelevance like French or Maths and you'll forget all about that sand, won't you?' He smiled. 'Until the next time. And next time,' he dismissed them with a wave of his arm, 'we'll discuss the conceptualisation of Hegel's dialectic. Good morning, boys and girls.' And another generation had come to know Mad Max.

* * *

Someone — and it was probably Roger Garrett, compiler of the calendar — had decreed that at the end of the first gruelling day of term there should be Department meetings.

Paul Moss was sufficiently a man of the people to provide biccies. Tea was on Anthea Edwards, third in the History Department. And the milk was provided by Sally Greenhow, gazetted from Special Needs, on account of how they had a fridge in Special Needs.

It had to be said that Matilda Ratcliffe didn't like the History Department using the library. After all, they had rooms of their own. But Paul Moss liked the ambience, the open spaces. Mildly claustrophobic, he'd been trying for three years to get off the first floor to grab the Modern Languages annexe for himself. The Head of Modern Languages, a rather reptilian creature with liver problems, had fought him off on rather spurious educational grounds.

They munched the Hob-nobs and sat around, loosely following Moss's agenda.

'Anthea,' he said, 'how did you find those new books?'

Anthea rolled her eyes upwards. 'Is it me,' she asked, 'or are the junior schools sending us thicker kids every year? Did you have a hand in the setting, Paul?'

'A rather furtive one, yes.' Her Head of Department grinned. He was mid-thirties, ambitious, with a boyish look and a mop of fair hair. 'But you know how it is. The English Department rules OK.'

'Ah, you've been listening to Mr Smith again,' Maxwell chuckled. 'The English Department does nothing OK.'

'I thought Geoffrey Smith was a friend of yours,' Anthea said. Ever the literal one, she'd never really mastered the ancient art of cynicism. It would keep her third in a department for ever.

'Oh, he is,' Maxwell humoured her. 'I'd go through the shredder for that man. But trust him to set the kids accurately? Or drive anywhere with him? I'd rather he set my broken arm.'

'What were the police doing here this morning?' Sally asked. They all looked at her. Sally Greenhow looked like a tall kid.

She still had the frizzy hair, round face and dimpled cheeks of a little girl — a sort of ten-year-old on stilts. Only the cigarette, endlessly twitching between her fingers, betrayed an adult's neuroses.

'They seemed to be checking the bike shed,' Anthea said.

'Why?' Moss asked.

'Don't tell me we've had a theft already?' Anthea poured herself a second cup of tea. It was quite stewed at the bottom by now.

'No, it's Jenny Hyde,' Sally said as though the walls had ears. Matilda Ratcliffe had, and they pricked up now as she busied herself filing behind her counter.

'What?' Maxwell asked.

'Well, they're looking for the bike.' Sally thought it was obvious.

'What bike?'

'They saw a bike parked outside the Red House on the day she . . . you know.'

'How do you know that?' Maxwell's Hobnob plummeted into his tea, the victim of over-dunking.

'I don't know.' Sally dragged deeply on her cigarette. 'Somebody told me.'

'I don't know how you tell one bike from another,' Moss shrugged.

'They were looking for cars, too.'

All eyes turned to the voice from beyond. Matilda Ratcliffe was still filing, her face downcast, but the words had definitely come from her.

'Did somebody come in?' Maxwell looked at his fellow historians.

'Oh?' Moss thought he ought to try to coax the librarian back to life. 'Were they?'

'I went out to get my packed lunch,' she told them, avoiding their gaze and suddenly hating the spotlight in which she found herself. 'They were noting down registration numbers.'

'Were they now?' Maxwell muttered.

'I thought it was the height of cheek, those reporters pestering kids this morning,' Anthea said. 'Did anybody see them go?'

'I think the rain drove them away,' Moss said. 'Certainly they'd gone by the time I went out for my lunch.'

'I'm afraid I talked to them,' Anthea confessed, pausing in mid-nibble.

'Really?' Maxwell beamed. 'I hope the Headmaster doesn't get to hear of this, Mrs Edwards.'

He watched her neck mottle and her lips miss the crumbs.

'You're such an arsehole, Max,' Sally scolded him. 'The rumour is they're only here because you shot your mouth off to the Advertiser anyway.' Here was one young, female member of staff who had no fear whatever of Mad Max Maxwell.

Maxwell sucked in his breath, and smacked his left wrist. 'Well, hush my puppies,' he said. So it was all-girls-together-week, he realised as he saw the fire in Sally's eyes. Twenty years ago, he'd have pulled her pigtails. Still, the rumour was correct. The old Leighford grapevine was working, well as ever.

'What did you say?' Moss wanted to know.

'Nothing.' Anthea was quick to defend herself. 'Nothing much. I only taught her in Year 9. I just said she was bright, conscientious.'

Maxwell inhaled sharply again. 'Well, that's it then,' he said. 'That'll be banner headlines in the *Sun* tomorrow. And I don't want to think what the *Daily Sport* will do with it.'

'For God's sake, Max!' Sally hissed. 'This isn't easy for any of us, you know. It was bad enough when Jenny went missing.'

Maxwell's cup hit the saucer unexpectedly hard. 'What?' he said.

'I said . . .' Sally enunciated slowly. Obviously the march of time had caught up with one geriatric Head of Sixth Form.

'That Jenny went missing. Yes, I heard that. When? Where?'

'Where,' she leaned back in her chair, 'I haven't the faintest idea. When, at the end of last term . . . But surely you knew that?'

'No.' Maxwell felt the ground vanish beneath him, an alienation perhaps everybody starts to feel when they're fifty-two. 'No, I didn't know that. How do you know it?'

'Special Needs,' Paul beamed. 'They always pick up the scandal down there.'

Sally laughed. 'Usually, yes. But not this time. No, it was Janet Foster, Jenny's form tutor. Apparently Jenny wasn't in during the last week of term. Janet followed it up.'

'Of course she did.' Maxwell was nodding, frowning at the same time. 'She would. She would. Damned good form tutor is Janet. Wonder why she didn't tell me.'

Sally shrugged. 'Slipped her mind, I suppose. You know what the last week of term's like. That quiet time when Years 11 and 13 have gone and we all have so many free periods.'

'That quiet time,' Moss took up the irony, 'when the timetable for September doesn't work even though three blokes and an entire computer network have been working on it all year?'

'Anyway, weren't you off yourself?' Anthea remembered.

'Er . . . from the Monday to Thursday, yes. My knee was playing me up. I had those physio appointments.'

'Well there you are,' Sally said, ever willing to defend the feminist right. 'I expect Janet saw Alison about it.'

'Alison?'

The Special Needs teacher leaned forward, as though coping with one of her most special charges. 'Alison Miller, your deputy. Are you all right, Max? Been a bit of a strain, has it, today?'

'All right.' Moss actually clapped his hands. 'Let's get back to some departmental business, shall we? Coursework for Year 10.'

And they all let out the inevitable, universal groan.

* * *

Bill Foster had left Janet nearly ten years ago. There wasn't another woman or anything like that. They'd just been incompatible from the start. She was a sculptress of talent, had exhibitions from time to time. He was a couch potato in an engineering firm. God knew what had brought them together in the first place, but time had driven them apart. He'd gone off with the stereo, half the furniture and no regrets. She'd got the house, which she'd converted into an enormous studio overlooking the sea, and a geriatric dog and the other half of the furniture. Regrets? She had a few. The nights were cold in the winter and the plumbing, in the rambling Victorian house, was a bitch.

'Max?' Janet looked quite deathly without her make-up. Her mousy hair was wrapped in a pink towel that made her look vaguely like Hogarth.

'I'm sorry, Janet.' He swept off his shapeless hat. 'I know it's late.'

She fiddled with the chain. 'No, no,' she flustered, closing the top of her housecoat, 'not at all. It's just that . . . Have you ever been here before?'

'Er . . . once, I think,' he told her, edging past into the hall. 'It was old Whatsisface's retirement. I'd had a few and Bill brought me here to dry out. Remember?'

'Oh, yes,' she laughed. 'Can I get you a drink now?'

'You can get me a cocoa,' he smiled. Then he saw the dog waddling lamely over to him. 'Hello, Dick.'

'Dirk,' she corrected him.

'Dirk.' He took the outstretched paw. 'Yes, of course. Charmed. How old is he now?'

'Nearly eighteen.' She padded into the kitchen. 'That's over a hundred and twenty in human terms.'

'Ah,' Maxwell mused, 'I'm not sure I'll be able to shake anybody's hand when I'm over a hundred and twenty.'

'What's the matter, Max?' She had her back to him, filling the kettle.

'Jenny Hyde,' he said.

'Yes.' She reached into the fridge for the milk. 'I thought it would be.'

'Did you?' He perched himself on one of her high stools at the breakfast bar. Beyond his reflection in the window he saw the lights twinkle on the sea and he knew the wind sighed in the dunes.

'You didn't mention her in assembly this morning.'

'It didn't seem the moment,' he said.

'Bit corny of Diamond, wasn't it?' she asked him. 'That ghastly one minute's silence. Anybody'd think he was a real Headmaster. Did you know he was going to do that?'

'If it's anything to do with the sixth form,' Maxwell told her, 'you can bet I'm the last to know.'

'Sugar?'

'Two, please,' he said.

'I thought you were dieting?'

'I am,' he told her. 'Two sugars is the diet.'

She laughed and shook her head. 'I went to the funeral, you know.'

'Yes,' he said. 'Thanks for doing that.'

She looked at him. 1 don't need thanks, Max,' she said. 'I liked Jenny. Everybody did.'

'Somebody didn't,' Maxwell reminded her.

Her face was suddenly older, sadder. 'No,' she murmured. 'Somebody didn't.'

'Who was there?' he asked her. 'At the funeral, I mean.'

'Oh, her family. Mum, dad. Others I didn't know. There were quite a few of the sixth form. Tim, of course. Tim Grey. They were going together, weren't they?'

Maxwell shrugged. 'What am I?' he asked. 'The Leighford High Lonely Hearts Club? I can't keep tabs on all these pubescent gropings.'

'Well, he was there, anyway.'

'I heard something today. Oh, thanks.' He took the proffered cup.

'Oh?'

'I heard Jenny ran away from home. Is that right?'

She looked warily at him. 'Who told you?' she asked.

'Doesn't matter,' he said. 'Did she?'

'Yes.'

'You didn't tell me.'

'I was told not to.'

'Oh?' His eyebrows and hackles rose simultaneously. 'By whom?'

'Mrs Hyde.'

'I see.'

'I'm not sure you do. I've told the police already.'

'You have?'

'Max, you weren't here,' she explained.

'I know,' he said. 'I'm beginning to feel like Ray Milland in *The Lost Weekend*, as though a whole chunk of my life is missing.'

'A whole chunk of Jenny's is,' she said, solemnly.

'I want to know,' he told her.

'I told Inspector Hall I wouldn't talk to anyone else,' she said.

'Janet,' he held her shoulder, 'I liked Jenny, too,' he said.

And she looked at him.

And she told him.

CHAPTER 5

There was no doubt about it, Janet Foster made a mean cup of cocoa. Maxwell blew the froth from the top until he realised that Janet was looking at him. Some days, when he felt at his most self-reflective, he began to make mental lists of the odd habits that bachelorhood had imposed upon him. Blowing on his cocoa was only the tip of the iceberg. He smiled at Janet, knowing he was sparing her from his bath-time rendering of the Everly Brothers' Greatest Hits.

'So what was it all about, then?' he asked.

'Jenny wasn't the confiding sort,' Janet said. 'She had that rather enigmatic smile, didn't she? A sort of Leighford Giaconda. God knows what sort of turmoil went on behind that placid smile.'

'But you had an inkling?'

Janet propped one leg up on Maxwell's foot-rung, balancing that by resting her towelled head on her elbow. 'Yes. Yes, I did. I don't suppose an old chauvinist like you believes in intuition, do you?'

'Is the Pope multi-lingual?' he asked her. This wasn't Anthea Edwards. He knew she wouldn't say yes.

'Three days, your writ says,' she murmured.

'What?'

'Three days' absence, then we have to send out a note to parents asking why their darlings have been away.'

'Diamond's writ,' Maxwell told her, 'not mine.'

'Well, anyway. It didn't come to that because I saw Mrs on the Wednesday night.'

'Mrs Hyde?'

'Yes. You know I run an evening class at the Tech?'

Maxwell didn't. There was a lot, he was beginning to realise, he didn't know.

'Just basic sculpture.' She offered him a cigarette. 'Oh, you don't, do you? Always surprises me, that. You may look dissolute . . .'

'Thanks!' He punched her gently in the shoulder.

'Oh, Max,' she laughed. 'You're a grand old man; you know you are. No, I think it's sexual.'

'What? Me not smoking?'

'No, the people at the pottery class. They like the feel of wet clay oozing through their fingers . . .' Her voice died away. For all Janet Foster was the one who'd introduced life drawing classes for the A level course, she had a rudimentary prudery somewhere.

'That's why Mrs Hyde joined the class?' Maxwell asked.

'It's possible.' Janet, while still defending her viewpoint, had retreated a few miles. 'She's a very attractive woman. More so than Jenny, wouldn't you say?'

Maxwell could barely remember the woman. He'd met her perhaps three times in his life, always across a cramped table during the melee of parents' evenings. Both the Hydes had radiated arrogance. Jennifer, it seemed, had decided against Oxbridge. Snobbery wasn't her forte. Wait until you're asked, Jennifer, Maxwell had thought. Not a single member of staff had mentioned the girl to Maxwell as somebody with a fighting chance at either of the country's oldest universities. The spires would not dream in the Hyde household. Perhaps sensing this, Jenny herself had turned them down, denying the world of academe the keen thrust of her biological mind. What a waste to natural science. And what a waste of Geoffrey Smith's time, too, when, in accordance with Mr and Mrs Hyde's wishes, he'd given up his own time to polish her English in readiness for the entrance exam. Even had her round to his house from time to time. As for snobbery not being her forte, that had a ring of truth. At Leighford, she was Jenny, ordinary, popular, gregarious. At home she was Jennifer, blue-stocking extraordinary. It was not the first time that Maxwell noted two utterly different kids — one at school, the other at home. Literally, in this instance, Jekyll and Hyde.

'Anyway,' Janet was cradling her cocoa in both hands. 'Marianne — that's Mrs Hyde to you — came up to me afterwards. She made small-talk for a while, then asked me if I'd noticed anything . . . odd . . . about Jenny.'

'Odd?'

'Yes. Apparently, just recently, two days or so before this, she'd become quiet, moody.'

'Had you noticed that?'

'No, I can't say that I had. 'Course, it's difficult when you don't actually teach them. And you can't count the tutorial period.'

That blissless state when every tutor at Leighford High spent fifty minutes a week in the company of twenty-five strangers, attempting to discuss the Great Issues of Life. No, Maxwell agreed, nodding; you can't count the tutorial period.

'It all came out in the wash that Jenny had asked to stay with Anne Spencer for that last week of term. They were working on some biology assignment or other and as Anne's house is out on the Shingle, it made some sense. They were doing something on seaweed or whatever. I happened to mention that I hadn't seen Jenny that week and Mrs H. turned quite pale.'

'She wasn't at Anne's?'

'Well, the next day I spoke to Anne in the corridor. No, Jenny wasn't with her. She'd never actually stayed with her, not overnight.'

'Didn't Mrs Hyde check with the Spencers?'

'She might have done after she talked to me. I don't know. The point was, though, that no one knew where Jenny was.'

He got up and wandered to the window. From here, he could see the headland called the Shingle, a black dragon lying prone in a silver sea, wrapped now in autumn's mist.

'Look, Max,' she followed him, 'I should have told you all this. I can't think why I didn't.'

He turned to her. 'Mrs Hyde asked you not to, didn't she?'

'Yes,' Janet said. 'That evening at the pottery class she said — and I'll never forget her words — she said, "Please don't tell anyone, especially Mr Maxwell."'

Mr Maxwell shrugged. 'Don't worry. It happens all the time,' he reassured her. 'Remember that Atkins girl a couple of years ago? I didn't know where she was living from one day to the next. She might have been on the game in Soho for all I knew. Did the Hydes call the police?'

'Well, I rang Marianne from school that morning. To tell her what she probably already knew, that Jenny wasn't at the Spencers'. Of course, two days later, they found her body at the Red House. Do you know the Red House, Max?'

'Not really,' he shrugged.

'We used to take kids sketching there.' She looked at their reflections in the window. 'It's hindsight, I suppose,' she shuddered a little at the memory of it, 'but I never felt quite at ease there.'

'Hindsight?' He leapt back in mock amazement. 'Look, do you mind? Leave that sort of language to us historians, please, young lady. I don't go around spouting nonsense about chiaroscuro, do I?'

It was her turn to swipe him round the shoulder. 'Oh, bollocks, Max,' she laughed. 'You'd pinch anybody's jargon without a second thought.'

He laughed with her and put his cup down on the draining board. 'I'd wash it up,' he winced, holding his head, 'but my old trouble's playing up again.'

But Janet was staring out at the Shingle too and at the line of the headland that led to the Red House. 'What happened, Max?' she murmured, not looking at him. 'What happened to Jenny?'

He crossed to her, hesitated, then put his strong hands on her narrow shoulders. 'She died, Janet,' he said softly. 'She just died.'

* * *

Perhaps that wasn't the best time to do it, but he couldn't sleep anyway. Maxwell made his excuses to Janet Foster and pedalled for the Shingle, crossing the road that winds uphill all the way. Now that it was autumn, the fudge-coloured ponies were locked away in warm, sickly-smelling stables and the riding school lay black and bleak under a fitful moon.

At the gate of St Asaph's, he swung from the saddle and parked White Surrey against the old tree that the storm of '87 had failed to uproot. There was a short-cut, he vaguely remembered, from the churchyard across the fields to the Red House, but the clouds were thickening from the west and the going would be rough in the dark. So he stuck to the road, that ribbon of moonlight that formed the sunken lane. In the shelter of the bushes here was a stillness he found eerie. You'd never think the sea was just over that hill. Or that the M27 thundered east and west only three miles away, juggernauts roaring through the night.

It was a steep climb by the road, but he made it and picked his way through the barbed wire some thoughtful soul had tangled round the old, rusted railings. He hadn't got a torch, but he could make out the sign that said 'Keep Out. Trespassers will be prosecuted.' Or strangled, he thought to himself.

The Red House was half a house, derelict, silent. The wind of early evening had dropped now, giving no explanation to the curiously stunted trees that slanted to the north, like something out of a Tolkien landscape. He knew enough about police procedure to know there would have been a blue and white tape stretched across here when they'd found her body. It was not there now, only tyre tracks of Range Rovers cut deep into what was once the croquet lawn. He ducked under the wild rhododendrons, free now to spread where they would without the cramping confines of human taste.

'Hello, hello, hello.'

The voice froze Maxwell's heart in the darkness. He felt his throat tighten and his skin crawl. And he spun round.

'I'd know that scarf anywhere. Returning to the scene of the crime, Maxie, me ol' mucker?'

There could only be one head that bald in the moonlight.

'Geoffrey, you total arsehole. I could have died.'

Smith laughed. 'Not you, Maxie, you're immortal. Shouldn't we exchange clichés about now? Like "What are you doing here?"?'

'All right.' Maxwell was still fighting the urge to throw up. 'I was about to ask the same of you.'

'"We'll ask the questions if you don't mind."'

'Yes, well,' Maxwell had tired of the game already. 'That's enough of that.'

'"That's enough of that." No,' Smith confessed, 'I don't recognise that one. Unless it's dear old Jack Warner, is it? *The Blue Lamp*?'

'I've stopped doing it now, Geoffrey,' Maxwell said, as though to a village idiot. 'It's not funny any more.'

'"Last night,"' Smith was giving his best Joan Fontaine, '"I dreamed I went to Manderley again . . ."'

'I said,' Maxwell grew louder, '"I've stopped doing it now."' He paused. 'Anyway, that's nothing like Laurence Olivier.'

'Ooh, you bitch. Nip?'

Smith had one of those walking sticks with a glass tot-carrier in the top. Reproduction, of course. 'No, thanks.'

'Good God, Maxim. Aren't you well?'

'Not as well as I was,' Maxwell confided, fumbling at his wrist, 'it's nearly midnight. What the bloody hell are you doing here?'

'I thought you'd stopped all that,' Smith observed, 'I could say I was walking the dog, but for one thing . . .'

'No dog.' Maxwell's finger pirouetted into the air.

Smith clicked his. 'It's easy to see how you became a senior teacher in a third-rate comprehensive no one's ever heard of. You, presumably, are out looking for your cat, Tiddles.'

'My cat is called Metternich,' Maxwell reminded him. 'And don't call me Tiddles.'

'*Airplane*.' Smith jabbed the sky at him. 'One of Leslie Neilson's lines. Why *is* your cat called Metternich, Maxie? I've often wondered.'

'Ah, well,' Maxwell's feet crunched on the gravel, 'if you'd followed a cultured discipline like History instead of wasting your time on English literature and similar crap, you'd know that Metternich was the Austrian Big Enchilada back at the Congress of Vienna.'

'Sort of Douglas Hurd?'

'Yes, but with presence and a brain.'

'Right.'

'He was a manipulator par excellence. Known as "the Coachman of Europe".'

'I knew that,' Smith told him.

'Well, then. If you've ever seen my Metternich playing with a mouse, you wouldn't have to ask.'

'I'm here,' Smith was suddenly serious, 'for exactly the same reason you are, Max. Because I couldn't keep away.'

Maxwell nodded. 'Thank Christ,' he said. 'I thought it was just me slowly going mad with this Jenny Hyde thing. Shall we?'

They did. Two grown men behaving like a percentage of the Famous Five. Or was it the Secret Seven?

'You didn't think to bring a torch, I suppose?' Maxwell asked.

'Sorry. Shit!' Smith's shin collided with something. 'Spur of the moment thing, really. I couldn't sleep.'

'Hilda?' Maxwell suddenly remembered the rather crabby little woman his old mate had inexplicably married years before.

'At her mother's. Tending to Godzilla.'

'I thought she was dead.'

'Wishful thinking,' Smith laughed.

'So you're a grass widower, then?'

'After a fashion. Where did they find her, exactly?'

Maxwell shrugged. They stood in the vestibule. High above them the sky broke bright through the shattered roof where the rafters jutted against the clouds. 'The *Advertiser* didn't say,' he said.

'Who uses this place, Max?' Smith batted aside the damp cobwebs.

'Winos, by the look of it.' His feet crunched on glass. He crouched for as long as his knee would let him. 'Strongbow.' He peered at the faded label.

'Not even well-heeled winos, then?' Smith commented.

'What did you expect?' Maxwell was at his elbow again. 'Moet et Chandon?'

'That's not what I meant. The nationals said this place was a favourite with local lovers.' He tapped a broken pipe that jutted through the wall. 'Must be pretty desperate.'

Maxwell tested the first stair. 'My guess is they found her up there.'

'Why?'

'I don't know,' he said. 'Let's have a look.'

'Maybe it's lighter up there. You know, this must have been quite a place in its day. I seem to remember when Hilda and I first moved here it was still lived in. Not that you ever saw anyone coming or going, but I remember it looked a sad place.'

'Sad?'

'Yes.' Smith reached for a banister that wasn't there as the stairs spiralled up to the left. 'Its windows looked like eyes, big with tears.'

Maxwell paused on the turn. 'Dylan Thomas?'

He felt his oppo's stick tap the back of his leg sharply. 'Geoffrey Smith, you bastard. And by the way, Maxie, this is me — Geoffrey. You don't have to come that cynical bit with me, you know.'

Maxwell smiled, anonymously and unobserved in the darkness. 'It's a mask I've worn for so long,' he said. 'I'm not sure I'd know how to drop it, now. Even with you. Here.'

'Where?'

'Did I ever tell you I was psychic, Mr Smith?'

'No, Mr Maxwell, you didn't.'

'That's 'cos I'm not. But even so . . .'

'What?'

The Head of Sixth Form crossed the slippery boards of the floor until Smith saw him silhouetted against the bay of the window. For an instant he looked like a still from the only film that had ever really frightened him — where the Devil rears up in shafts of light over the little girl's bed in *The Exorcist*. Then he shook himself free of it.

'Even so?' he said.

'Hmm?'

'You said you weren't psychic, but even so.'

'Even so, I think it was in this room.'

'That she died?'

Maxwell nodded. He turned into the room. The moon had come out and it threw shadows across the floor and to the far wall. Smith's skin was a patchy grey under the clouds, his eyes and the handle of his stick flashing in their brightness. Maxwell knelt down again. 'Jesus, I've got to stop this sleuthing bit. I hadn't realised that kneeling was a job requirement for the fuzz. What do you make of this, Watson?'

Smith knelt opposite him, delivering his best Nigel Bruce. 'It's a floor, Holmes,' he said.

'Capital, my dear fellow.' Maxwell's Rathbone flared his nostrils. 'But I'm talking about this discolouration.'

'Discolouration? Oh, yes.' Nigel Bruce had vanished. Geoffrey Smith was back. 'It's a square shape. No. A rectangle. Bed?'

'Thanks for the offer,' Maxwell muttered, 'but it's just 'cos Hilda's away and you're a funny age. Not a bed, but a mattress.'

'So?'

'So who used it? Jenny?'

Smith looked up at him. 'Was she that sort?'

Maxwell leaned back on his heels. 'She was a woman, Geoffrey, albeit a young one. What do I know about hormones? Sexual urges. I was never seventeen, let alone a woman. What made her run away?'

'She ran away?'

Maxwell nodded. 'I'm glad I'm not the only one not to have known these things. She'd been gone for at least five days. She left home at some time between the Friday and the Monday. She told her parents she was staying with Anne Spencer, which she wasn't. The Hydes realised it on the Wednesday and they probably notified the police that day.'

'The police?'

'That's what I'd do if I had a seventeen-year-old who'd done a runner. Wouldn't you?'

'I've got two boys, remember, Maxie; one in Australia, one in Canada, bringing a civilising influence to the colonies. I realised the impossibility of having a daughter.'

'You may have a point,' Maxwell said, suddenly elsewhere; another time; another place. 'They found her Friday night.'

'Hall,' Smith remembered. 'Chief Inspector Hall.'

'Yes, we've met.'

'Oh, you're honoured.'

'Am I? Help me up Geoff, will you?' Maxwell was stuck.

'"Can't feel your legs, Douglas?"' Smith's Kenneth More as Douglas Bader needed work, but Maxwell was too good a friend to say so. He just groaned as the pins and needles ran riot up and down his calves.

'God, interview leg,' he hissed, hopping around.

'What?'

'I must have told you. When I went for that Deputy job in Chichester. I was leaning so hard on my left leg, trying to be casual and in control, that when I stood up I fell over. I didn't get the job.'

'Well, of course not. There are enough dipsomaniacs in Chichester as it is, without you adding to their problems.'

Maxwell turned to the window. In the early hours of Wednesday morning under the coldness of the moon he saw the lawns fall away to the sea and the huddle of houses on the far hill where Janet Foster had put her lights out and would be sleeping now, with Dirk at the foot of her bed. Was this, he wondered, Jenny's last view?

'Who's got the mattress now, Geoff?' he asked.

'The law.' Smith was beside him. 'If you're right about a mattress in the first place. If she was lying on it, they'd take it away for forensics. God, Max, don't you watch any television?'

'Too busy marking.' Maxwell stared out to sea. 'That's it, then.' He turned to his old comrade of the chalk face. 'I've got to go to the police.'

'Are you mad?'

'Why?'

'It may have escaped your attention, dear boy,' Smith folded his arms, suddenly cold now at this hour, in front of these glassless windows, 'but there's a juvenile crime wave going on out there.'

'Cobblers,' Maxwell growled. 'The only crime wave is the rate at which those doom and gloom merchants in the media churn out scaremongering stories.'

'And who do people blame for the juvenile crime wave?' Smith ignored him. 'The police. And who do the police blame?'

'Juveniles?' Maxwell decided to humour him.

'Too simple,' Smith chuckled. 'Where's your psychology, man? The police blame the people who create the delinquents. "The Lord, he lays it on Martha's sons."'

'Ah, the parents.'

'Oh, ye of little faith.' Smith clicked his tongue and shook his head. 'Us, dear boy. The teachers. Oh, yes, we don't get 'em till they're eleven and we see 'em for seven hours out of twenty-four, but it's bound to be our fault.'

'I'm game for the odd diatribe,' Maxwell told him, 'even at . . .' he checked his watch, 'nearly one in the morning. But what is your point? That the police won't be very helpful?'

'I knew you weren't listening to the clichés when we got here.' Smith turned to peer down into the shadows of the garden, where the nettles jostled each other to reach the sky.

'They ask the questions; they don't answer them. You don't want to end up as a suspect, do you?'

'Come on!'

'I'm serious, Max,' Smith said. 'When a wife dies, the husband's suspected. And vice versa. But when a kid dies . . .'

'The father,' Maxwell said.

'Yes, I should think Mr Hyde's been through the mill a tad recently. But what about the kid's teachers?'

Maxwell looked at him. 'I had no idea you were that paranoid in the English Department.'

'Paranoia, dear boy,' Smith edged his way across the floor, 'is in the eye of the beholder. Stay away from the filth, Maxie. Or they'll have you. Anyway,' he called back from the dark of the landing, 'we can bypass the buggers.'

'Oh?' Maxwell crossed the floor too. 'How?'

'Does the name Jim Astley mean anything to you?'

'Not a lot. Why?'

'We were at university together.'

'Oh, yes,' sneered Maxwell. 'Reading. Bad luck.'

'Of course, he was on a longer course than me.'

'Joined-up writing?'

'Medicine. He's the local police surgeon, here in Leighford.'

There was a silence as Smith reached the bottom of the stairs. He counted to three before he heard it, deep, growling.

'You absolute bastard!'

'"Don't you just love being in control?"' Smith chuckled.

It had been a long time since the Red House had heard laughter. But as they left it, neither of them cared to look back.

'Give you a lift, Max?' Smith fumbled for his keys.

'No, thanks,' Maxwell said, 'I promised the History Department I wouldn't.'

'Wouldn't what?'

'Squander my young life by placing it so utterly recklessly in your incompetent hands.'

'Well, then,' Smith's Bette Davis was a gem, 'on yer bike!'

* * *

Two men, the report said. At the Red House. Spotted by Car Polka Bravo Nina at one thirteen. One drove away in a Capri with a bit of wellie under the bonnet. The other got on to a bike. Polka Bravo Nina hadn't been able to get close enough to identify either man, but suspect on bike wore hat and long college-type scarf.

The file lay buried in somebody's in-tray in the Tottingleigh incident room.

Whoever it was, that somebody was not Detective Inspector Johnson.

CHAPTER 6

Jim Astley couldn't have told you, if you'd asked, how he'd got into the morbid anatomy business. There was a time, he vaguely remembered, when he saw himself as a Lister or a Barnard and his mother used to make jokes about her son, the brain surgeon. Somewhere along the line, he'd lost all that and the how and the why of people's deaths came to mean more to him. Not that many others could see it. Walking hand in hand with tragedy was not something most people did out of choice. Unless they were pathologists; or policemen; or firemen. Or two teachers, longish in the tooth, standing in the low, beamed kitchen of Astley's home.

'You've done all right for yourself, then, Jim.' Smith nodded, accepting the tea with alacrity. A Siberian wind had killed the Indian summer and leaves were eddying in tight little circles across the patio.

'It's a living,' Astley said.

'I always warned you I'd drop in one of these days.' Smith beamed, hoping it didn't all sound too artificial.

'Yes,' Astley smiled. 'A bit like rabies, really. I never thought it'd actually happen to me. Sugar, Mr Maxwell?'

'Max,' the Head of Sixth Form said. 'Call me Max. Everybody does.' He accepted Astley's bowl.

'Really?' the police surgeon said. His children had gone to private school. He'd never heard of Maxwell at all.

'How's Marjorie?' Smith lolled back on the Windsor chair, his right arm dangling almost to the block floor.

Astley looked at his watch. 'Filling the bottle bank with her empties. Look, Geoffrey, I don't want to seem inhospitable. But . . .'

'But,' Smith looked like a little boy who'd been caught scrumping apples, 'apart from one Scotch last Christmas and a casual "What ho" in the High Street, you and I haven't exchanged half a dozen words in thirty years; yes, I know.'

'You always did have a way with words,' Astley smiled. 'I hope I haven't been overly offensive, but what the buggery do you two want?'

'Well . . .'

'Cause of death,' Maxwell saw his opening. 'Jenny Hyde's, that is . . .'

Only Astley's clock answered, and all it said was 'tick, tock'.

The police surgeon looked at them both. Then he ran both his hands down his goatee and waded into Maxwell. 'I presume,' he said, 'that you have ethics in your profession?'

'We do.' Maxwell's eyes burned back into Astley's.

'And that if I wanted to see a confidential file on some child, you'd tell me where to stick it.'

'We don't have confidential files,' Maxwell pointed out. 'This is John Major's England, Dr Astley. The People's Charter. The classless society. You may have heard of the Freedom of Information Act. We are obliged to do something about it.'

'So sensitive information is available to everybody, is it?'

'I didn't say that.'

'You implied it.'

'Boys, boys,' Smith threw up his hands, 'I think you'll find we're on the same side.'

'Are we?' Astley asked, raising an eyebrow. 'I wonder.'

The clock again made answer and Astley's red setter whined in its dreaming sleep and turned over in its basket.

'Look,' Maxwell was more conciliatory now, 'Dr Astley, you face this all the time in your line. Sudden, violent death. We don't. We're on the edge of something here. Something, when you come right down to it, so appalling it doesn't bear thinking about. But we are part of it. Nobody asked us if we wanted to be. It just happened that way. We're part of it, but we're outside it. It's like . . . like watching something from a train. You see it happening, but you can't get to it. It's a moment; then it's gone. Jenny Hyde was one of my girls. I just . . . well, I just feel responsible, that's all.'

Astley looked at them both, the steady, grey eyes of Peter Maxwell, the sallow, balding features of Geoffrey Smith. Then he sighed and leaned back. 'The conversation that is about to take place never happened. Is that clear? I'm putting my job on the line for you two and I'm damned if I know why. If this ever gets out . . .'

'It won't,' Maxwell was quick to assure him.

Astley nodded. Every instinct he had made him doubt what he was about to do, but he did it anyway. 'What do you want to know?'

'Everything.' Maxwell leaned forward, both elbows on the table.

The doctor began the litany. 'I was called at seven thirty. I'd been fishing all day but the buggers stopped biting during the afternoon. I confess I'd dropped off. Ever carried one of these?' He tapped the mobile phone lying on the table.

The teachers shook their heads.

'Worst bloody invention known to man. It must have been . . . ooh, nearly twenty minutes before I got to the scene of the crime.'

'The Red House?' Maxwell checked.

'I believe some people call it that. A less than noble pile behind the Shingle, on the way to Leighford Cross.'

'Front bedroom?' Maxwell said.

Astley was taken aback for a moment. 'How did you know that?' he asked.

'I didn't,' Maxwell told him. 'I'm guessing.'

'There was a stain on the floor,' Smith explained. 'Looked as if a mattress or something had been there.'

'That's right,' Astley said. 'There was.' Something inside him was screaming at him to stop. Not to say any more. But somehow, it was too late for all that. 'How did you know about it?'

'We've been there,' Smith told him. 'Sleuthing.'

'She was strangled?' Maxwell was having to make all the relevant running.

'Yes. With a ligature. Probably a pair of tights.'

'How do you know?'

Astley moved his chair a little away from the table so that it scraped on the floor. The dog gave a little whimper and went back to sleep. That she'd been strangled? Because there were all the classic signs. 'Her lips and ears were blue, there was a little froth around her mouth, although most of that had been washed away by the rain. The room where she died is open to the sky at that point. Her nails had changed colour. In cases like this the actual cause of death is asphyxia due to constriction of the neck.'

'Jesus,' Smith whispered.

'And how do you know it was tights?' Maxwell batted aside the revulsion he knew Smith felt too. Somehow he sensed there wasn't time. He needed to know more; to know all.

'The knot marks,' Astley explained. 'Usual groove around the neck and the mottling above it — petechiae, as we say. The bruising was more severe to the left of the thyroid cartilage — the Adam's apple to you boys.'

'But the tights weren't left there?'

'No. Whoever the murderer was, he untied the ligature and took it with him.'

'So they could have been Jenny's tights?' Smith proffered.

Astley shrugged. 'They could have been,' he said.

'Did she put up a fight?'

'Difficult to say. You can certainly forget the nonsense about debris under the fingernails and that all the police have to do is find a guy with scratches on his cheek.'

'It doesn't work like that?' Maxwell asked.

'Oh, it can,' Astley told him, 'but not in this case.'

'So what do you conclude?'

The doctor stirred his tea with a lazy, thoughtful motion. 'This is all off the record, of course,' he murmured.

'Absolutely.' Maxwell crossed his heart and put his finger to his temple, Boy Scout style.

'Well, the post-mortem was interesting.'

'Why?'

'Normally in strangulation, even strangulation with a ligature, I'd expect the hyoid to be snapped. Especially in a young person.'

'And it wasn't?'

'No. Plenty of damage to the thyroid and the cricoid, but that you would expect.'

Maxwell looked at Smith. 'Which means?'

'Which means that, if there were obvious signs of it, I'd say Jenny put up a terrific struggle.'

'But you just said . . .'

'That there weren't obvious signs, quite.'

'So?'

'So the other possibility is that her attacker wasn't very strong.'

'Do the police have anybody in the frame?' Smith asked.

Astley shrugged. 'You'd have to ask Henry Hall that one,' he said, 'and I don't somehow think you'd get much of an answer.'

'Was she sexually assaulted?' Maxwell asked.

'Yes and no.' Jim Astley could be as cryptic as the next man when the mood took him.

'By which you mean?' Maxwell prompted him again.

The doctor got up and crossed to find his pipe, 'When I got there, she was lying on her back. If I remember rightly, her arms were above her head, almost as though they'd been held there, out of the way.' He shut his eyes to recall it specifically. 'Fists clenched. Her blouse and bra had been torn open. It was a front-fastening job, so there was no excessive strength needed there and there was no need to fumble behind her. She had one leg — her left, I think — bent out to the side. Her skirt was pulled up around her waist, but — and this is where it gets interesting . . .' He began to cram the dark brown mixture into his pipe bowl, savouring the moment, savouring his expertise. 'Her knickers were still there.'

'So?' Temporarily at least, Maxwell was lost.

'No obvious signs of sexual interference. The post-mortem confirmed it. No semen traces anywhere. Vagina. Anus. Ears. All clear.'

'So . . .' Maxwell hadn't caught him up yet.

'So,' Astley's face blurred for a moment behind the smoke and he puffed on the stem, 'a number of possibilities. We could be looking for a pervert. Strangulation is very common in cases of rape.'

'But you said . . .'

'There was no rape. Right. So perhaps our friend was interrupted.'

'By this tramp . . . what was his name?'

'Guthrie,' Smith remembered, 'Dan Guthrie.'

'Right.' Maxwell clicked his fingers. 'Or?'

'Or,' Astley took the reins again, 'when it came to it, he wasn't able to perform. That's quite common too. Of course, if he ejaculated with his trousers on, we'd have nothing to work on.'

'Ah, genetic fingerprinting,' Smith beamed.

'Exactly.' Astley joined the pair at the table again. 'But for that to work, you need a specimen — blood, semen, sweat, something. We had nothing.'

'Wasn't it wet?' Maxwell seemed to remember. 'On that Friday?'

'By the time they found her, yes. But I estimated the time of death at between three and five.'

'Broad daylight?'

'Yes,' Astley nodded. 'It was fine until six or seven. You're thinking about footprints?'

It was Maxwell's turn to nod.

'I don't know what the scenes of crime lads got,' Astley said. 'I think they picked up a few partial prints on door frames and so on. But you've got to remember how many people must have used that place over the years. Kids. Winos. Courting couples. Short of fingerprinting the entire town . . .'

'That's been done, hasn't it?' Smith asked.

'Once or twice, yes,' Astley told him, 'but it's an unusual step and you can't force people. Anyway, who's to say our man lives in Leighford?'

'You're sure it's a man?' Maxwell asked.

Astley looked at him. 'Ninety-five per cent,' he said. 'Statistically, women don't kill at close quarters. Not by strangulation. They poison. They shoot. Lizzie Borden chopped. But they don't strangle.'

'I thought Lizzie Borden got off,' Smith said.

'Yes,' Maxwell smiled, 'like you and I get off buses, but she did it all the same. Seen the photographs? She was a chunky little lady. Biceps like wardrobes.'

'Look,' Astley brought them back to modern crimes, 'let me say this again. This conversation never took place. You know as much as I do now about the death of little Jenny Hyde. Though, frankly, if the law isn't getting anywhere, I don't really see . . .'

'Well,' Maxwell stood up and extended a hand, 'thank you, doctor, for your candour.'

'We must do this again sometime.' Smith shook his hand too.

'Yes,' Astley growled, 'in another lifetime, preferably.' He saw them to the door. 'My advice,' he said, 'would be to leave well alone.'

'We can't do that,' Maxwell said. 'There are too many unanswered questions.'

'Yes, there are,' Astley nodded, chewing his pipe, 'but you might not like the answers very much.'

On the way to Smith's car, Maxwell opened the gate. 'I'm surprised,' he said.

'What about?' Smith asked.

'That the good doctor confided so readily. In fact, I'm surprised he confided at all.'

'I'm not,' Smith chuckled. 'I knew he couldn't resist showing off. He always was an arrogant bastard. Couldn't pass up the chance to blind us with science. You know, he actually volunteered to take part in University Challenge?'

'No.' Maxwell held his fingers upright in the sign of the cross. 'Did you win? Your team?'

'Christ, no. We were against Gonville and Caius. You're bikeless, Maxie,' Smith observed. 'I'll run you home.'

'Fine,' beamed Maxwell. 'As long as we stick to running.'

'I did drive you here,' Smith reminded him.

'Did you?' Maxwell asked. 'I was shitting myself at the time and signally failed to notice.'

'Get in!' Smith pushed his Old Contemptible into the car.

And the tyres screamed into the night.

* * *

In Scotland they call them janitors. In some parts of London, school keepers. To most of us, they are caretakers. But whatever they call them, they are the backbone of a school. The governors don't run it; the Headmaster doesn't; not even the school secretary. The caretaker does. Cross him and you're buggered. There'll come a day when your classroom's freezing, when you can't unlock your office door, when you're desperate for someone to put the chairs out for an evening meeting. That day, you'll thank your God for the caretaker.

At Leighford High that man's name was Martin. Those he reckoned called him Bob, after the canine tablets. The kids called him, out of earshot, Doc, after the boots. Only Maxwell called him Betty after 'all my eye of a yarn and,' but then, Maxwell was a law unto himself anyway. Bob Martin wore a blue boiler suit most of the time and when he made his rounds late at night, walked with a vicious-looking mongrel on a short leash. It didn't exactly deter burglars. They still hit the school on average three times a year looking for the petty cash from the tuck shop or any piece of computer hardware that wasn't nailed down. He looked as if he'd never owned any hair and he blinked slowly while chewing a seemingly endless piece of gum.

He only ever bothered people when he wanted to complain. And he was bothering Peter Maxwell at nine o'clock the next morning.

'Hello, Betty.' Maxwell was facing the third day of the new term. It had been a long week.

'I was turfin' out them old lockers,' Martin said, never one to stand on ceremony, 'and I found this.'

Maxwell squinted at the man framed by his office door. 'What is it?' he had to ask.

'Well,' Martin coughed with the volume and precision of a thirty-a-day man, 'in my day we called 'em nodders or French letters. They seem to 'ave invented a new name for 'em now — condoms.'

Gingerly, Maxwell took the packet, eternally grateful that it didn't seem to have been opened. 'Ah, so it's that Condom Moment?' Betty Martin wasn't smiling. 'And this was in a locker?'

'Be'ind, to be precise,' Martin told him, 'along wi' this.'

'This' was an exercise book, blue, with a marked crease down the centre, as though it had been wedged somewhere tight for some time.

'Bin it,' Maxwell shrugged.

'I'm not sure that's such a good idea,' Martin said and threw the book on to Maxwell's desk. 'Not when you read the name on the front. You 'avin assembly again this mornin'?'

'No, thanks, Betty,' Maxwell frowned. 'Thursday this term.'

'Just as long as I know.' Martin was clumping away down the corridor. 'Chairs don't get put out by their bloody selves, you know.'

'Indeed not,' but Maxwell wasn't thinking about chairs. Or who put them out. He was reading the name on the book's cover. The name Jenny Hyde.

* * *

Sylvia Matthews, when she wasn't sorting out other people's period pains and whizzing the odd dislocation in PE lessons down to the Casualty Department at Leighford General, was an addict of those nasty little booklets that purport to carry logic puzzles. Not the kind of logic that Sherlock Holmes was addicted to, but the sort of methodical reasoning where you put crosses in boxes to eliminate the obvious. And she was cerebellum-deep in one of these when her door bell rang.

'Max?' She saw his distorted profile in her door-lens. But he wasn't carrying flowers this time, not even her own. She opened the door to him. 'The start of term was three days ago. Max, we've had our annual nosh,' she said. 'What's the matter?'

'Girls,' said Max, brushing past her with the air of a man whose mind was elsewhere. 'Tell me about girls,' and he threw himself down uninvited on Sylvia's settee.

'Well,' she widened her eyes, 'it depends on which version you want. If it's the Biblical one, they came after boys. An afterthought made from Adam's spare rib. If it's the biological one . . .'

He screwed up his face at her. 'You too saw the Spencer Tracy last Sunday,' he nodded.

'The what?'

'*Inherit the Wind* — a rattling good yarn based on the "monkey trial" in Tennessee in the '30s. Spencer Tracy was Clarence Darrow . . .'

'Max,' she sat opposite him, 'what are you talking about?'

He ran his hands through the shock of barbed wire hair. 'Buggered if I know, Sylv,' he said. 'Let me be more specific. Don't tell me about girls. Tell me about girls and their diaries.'

'Ah.' She raised an eyebrow. 'That's something else entirely.'

'Is it?'

'I kept one. Didn't you?'

'No time,' he shrugged. 'Not when you're making dens out of grass and rushing around the streets carving a Z for

Zorro on people's walls with your plastic rapier. Boys don't have time.'

'Well, there you are.' Sylvia sat back. 'It's precisely because boys don't have the time — or inclination — that we girls confide things in our diaries.'

'I last read psychology nearly thirty years ago, Sylv,' he apologised. 'I think you'll have to pass that one by me again.'

She looked at him. 'A crusty old bachelor like you wouldn't notice,' she observed, 'but girls develop earlier than boys. Hormones and so on.'

'With you so far, Matron mine,' he nodded.

'They have crushes on people while boys are still kicking footballs or doing whatever Zorro did — whoever he is.'

Maxwell sucked in his breath. 'That was barbed, Nursie,' he said, shaking his head. 'Barbed.'

'Now, a love-struck young girl can confide in her mother — if her mother is the understanding sort. But so often she's not, so she doesn't — if you follow me.'

Maxwell nodded.

'She can confide in her friends — but there's a problem there. What if her friends laugh at her? Worse, what if they're love-struck over the same boy?'

'It's a bitch.' Maxwell saw the dilemma.

'So, she confides to her diary. The one thing that won't laugh or answer back. That's no rival. No threat. That's where you'll find the secrets of her heart. Mine had a lock on it.'

'Your heart?'

She threw a cushion at him. 'My diary, idiot!'

'Because your mother didn't understand?'

'I don't know.' Sylvia shrugged. 'I never told her. I suppose I thought she wouldn't. That's the other thing, of course. When you're thirteen, you tend to misunderstand people yourself. Then, my mother seemed positively ancient. I couldn't believe she'd ever been through anything like this herself.'

'What about when you're seventeen?' Maxwell asked her.

'Seventeen?' Sylvia sighed, remembering. 'No, I was too busy myself by then.'

'Fighting them off, eh, Sylv?'

She attempted a laugh, but it didn't come off. 'That's right. And there were A levels and my dad died that year. No, there didn't seem a place for "Dear Diary" in all that. I'd just grown up, I suppose.'

'Hmmm.' Maxwell chewed his lip. 'Maybe Jenny Hyde hadn't.'

'Jenny?' Sylvia sat up. 'What's this got to do with Jenny?'

'Betty Martin found her diary today.'

'Her diary?'

'Back of some lockers.'

'Where is it? Have you got it?'

'No,' Maxwell told her. 'It's at home.'

'Did you read it?'

'Of course.'

'Well, good God, Max, don't sit there like some bloody Buddha. What did it say?'

'I don't know where to start, really. Your diary — what did it look like?'

'Mine? Why are we talking about mine when you've got Jenny's?'

He lapsed into his best *Dragnet*, long before Sylvia Matthews' time. 'We'll ask the questions, ma'am.'

'Oh, all right,' she humoured him. 'I told you. It had a lock.'

'Sort of purpose-built, then?'

'Yes. I bought it in Boots. It had a red leatherette cover and gilt clasps. It'll probably turn up on *Antiques Roadshow* one of these days.'

'And you never used an exercise book?'

'For personal, bottom-of-my-soul secrets? I should say not.'

'Why not?' he harried her.

'Because it might be found,' she told him. 'Read by Tom, Dick or Harry.'

Maxwell smiled broadly, his tongue appearing in the gap between his front teeth. 'Sylvia Matthews, I love you,' he said.

Her smile vanished. For a second, she stared at him, willing the moment to be different. Maxwell sensed it too and his smile changed, to one of regret. To one that said, 'Never mind.'

'In my experience as an historian,' he said, 'diaries are written for two purposes. There's the sort pretentious people write purely for publication purposes. Oscar Wilde knew that. Sadly, he didn't know much else.'

'I don't follow.'

'There's a kind of arrogance,' Maxwell said, leaning back, 'in Evelyn, Pepys, even Queen Anne, stupid, rheumy, gout-ridden old cow that she was, that makes some people say, "Listen to this, everybody. This is worth hearing. Or reading. Because I wrote it."'

'Are you saying that Jenny's diary . . .'

'Was written in the knowledge — or at least the hope — that somebody would find it, yes.'

'But . . .'

Maxwell's mind was racing ahead. 'She didn't leave it lying about at home. She left it at school. Why?'

'I don't know,' Sylvia admitted.

'Neither do I. Except . . .'

'What?'

You always knew when a new idea had filtered into Peter Maxwell's mind. He frowned and his eyes went distant, cold. 'Except I think her death had something to do with . . . school.'

'With school?' Sylvia took time to digest it. 'What?'

Maxwell had anticipated the question and was already shaking his head. 'Buggered if I know, Nursie,' he muttered.

'You haven't told me what was in the diary,' she reminded him.

'Why wasn't it in her locker?' He was asking himself really.

'Too obvious?' she suggested. 'Max, you've got to tell me what the diary said.'

He looked at her. 'Not yet,' and he was on his feet, making for the door.

'Peter Maxwell, you're a bastard,' she scolded him.

'Yes,' he concurred, 'and I'm a mean one as well.'

'At least,' she said, 'you must take it to the police.'

He stopped at the door. 'Must I?' he asked her.

'Of course.' She frowned, suddenly frightened. 'Max. Of course. You must.'

But he couldn't hear her as he reached the bottom of the stairs.

'Max. You must.'

He'd wanted to ask her something else, he realised, but he was in the saddle of White Surrey now, pedalling up Overdale Hill like a thing possessed. He never noticed these things himself, but perhaps an observant female like Sylvia Matthews would.

He wanted to know if, at the end of a hot July, it was likely that Jenny Hyde had worn tights.

CHAPTER 7

Metternich the cat circled Maxwell's lap, head down, tail up, searching in that inscrutable feline way for the optimum position to sleep. Each time he turned, his claws raked Maxwell's trousers and sank to the skin.

'I know what this is all about, Count,' Maxwell murmured, lifting the book to accommodate the animal, 'it's revenge, isn't it? Revenge for the fact that I had you bricked. Well, I'm sorry. But I couldn't have you over-populating the neighbourhood, could I?'

Metternich looked at his master, utterly unconvinced.

'People would be endlessly bringing me baskets full of kittens with black and white markings saying, "Yours, I believe." And anyway, you'd make the whole place smell like a knacker's yard.' He grimaced and twirled the cat's tail so that it had to change position. 'Thank you, Count,' he said, 'but there can be few less entrancing sights in the whole world than a close-up of a cat's bum. Will you sit down?'

All in his own good time, the animal did and proceeded to doze on the Great Man's knees. Maxwell was back where he'd started, all those years ago, at Jesus College, Cambridge; back where he was happiest, really, handling original documents. But these documents were different. They were among the last recorded memories of a dead girl. Nothing odd about that — many historical records could be described in that way. But these were the collected works of Jennifer Antonia Hyde and she'd been murdered. He recognised the distinctive loops she gave her Ts and noted how she still continued that silly habit of making flowers of the dots of her 'i's. Nice to have the time, he thought. Then again, the whole thing seemed rushed, hurried, cobbled together without patience or reflection. Inevitable, he supposed, in a seventeen-year-old who had not yet learnt the value of wisdom or known the immensity of silence. Maxwell knew it, but he doubted if he'd ever truly be wise.

He began to note mentally the jumble of events that lay scattered over the pages. *'Quarrel with Tim.' 'How can he be such a bastard?' 'Went to K's.' 'He's lovely.' 'K told me he loved me.' 'What shall I do about P? Why do I always fancy the married ones?'*

He found himself chuckling as he reached the bottom of the page. *'Mad Max had a go at me today over deadlines. He's such a shit.'*

'Thanks, Jenny,' the Head of Sixth Form murmured. 'Glad we're on the same side.'

* * *

It had to be said that Anne Spencer wasn't Peter Maxwell's favourite sixth-former. There was something in the way she carried her head, wore her hair, affected a viceregal iciness that froze blood. She was sitting the next day in the common room, that sprawl of vandalised furniture and unwashed cups that was home to the sixth form. A couple of the Year 13 hardmen loafed with her, skiving, had Maxwell had time to check the register, from private study in the library. He hooked a finger at her and beckoned. She rolled her eyes heavenward in an open gesture of contempt that Max would have felled her for once. Not now. It wasn't worth the blood pressure. He motioned her into his office, the ex-classroom that gave him space to pace, room to boom, whatever tactic he needed to use on whoever was in The Chair.

But he didn't offer her Old Sparky, the grim, upright job he reserved for troublemakers. Instead he offered her the low, mock-leather number for those in trouble. It's doubtful if the Anne Spencers of this world recognised the difference. And if they did, they weren't letting on.

'Well, Anne.' Maxwell sat opposite her, the low coffee table between them. 'Time we had a little chat, I think.'

'What about?' She pouted her dark lips at him and tilted her head to one side, which gave him the distinct message that she was doing him a favour by talking to him at all.

'About Jenny,' he said softly.

For a moment her eyes flickered, then she was outstaring him again. 'What about her?' she challenged him.

'It must have been a terrible blow for you,' Maxwell said. 'You being her best friend.'

'Yes,' her voice was iron-hard. 'Yes, it was.'

'Have the police talked to you?'

She nodded. 'They came to the house,' she told him, 'a couple of days after they found her.'

'Anne,' Maxwell leaned over his knees, looking as deep as he dared into her eyes, 'Jenny ran away, didn't she?'

Anne shrugged; enigmatic; non-committal. 'Did she?'

It only took so long for Peter Maxwell's hackles to rise. He could feel them now, wherever men keep their hackles. It started as a rush in the chest, a crawling along the nape of the neck, a vibration up the scalp. But he held it all in check. 'I think you know she did,' he said. 'Didn't the police ask you about it?'

'They may have done.'

He chuckled and she sensed the irony of it. 'Look, it was weeks ago, right?

'I don't remember.'

'Your best friend is killed, strangled to death six weeks ago and you don't remember?' When the moment came, Maxwell could be deadly.

'Yeah, all right.' Anne was rattled, her voice loud, her colour high. She'd uncoiled her nubile body and was toe-to-toe with Maxwell. Or she would have been, if the coffee table hadn't been in the way. 'All right. I know she's dead. That's bloody obvious. But I don't know nothing about why, all right? I don't want to get involved.'

'But you are involved, Anne.' Maxwell was calmness itself. 'Whether you like it or not. Because Jenny told her parents she was with you in the last week of last term.'

'Well, she's a bloody liar, then . . . isn't she?' Anne wasn't just loud now; she was shouting, her eyes wild. 'Keep out of my bloody life, you old bastard!'

And she was gone, crashing out of the office, barging aside the Year 12 couple looking for the right room for Business Studies. There was a time when Maxwell would have gone after her, worrying, searching. He'd have found her distraught in Nursie's arms or curled up in a loo somewhere, lips quivering too much to light the calming fag. Now, he'd let her go her own way. Find her own salvation. In the event, Alison Miller put her head around the door.

'Is everything all right, Max?' she asked. She'd never heard anyone call Maxwell a bastard before. Not to his face anyway. And certainly not a kid.

'I'm losing it, Alison,' Maxwell sighed, crossing to his desk.

She came in and closed the door. 'What did you expect?' she asked him. 'From Anne Spencer of all people. I was always amazed the Hydes let Jenny mix with her. She was always in trouble in the main school. I tried to teach her Biology once . . .'

'I remember that day,' Maxwell chuckled. He looked at his Number Two. Like some fifteenth-century damsel, with the high waistband to accentuate her fecundity. 'How are you, Alison?' he asked. 'Did you have a good summer?'

She smiled so that her teeth showed, a rare phenomenon for sad little Alison Miller. It was a standing joke between them, being too busy in the first days of the academic year to have time for the pleasantries of life.

'No,' she said and her pale face crumpled like paper. She drove her head into Maxwell's chest and he folded his arms around it, burying his face into her frizzy dark hair. As she sobbed painfully, uncontrollably, he gingerly extended his right leg and made sure the door was closed.

'What's the matter?' he whispered and the sound of it carried her back. Back to the childhood she'd left behind, the childhood she'd passed to her own children. But Alison couldn't tell him. Not in any detail. All she would say, could say, was her husband's name, over and over again — 'Keith. Keith.'

* * *

Mrs B. was there as usual by quarter-past four, wrapped in her regulation contract maroon overall, mop and duster at the ready. She peered around Maxwell's door and he prayed again, as he did every day, that she wouldn't actually say, 'Can I do you now, sir?' But Mrs B. — Maxwell didn't have a clue what the woman's name was — didn't go back as far as ITMA, so he really needn't have worried.

'Hello, Mr Maxwell,' she called, 'it's only me.' Sadly, Mrs B. did go back as far as Harry Enfield. 'Did you have a nice holiday? Ain't it a bleedin' shame about that girl? She was raped, you know. Well, it's the times, ain't it? What can you expect?'

Maxwell blinked smilingly. But he was a past master at Mrs B.'s barrages and he turned to answer her steadily. 'Yes, thanks. Yes, it is — a bleedin' shame. I know. Yes, I suppose it is. I don't know.' He mentally ran through the number of rhetorical questions on his fingers. Yes, he thought he'd covered them all.

''Course,' Mrs B. moved his jacket so that her duster could reach the parts other cleaners couldn't, 'you know who done it, don't you?'

'No.' Maxwell was all ears. Chars with verbal diarrhoea and hearts of gold might yet solve the mysteries of the universe. 'Who?'

'That bleedin' tramp, that Guthrum.'

Now Maxwell knew that Guthrum was a Danish king of Mercia defeated by Alfred at Edington, but he guessed that

Mrs B.'s scholarly grasp of the Dark Ages was less than his own and he let it go.

'Excuse me.' The promising conversation was interrupted by a big-shouldered intruder who filled the doorway. 'Could you leave us? I'd like a private word with Mr Maxwell.'

'Well, pardon me,' snorted Mrs B., never a respecter of persons, and she clattered out into the corridor with the maximum of fuss, crooning loudly, 'The minute I walked in the joint, boom, boom . . .' and waggled her overalled bum at the visitor.

'Esmerelda.' Maxwell launched into his Charles Laughton impression, twisting his lips and nose and dragging his left leg. The woman before him didn't react. Didn't move. Her face remained cold. Impassive. 'Oh.' Maxwell straightened up. Even then he was barely level with her nose. 'Not a social call, then, Deirdre?'

Deirdre Lessing had invented power-dressing. She swept past the Head of Sixth Form and sat down, uninvited. 'It's about Anne Spencer,' she said.

Maxwell looked at the pearl-grey suit, the padded shoulders, the upswept hair. Was she really, he wondered again, an ash-blonde? Rumour had it that there were several men along the south coast who could answer that one and none of them was her hairdresser. And Mr Lessing? Rumour had it that he had died of shame years ago, what with his wife wearing the pants and removing everybody else's. But that was only speculation.

'Anne Spencer.' Maxwell sat opposite her. 'You do surprise me.'

'Do I, Max?' Her grey eyes burned into his, her voice like a razor's edge. 'Let's be quite clear on this, shall we? You've always resented me, haven't you?'

Maxwell smiled. 'Resentment is too strong for it, Deirdre,' he said.

She pursed her lips. 'What word did you have in mind?'

He scanned his mind and his bookshelves for an answer. 'Ooh, I don't know,' he said, stroking his chin. 'Indifference, perhaps.'

For a moment it seemed as though Deirdre Lessing was going to hit Peter Maxwell. In the event, she crossed her formidable thighs and took several deep breaths, any one of them blouse-threatening. 'I *am* Senior Mistress,' she reminded him.

'Indeed.' Maxwell's smile could be as inscrutable as a Ming Emperor's when he wanted it to be. 'Whose?' was the question that sprang to mind, but he was too much of a gentleman to ask it. He remembered suddenly that his old oppo Geoffrey Smith referred to the lady as 'The Senior Mattress' and prophesied, when he'd had a few, that she was likely to be buried in a Y-shaped coffin.

'I am in charge of girls' welfare,' Deirdre went on, mercifully ignorant of the depth of Maxwell's scorn. 'Anne Spencer came to me very upset.'

'Yes,' said Maxwell. 'That's how she left me.'

'Well, can you wonder at it?' Deirdre asked.

'Look, Deirdre.' Maxwell leaned across to her. 'One of my sixth form — one of your girls, come to that — was murdered a few weeks ago. Nobody seems to give a tinker's damn about that.'

'Rubbish, Max,' she snorted. 'We all do. You're taking this far too personally. Jenny Hyde was, as you say, one of my girls too. She belonged to all of us. You can't go around bullying people. What do you hope to achieve?'

'Answers,' he told her.

'But the police . . .'

'Deirdre, Deirdre.' He found himself chuckling at her naivety. 'Did I ever tell you I taught in Bermondsey?'

'No,' she confessed, 'you never did.'

'Well, it's not something I bandy about generally, but I did.'

'So?'

'So until I went there, I believed in the police. Something to do with asking the time and trusting the boys in blue and hearing dear old Jack Warner reminding me to look after dear old mum and so on.'

'And Bermondsey changed all that?'

Irrevocably,' Maxwell said. 'Because I met parents — honest, hardworking parents — who had information on the police. I saw it myself one night. There was an old girl loitering in a doorway. I was on my way home from one of those interminable moderation meetings we used to have in those days. All right, the old girl was giving the law a hard time. She was drunk. She was shouting, cursing them up hill and down dale. Then they started hitting her. One of them kept thumping her in the stomach until she went down.'

'What did you do?' Deirdre asked.

'Got off my bike and went up to them.'

'And?'

'And — if I remember the words aright — the constable told me to piss off. It was, he said, none of my effing business. They bundled the old girl into a Maria.'

'Disgraceful!'

'I've never quite felt the same about the upholders of the law since then.'

'That was a one-off incident, Max.' Deirdre had rationalised it. 'One division of one police force. You can't generalise and you don't know what sort of provocation . . .'

'I know, I know.' He raised his hands in agreement. 'But people do generalise, Deirdre, you know that. Rightly or wrongly, dear old Jack Warner became Mr Nasty Guy. Nobody talks to the police because they don't trust them. Perhaps, I thought, perhaps Anne Spencer wouldn't have talked to them. Just because they're the police. And perhaps, I thought, just perhaps, she might talk to me.'

'Well, you were wrong,' Deirdre told him. 'Anne doesn't think you have a right to probe and neither do I.'

'Good God, Deirdre, we only exchanged half a dozen words. I think Anne knows something. Something she hasn't told the police. Something she hasn't told anyone.'

Deirdre Lessing stood up. 'I think you're clutching at straws, Max. This isn't an Agatha Christie, this is reality.'

Maxwell stood up with her. 'I'm not trying to be Jane Marple,' he told her. 'I'm fifty-two years old, Deirdre, and

I've never known someone I know be murdered before. Some people might shut their eyes. Shudder. Go back to sleep. Get on with their lives. I can't do that. I've got to be out there, pitching.'

She turned on her way to the door. 'Well, take my advice,' she told him coldly. 'Pitch somewhere else, because I've got a feeling about this business. I think you're going to end up in a lot of trouble, one way or another.'

And she left.

Peter Maxwell put his head around the door and looked down the corridor to where Mrs B. was raking the discarded cigarette ends out of the crack between the wall and the floor of the boys' loos. 'Who's your money on again?' he called.

'That Guthrum,' she said. ''E done it.'

Maxwell reached for his hat and scarf.

'And if 'e didn't,' he heard Mrs B. bellow as he made for the stairs, 'she did.'

And he didn't have to see Mrs B. scowling out of the window at the briskly departing figure of the Senior Mistress, to know whom she meant.

* * *

Jack London, the journalist, had called them the People of the Abyss. That was ninety years ago, but they were still there. And over those ninety years, others had joined them — the Great Unwashed of the '60s, the New Age Travellers of the '80s. But these were groups who had an identity, a label. They made statements about themselves and however much retired colonels of Tunbridge Wells might thunder 'layabout' as a blanket term of contempt, they were deliberate choosers of the Alternative Society. Strangers to soap and work and law, they brought litter and fear to the heartlands of the rich and the inherited. Their smell was indescribable.

But it wasn't one of these that Peter Maxwell was looking for. It was raining as his feet crunched on the shingle that Sunday, the first weekend of the autumn term. He knew Dan

Guthrie by sight. Everybody did. He could have been anything between thirty and sixty, with a pepper-and-salt beard and straggly hair and a mouth full of brown, uneven teeth. Dan Guthrie made no statement about himself. Unless it was to ask in his thick Scots accent for the price o' a cuppa tea.

Margaret Thatcher's England seemed to have increased the number of Dan Guthries wandering the country's green and pleasant land. They haunted the university towns where the young and the hopeful still felt sorry for them and dug into their frozen grants to give them their small change. Brighton was their capital, on the coast at least. When dusk fell on the Sodom of the south, they crept from their holes, squatting in doorways and cadging fags, menacing tourists with their shaved heads and Doc Martens. The men were just as bad.

Somebody said the best time to find Dan Guthrie was Sunday morning as the bells told the faithful to get out the Morris Minors and head for church. They were on their way as Peter Maxwell swung out of the saddle of White Surrey in the dunes before the sand forced him to stop, and he watched them staggering into St Asaph's, their Sunday-best umbrellas aloft. The weather was a bitch as he left the shelter of the sand and tufts of coarse sea-pinks. He held on to his hat and put his shoulder to the wind, hearing his feet crunch and feeling his ankles at risk from the slippery stones.

Along the line of black, tar-coated seaweed that marked the upper reaches of the tide, he saw a huddled something in the lee of a breakwater — Dan Guthrie under canvas.

'Mr Guthrie?'

However old the down-and-out was, today he looked all of sixty, perhaps more. He squinted up at Maxwell under the tarpaulin sheet that was his only roof. 'Who are you, mister? Are you the police?'

Maxwell recognised the inflection of the word — Glasgow. He'd watched too many Taggarts for it to be anywhere else.

'I'm Peter Maxwell,' he said, extending a hand and kneeling on his heels. 'No, I'm not from the police.'

Guthrie hesitated for a moment, then reached out with a swarthy, leather-brown hand and caught Maxwell's. Powerful grip, the Head of Sixth Form thought. Powerful enough, perhaps, to strangle a girl of seventeen years and four months.

'Ye got the price of a cuppa tea?' It was the first question Dan Guthrie usually asked anybody. In fact it was the only question he usually asked. But when a crusty old gent comes up to you unannounced, when you're having a lie-in of a Sunday morning, there are more pressing things to ascertain.

'I think so.' Maxwell threw dignity to the wind and sat next to his man. 'Mind if I share your tent?'

'It's a free country,' Guthrie observed without much recourse to the facts.

Maxwell fumbled in his pocket, resisting the urge to throw up at the smell from Guthrie's mobile home. He pressed a warm, brass coin into the man's hand.

'Ta.' Guthrie pocketed it. Maxwell was vaguely surprised he hadn't bitten it first, just in case.

'I've been looking for you, Mr Guthrie,' he said.

'Oh, aye?'

'Do you mind if I call you Dan?'

Guthrie shrugged. 'That's up to you,' he said. 'What is it you want?'

'The murder.' Maxwell got straight to the point. 'Jenny Hyde.'

Guthrie looked out to sea where the grey breakers swelled under the autumn rain and a solitary herring gull circled over them. 'I dinna know nothing,' he said.

There were always rumours about men like Dan Guthrie. Anyone odd, anyone who didn't conform to society's norms, was always likely to generate speculation. Some said he was a millionaire who'd turned his back on his millions, exchanged the country seat for a doss house or a doorway. Others that he was a professor of languages who'd had a nervous breakdown and fled Oxford for the freedom of the roads. Suddenly, Maxwell knew that neither of these was true.

'That's more than I know,' he said. 'I was her Year Head, Mr Guthrie — Jenny's teacher. I want to know why she died.'

There was a long pause. Guthrie stared at the sea, silent, enigmatic. 'I told you,' he said. 'I dinna know nothing.'

Maxwell stared at the grey rollers too. 'I saw you on television,' he said.

'Television?' Guthrie turned to him, squinting out of one eye, the other almost closed.

'I don't suppose you'll have seen the programme,' Maxwell said. 'It's called *Crimewatch* — Nick Ross and Sue Cook are the presenters.'

'Oh aye.' Guthrie turned away again. 'I wouldnae speak to them.'

'Why not?' Maxwell asked.

Guthrie spat copiously at the already wet stones. 'No bloody point,' he said. 'They'll never catch him.'

'Who?' Maxwell was quick to ask. Was this a chink in the drop-out's armour?

Guthrie turned to him. 'Whoever killed the wee girl,' he said.

Why did Maxwell get the impression that he'd spent the last week talking to himself? All he got was an echo. Hollow. Empty. Hopeless. 'Well, when I say I saw you on television,' Maxwell corrected himself, 'that's not exactly true. Nick Ross mentioned you. Said you'd found the body . . .'

Guthrie blinked, glancing furtively left and right. 'Not me, mister,' he said, fixing his gaze out to sea again. It wasna me.'

'What were you doing at the Red House, Mr Guthrie?' Maxwell badgered his man now, sensing that he was rattled.

'It was raining,' the tramp told him. I needed somewhere to stay. Somewhere to go.'

'It's raining now,' Maxwell said. 'Yet here you are on an open beach.'

'I was in the neighbourhood.' Guthrie was louder now, standing his ground.

'And what did you see, Mr Guthrie? At the Red House? Did you see her? Jenny? Was she alive or dead? Come on, man! I need some answers!' Maxwell was screaming above the wind.

'A car!' Guthrie shouted back, his lips curled, the gaps visible in his teeth. 'I saw a car.'

Maxwell subsided. There was talk in the staff room of a car. That the police were looking for one. 'What sort of car?' he asked softly.

'Man, I dinna ken.' Guthrie shook his head. 'They're all the bloody same to me.'

Maxwell nodded. He knew how Guthrie felt. 'All right,' he said, 'what colour was it?'

'I dinna remember,' the man mumbled.

'Think!' Maxwell was sharp again, but he felt the drop-out flinch and he subsided. 'Think back, Mr Guthrie. It was a Friday, wasn't it?'

The days were all the same to Dan Guthrie. It didn't help. 'It was evening,' Maxwell prompted him. 'Raining.'

'Aye.' Guthrie's face twisted with the effort of remembering. 'It was dark. Fearful dark for July. Man, the skies opened. I was caught oot in it. I remember . . . I remember runnin' to the hoose. The Red Hoose. An . . .' He looked at Maxwell. 'Y'ken, it's been a while since I ate.'

'What?' Maxwell had lost the man's drift. 'Oh. Oh, right,' and he caught it again, hauling a tenner out of his wallet.

Guthrie snatched it and stuffed it away eagerly. Exactly where, Maxwell didn't care to enquire too closely.

'You were making for the Red House,' he reminded him.

'Aye, the Red Hoose. That's right. There was a car. Away doon the lane. I could see its lights in the rain. It was awful dark overhead.'

'What time was this?' Even as he said it, Maxwell realised the futility of the question. Men of Dan Guthrie's lifestyle don't exactly live by their Rolex. The tramp just shrugged at the irrelevance of it. He knew the seasons. He had a reasonable grasp of the months. Beyond that it was all just night and day. And they were all the same.

'It was a light-coloured car,' Guthrie said.

'Could you see the driver?' Maxwell asked.

The drop-out shook his head. 'I went in,' he said. 'That place has got more holes than a bloody sieve but I found a dry spot.'

'On the ground floor?'

'Aye. It stopped raining after a bit and I was going up to Barlichway to sleep.'

'Barlichway?'

'That vicar bloke. Young, he is. Not oot o' nappies. But he runs this sort o' shelter for us travellers. Ye can get a bowl o' soup and a crust o' bread too. Not a bad bloke. He's aboot the only one I wouldn't piss in his font, anyhow.'

That at least was gratifying.

'This bloody dog came in.'

'To the church.'

Guthrie looked oddly at him. 'To the Red Hoose,' he explained, as though to the village idiot.

'Mr Arnold's,' Maxwell nodded.

'Bloody thing came sniffin' round me. I kicked it. And it buggered off.'

'Then you left.'

'Aye. The bloody dog went upstairs.'

'Did the police talk to you, Mr Guthrie?'

The man spat again, if anything more volubly than before. 'Bastards,' he grunted.

'Who did you talk to?'

Guthrie shrugged. 'I dinna ken. They're all bastards. Always movin' ye on.'

'You don't like the police, do you, Mr Guthrie?' Maxwell smiled.

'If one was afire, I wouldn't piss on him to put it oot,' the tramp said. 'But . . .' and for the first time Maxwell saw him smile, 'they do a pretty mean cuppa tea, for coppers, I mean. And ye get to look up a woman policeman's skirt. So it's no' all bad.'

CHAPTER 8

He'd put it off once before. Five days ago. When it was raining. It was still raining. But he wouldn't put it off any longer. Maxwell had grabbed a bite at the Nag; something they'd chalked up on a board as Navarin of Lamb, but it could have been anything. Still, they drew a decent pint at the Nag and it gave him time to marshal his thoughts.

The truth of it was, of course, he told himself as he buried his upper lip in froth, that when it came to murder, Peter Maxwell was an amateur. Like most people, his knowledge of crime lay with the odd flight of fantasy. Well, then. How did it happen in English cosies, the thrillers he'd been brought up on? There was a body in the library or a death at the vicarage and some incredibly unlikely old fusspot, who was terminally ga-ga but had a mind like a laser, sorted it all out, muttering things like, 'Of course, how preternaturally stupid of me.' Joan Hickson was no doubt more immaculate as Jane Marple, but dear old Margaret Rutherford was infinitely more fun. All right. What about the Americans? The hard-boiled school of pulp? In all those, the hero had a seedy down-town office with badly fitting blinds and a perfectly dreadful taste in fedoras and trench coats. Some broad always came in, looking sultry or like Veronica Lake, whichever came first, and the rest was all knuckle sandwiches and lead poisoning. At least that was how they did it in the '50s and he found it so depressing, as an attempt at literature, he hadn't read anything hard-boiled since. Save it for eggs, he thought to himself.

And what about reality? Christie, Chandler, other exponents of the murder genre cheated. They dreamed up their crime, their victim, their killer, then worked back with lesser or greater degrees of logic. But real life wasn't like that. Real life was a seventeen-year-old girl lying dead in a wet, old house and no one knew who or why. What did he have? He lolled back in the snug while two old boys in the corner played shove ha'penny with a deadly accuracy and discussed Maggie Thatcher's memoirs.

Medically, he had a girl who'd been strangled, probably with a pair of tights. Hers? Somebody else's? She'd been assaulted, but she hadn't been assaulted. Why? Did someone want to make it look that way? To give the appearance of a maniac on the loose? Did that mean he wasn't a maniac? That his purpose was all the more rational, controlled? But who but a maniac kills a young girl anyway? And was there anything rational about murder? Whichever way he looked, he had nothing but questions. And hardly an answer in the world.

* * *

The Range Rover wasn't there. Were they out? A Sunday afternoon, in early September. Piddling down with rain. The season was all but over. There'd be the final flutter of the factory fortnight. The amusement arcades would thump out their glitzy resonance one more time before the whole place died again for the winter, and a plastic chimp covered in fur fabric would, for one more time, laugh electronically and promise the punters a prize every time. He swung out of White Surrey's saddle and wheeled it up the gravel path. His tyres hissed softly on the crazy paving and he leaned the bike against the wall, under the rain-beaten hanging basket which no one had tended since July.

He didn't know what to expect when he rang the bell. Perhaps they were out. He half hoped they were — that way he'd be able to stop the pounding in his chest. God, he felt dreadful. What do you say to a mother whose girl is dead? Left like a broken doll on a filthy mattress, naked to the world? Then he saw a ragged silhouette behind the frosted glass and it was too late to run.

'Mrs Hyde?' Maxwell tipped his hat. 'I wonder if I might have a word?'

She looked younger than Maxwell remembered her and, without make-up, ill and tired. There was no shine in her eyes, no warmth in her face.

'If it's not convenient . . .' Maxwell looked desperately for a way out.

'No,' she said, 'it's all right. You'd better come in. You're soaking.'

He was. He dripped in her hallway, uncomfortable, embarrassed. For once in his life, Peter Maxwell couldn't think of a damned thing to say.

'I've been expecting you,' she said, helping him off with his hat, his scarf, his coat.

'Have you?'

She hung up the wet things in the cupboard under the stairs. A girl's coat hung here too. Jenny's.

'You'll want to see her room,' Marianne Hyde said, as though she was an estate agent or a landlady whose heart wasn't really in her job.

'No, I . . .'

'Yes.' Her voice was brittle, sharp. Then softer. 'Yes, it helps me to talk about her. You have come to talk about her?'

Maxwell nodded.

She led him up the stairs, past the rather awful Picasso prints, and turned left on the landing. There was a pile of towels on the floor, holding open the door of the airing cupboard.

'Sorry,' she said. 'I always wash on a Sunday.'

He smiled awkwardly and still managed to stumble over the towels. Then she walked into Jenny's room. They stood, both of them, looking at the bed with its grey duvet cover; the posters, culled from *19* magazine and whatever else young girls read these days, of blond young men in T-shirts and state-of-the-art acne. The room was stifling with memories. On the top of the bookcase a fluffy clutter of cuddly toys, some old and grubby, others new, in lurid pinks and yellows. Draped over the chair was a school blazer, the badge of Leighford High emblazoned on the pocket.

'She still kept it,' Marianne Hyde said as she saw Maxwell's eyes find it, 'even though it wasn't the uniform in the sixth form. I like uniform, Mr Maxwell. Even for the sixth form. I think it's important.'

'About Jenny . . .' he said.

She sat on the bed, folding and refolding her daughter's school scarf. Maxwell remembered the girl wearing that last winter, no school uniform in the sixth form or not.

'May I?' Maxwell gestured towards the chair. He hated touching it, moving it. This bedroom was a shrine to the murdered girl. He felt as if he was demolishing the Wailing Wall, stone by stone; as if he'd barged his way into Peking's Forbidden City.

She just nodded and he perched there, wetly. 'Mrs Hyde,' he said, 'I should explain.'

She wasn't helping him now. So far she'd led, controlled. Now he was in the driving seat. Maxwell was a leader of men. That was where he usually was. Liked to be. But at that moment, he'd rather be anywhere else.

'I want to help,' he said. 'I want to find whoever is responsible.'

She looked at him curiously and he recognised the old hostility he'd seen in her before, at parents' evenings. 'Do you have any qualifications for that?'

'None,' he admitted, realizing the futility of a master's degree in the real world. 'Except . . .'

'Yes?'

'Except I'm not a policeman.'

'Does that help?'

'It might.' Maxwell was warming to it now, thinking on his feet. 'People might talk to me where they wouldn't talk to the police.'

She nodded. She could see that. 'Is that it?'

'No.' he looked at her levelly. 'I'm not as distant as the police and I'm not as close as you and your husband.'

She paused, frowning. 'You're a sort of go-between.'

He nodded. 'The happy hunting-ground in the middle,' he said. 'Although there's actually nothing happy about it.'

'My husband and I talked about hiring a private detective — when Jennifer went missing, I mean.'

'Mrs Hyde,' Maxwell leaned forward, as close to her as he dared. 'I don't have the right to intrude. Jenny was your daughter.'

'Do you have children, Mr Maxwell?' she asked him.

He jerked back suddenly, as though she'd slapped him. For a second a wet road blurred across his vision. There was a roar and a scream in his ears. A shattering of glass. 'No,' he said. 'No, I don't.'

'Do you think you can help?' She leaned forward to him. 'You see, I want this man dead. People say . . . I've read magazines, when parents lose children, they just feel numb. Dead. They don't blame. Don't want revenge.' She stood up abruptly, crossing to the window, winding and rewinding the scarf until it was a knot in her cold, white hands. 'But I do. It's not that I'm a vindictive person, I'm not. But if the police find him . . .' She turned to look at him. 'If you find him, I'll kill him. I don't know how. I don't understand these things. But I promise you, I'll kill him.'

Maxwell felt his hair crawl. It wasn't what the woman was saying that frightened him. It was the way that she said it. Cold. Passionless. Her emotions drained and wrung out like the scarf in her hands. As tight in her fist as the ligature around Jenny's neck. He broke the silence for them both, like a spring snapping. 'There are things I need to know,' he said.

She sat down again, composing herself, arranging the chaos that had been her mind since that day in July, that day when her only child had walked out of her life.

'I didn't notice it at first,' she told Maxwell. 'How Jennifer had changed. She was . . . I don't know . . . distant, withdrawn.'

'When was this?'

'It was on the Saturday. I suppose, looking back, I'd been aware of a strangeness for two or three days. No more. On the Sunday I tackled her about it. It was over breakfast. Clive lost his temper with her. It's sad, really, I don't think he's ever forgiven himself. Oh, they'd patched it up by that night, but even so . . .'

'Jenny was supposed to be staying with Anne? With Anne Spencer?'

'That's right. Jennifer rang her that Sunday morning. I'd got nowhere with her over breakfast and when she'd got off the phone, she said that Mrs Spencer had asked her over for a couple of nights, so that they could work together on some project.' Marianne Hyde looked at the Head of Sixth Form. 'She was a clever girl, my Jennifer, Mr Maxwell, but you know that.'

He nodded. 'What did you think of this idea?' he asked her. 'Had Jenny stayed at the Spencers' before?'

'Not for a while. Not since her GCSE year, in fact. And never overnight. But they were closer then. To be honest,' she crossed to the window again, looking backwards and forwards across the front lawn, as though she half expected Jenny to appear any minute, swinging her school bag on her way from the bus, 'I didn't care too much for Anne Spencer. We began to hear things.'

'Things?' Maxwell's eyes narrowed.

'Yes.' Marianne Hyde was staring at the lowering Sunday sky and the vague reflection of herself in the double glazing. 'Oh, I don't know how much faith you put in these things, Mr Maxwell. Let's just say that Anne . . . slept around. There was talk of married men.'

'Ah,' Maxwell nodded. 'The world is full of them, of course.'

'Well, I don't know how true it is, but some girls . . . well, I just didn't like my Jennifer mixing in those circles.'

'So you said she couldn't go?'

'No.' She turned to face him. 'No, I didn't. My daughter was a headstrong girl, Mr Maxwell. I won't say wilful. She wasn't that. But she had a mind of her own. We'd already had words over her sullenness, at breakfast. I didn't want it all again, so I said she could go. She threw a few things into an overnight bag and that was it.'

He saw her eyes fill with tears, her lip tremble, just for an instant. 'I never saw her again,' she said. 'Not until . . . not until the police found her. And then, when Clive and I saw her, on that slab I mean, it wasn't her. Not any more. It wasn't our Jennifer.'

'Did you notice, Mrs Hyde,' Maxwell asked, 'if Jenny took her school uniform with her?'

'She took what she wore for school, yes.'

'Did she take a pair of tights?'

'I don't remember.'

'And her books?'

'I assume so. The police . . . haven't found her school bag. I've looked high and low here. There's no sign of it.'

'What time did she leave on Sunday night?'

'Just before seven.'

Maxwell scanned her face before he asked the next question. 'Did she say anything? Before she left, did she say anything . . . important?'

Marianne Hyde walked back to the bed, careful to keep her back to Peter Maxwell. 'It was all important,' she said to him. 'When they're the last words you hear your child say, every one of them becomes etched on your memory. She said, "It's all right, mum. I know exactly what I'm doing." And then she kissed me.'

'Did you know what she meant?'

The woman shook her head, 'Not then,' she said. 'Not now. I presumed it had something to do with her strangeness, but . . .' and he heard her sigh, 'I'll never know now.'

He let a moment go. 'When did you first realise she wasn't at the Spencers'?'

She curled up on the bed, her knees under her chin, her hands clasped round her ankles and her ankles wrapped in Jenny's scarf.

'Janet Foster told me,' she said. 'I attend her pottery classes up at the college. She asked me — it must have been the Tuesday. Jennifer should have been back that same evening, but I assumed we'd missed each other. I told Janet that she was at home as far as I knew.'

'But she wasn't?'

'No. When I got back, Clive was pacing up and down. He'd rung the Spencers. They hadn't seen Jennifer at all.'

'So she never got there?'

Marianne shook her head. 'Mrs Spencer knew nothing about it. I rang her straight away.' She looked at Maxwell. 'On reflection, I think that hurt Clive. Somehow it meant that I didn't trust him. But I wasn't reflecting then. Wasn't thinking. It's a sort of blind panic, Mr Maxwell. You can't know. You haven't got children. You can't know. I remember once, ooh, a long time ago when Jennifer was small. I left her in her pram. Outside the library, it was, before they built the ramp. I'd only returned a book and when I came out, she'd gone, pram and all. It was all right, of course. Some old dear had noticed that Jennifer was in the sun and had moved her into the shade. She was still there, billing and cooing, when I came tearing along. I was all set to fell the old trout with my holdall, but . . . well, you can't, can you? For that second, though, that second before I saw her . . . It's not a feeling I can really put into words. Your heart just thumps as if . . . as if it's going to explode. Your hands feel heavy, really heavy; your wrists . . . Well, that's how I felt when I phoned Mrs Spencer. I don't really remember what she said exactly. Except that Jennifer wasn't there. She hadn't seen her for weeks. I asked to speak to Anne. She wasn't in.'

'What then?' Maxwell didn't really have to cut in. Marianne Hyde was there now, reliving it like some ghastly action replay on the telly.

'Clive went round there. I stayed by the phone. I rang my sister in Orpington. A cousin in Wakefield. Friends. Anyone I could think of. Jenny had been gone for forty-eight hours and I hadn't got a clue where she was. When Clive came back, we called the police.'

'Helpful?'

'They were very quick. I was surprised by that. A plain-clothes officer and a WPC. She was pretty, I think. We never saw her after that first night. Do you know, it's funny,' but neither of them laughed, 'I'd never talked to a detective before. He was calm, solemn even. He asked if we'd had a row. If we had a recent photo. I hadn't got one that recent, but they said they'd take it all the same. It might help. Might jog someone's memory. The WPC made us all a cup of tea. I couldn't have found the kitchen that night, never mind the kettle. The detective asked if Jennifer had been in trouble. Clive got . . . difficult then and asked him what he meant. It was all so silly. We were all on the same side, after all, weren't we?'

Maxwell nodded.

'"Boys," the detective said. "Drugs." I thought Clive was going to go through the roof.'

'Boys,' Maxwell repeated, assuming the policeman's role.

'There's Tim,' Marianne told him. 'Tim Grey.'

'I couldn't think of a nicer boy,' Maxwell assured her.

'I don't think that's what the detective meant.' Marianne looked up at him, her chin between her knees. 'He meant sex. Was Jennifer mixed up in sex?'

'And drugs?'

For a moment it looked as though Marianne Hyde almost smiled, but it must have been a trick of the leaden September light. 'No,' she said, 'not our Jennifer. She was a good girl, Mr Maxwell. Sensible. We'd always discussed things. She knew how dangerous drugs were. Clive has a thing about them.'

'What else did the police ask?'

'They insisted on seeing this room.' She looked around, at the ceiling, the walls, trying to imagine the impact they would have on strangers seeing them for the first time. 'They stood near the door while I went through her things. It was then I realised that her money had gone.'

'Money?'

'She had . . . well, here it is, a piggy bank.' She passed him one of those porcelain pigs that the Nat West had been promoting a few years back. It had a porcelain nappy on, held in place by a porcelain pin. 'We gave her an allowance, Mr Maxwell, once she turned sixteen.'

'Do you know how much money she had?'

'In her actual bank account, a little under a hundred pounds. The police told me the next day that she'd drawn almost all of it out. Just left in the nominal pound to keep it open. In the room here, she had . . . I don't know, perhaps ten. I kept asking the police what had happened. I expected answers. They must have done this before, I remember thinking. Talked to parents in similar situations. They must have some answers. But they didn't. They just said it was a good sign. It was a good sign that she'd taken clothes and money because that meant she'd just run away.'

'They couldn't tell you why?' he asked.

She shook her head. 'They had all kinds of statistics. I couldn't take them in. Couldn't think. Neither of us slept that first night. Nor the second. The WPC had told us not to worry. That's like saying, "Don't breathe." We just sat, each side of the phone. Clive's not a very responsive person, but we held hands, all night. Both nights. Like kids on our first date. Another WPC came back the second morning. They'd tried various avenues, apparently, various contacts. This woman was harder than the first, not as caring. Well, I thought so, at least. She said that legally Jennifer could leave home whenever she liked; she didn't have to ask our permission to go nor to tell us where she'd gone. She kept patting my hand saying, "She'll be back. She'll be back. It'll be some boy. You'll see. Girls of today . . ." She was only a slip of a thing herself. How can they become so ingrained?' She frowned at him, perhaps even hoping for an answer. She didn't get one.

'I suppose they see so much of it.'

She shrugged. Marianne Hyde was an intelligent woman. She'd worked that out for herself. 'Then came the sighting.'

'Sighting?'

'Three, in fact. All at once. Or that's how it seemed. A car towards Hincham way spotted a girl who could have been Jennifer. It wasn't. An elderly couple gave a lift to a hitch-hiker answering her description on the A27. And someone saw her talking to a boy on the Dam.'

'That was on *Crimewatch*.'

'Was it?' Marianne nodded. 'I don't know. We couldn't watch it. After they . . . after they found her, we just . . . well, I don't know. It's all rather a blur. I don't really remember. I remember walking up to the Cross, where she used to get off the bus. I did that every day until the Friday. On the Friday night, they told us she was dead.' Her eyes were clear now, her face cold, blank. 'The WPC was there again, the second one. But it was a different detective. A Chief Inspector Hall. I hit him.'

'You hit him.'

Marianne nodded. 'Dreadful, wasn't it?' Maxwell watched a single tear roll down the woman's left cheek. 'It was a stupid, pointless, cruel thing to do. A release of tension, Clive called it. As soon as Hall had broken the news, I just slapped his face. Snapped, I suppose. He just stood there, rearranging his glasses. I think Clive and the WPC put me to bed. It certainly wasn't until the next day that we went to identify her.'

'Jesus!'

Maxwell spun round at the sudden interruption. In the doorway stood Clive Hyde, an open anorak dripping on to the landing carpet.

'What the bloody hell are you doing here?' he bellowed.

'Clive . . .' Marianne let the scarf go for the first time, but only with one hand.

'I'm talking to him.' The dead girl's father had filled the door with his bulk.

'Mr Hyde.' Maxwell was half a head shorter than Clive Hyde and ten years older.

'Don't say anything,' Hyde snapped, his jaw flexing. 'Just get the hell out of my house.'

'I was just . . .'

'You were just going,' Hyde finished the sentence for him. As Maxwell brushed past, he felt his lapels being ripped forward and Hyde was snarling in his face, crimson, furious. 'You leave us alone, you degenerate old bastard. Do you hear? Leave us alone!' and he bounced Maxwell off the door frame.

For a second, Peter Maxwell looked at Marianne Hyde. She was still sitting on her daughter's bed, still holding her ankles and with one hand on the scarf. And she looked at the two angry men in front of her as though she were watching wrestling on the box. It was all a show, theatrical and far away.

And both men were angry, not with each other, but with the same thing. Their little girl was dead and neither of them knew why. Maxwell shook himself free of the distraught father and stumbled for the door, remembering to fish out his coat, hat and scarf as he went.

* * *

He lay in the bath that night, mulling over the day. In the steam Dan Guthrie squatted on the squally beach, the seaweed thick and brown after the storm. His mouth hung open with his gappy gape, his good eye burning into Maxwell's soul. And Marianne Hyde, her face a ghastly white, sat rocking on the shingle, Jenny's scarf pulled tight around her own throat. And through the swirling blur, Clive Hyde, big, roaring, loomed over them all, his hands huge and his fingers curled as though around a young girl's neck. He shuddered and spent the next few minutes trying to find the soap, somewhere under the suds.

Then a thought occurred to the Head of Sixth Form, 'Metternich?' he shouted through to the lounge. The cat snored on, unperturbed. 'What did Clive Hyde mean when he called me a degenerate old bastard?'

CHAPTER 9

People forget. Even about murder, people forget. Or life has to go on, whichever cliché you prefer. So it was that Monday morning at Leighford High. There was the usual queue of malingerers outside Sylvia Matthews' door, wanting everything from tea and sympathy to morning after pills. The usual log jam in the corridors as friends met up to spread the gossip of the weekend. The usual gridlock when the bell went as the flow from Modern Languages hit the contraflow from the Science block. The hapless members of staff who had mistimed their own movements now found themselves, an island of calm in a sea of trouble, slowing kids down, tapping shoulders, pointing fingers. Jim Diamond had the usual urgent business in his office which meant that his door was firmly shut against all the hullabaloo. And so the day began as the days usually did.

Peter Maxwell had to see Geoffrey Smith. Metternich the cat was a good listener, but short on repartee and singularly mum when it came to advice. In the oddly lonely world of Mad Max, he needed a human being to bounce his ideas off; not that he'd ever, in public, end a sentence with a preposition.

'I can't hear a word,' Smith was roaring, the sun slanting in through the Drama studio windows and glancing on his bald head. 'Give it some wellie, Morrison. You have the misfortune to live in a sleepy little resort on the south coast of England. That means that a good fifty per cent of your audience will be geriatric. What does that mean?'

The luckless Morrison shifted his weight from leg to leg. 'Old,' he said.

'Not precise enough,' Smith countered. 'For your purposes, it means deaf. Mutter at them and even the immortal lines of the Bard will go right out of the window. Ah,' Smith heard the scrape of a chair behind him, 'Mr Maxwell has come to spot talent. I fear he'll have a rather long wait.' He threw himself down in the chair next to the Head of Sixth Form. 'From the top,' he sighed. 'And Davina, dear, I know it's difficult to empathise with a Renaissance Italian merchant prince, but not even Wops stand like that. Do try to stay in character. Go on.'

And as GCSE Drama rehearsals slowly limped on, Smith did what he was brilliant at, he divided his attention in at least two directions. 'Morning, Maxie. Come for a spot of team teaching?'

'I'd rather die than teach with you, Geoffrey,' Maxwell smiled. 'You know that.'

'To what do I owe the pleasure, then? Oh, come on, Glenda,' he suddenly bellowed, 'have I taught you nothing since Year 7? Project!' He leaned his head in the direction of Peter Maxwell. 'Singularly cruel of Mr and Mrs Jackson, don't you think? Saddling their youngest with the sobriquet Glenda. So much to live up to, somehow. You're going to tell me you've solved the Jenny Hyde case, aren't you?'

'I don't know what I'm doing, Geoff,' Maxwell shrugged. 'Remember when they brought in CPVE?'

'Er . . .' Smith wrestled with the letters. 'Certificate of Pre-Vocational Education, wasn't it?'

Maxwell slapped his wrist. Shylock and Bassanio lost their lines for a moment. 'Don't get arch with me, Geoffrey. That bloody course dominated our lives for four years. I seem to remember you had hair when it started.'

'That's a gross calumny,' Smith said blandly, 'I was born without hair. What's Jenny Hyde got to do with CPVE?'

'Nothing,' Maxwell confessed, 'except that I remember sending a memo to Legs which said, "I don't know what I'm doing. I don't know what you're doing. You don't know what I'm doing. What are we all doing?"'

'And you feel you're at that point with the Jenny Hyde thing?'

'Worse,' Maxwell moaned.

'Well, well. While these two wooden herberts get splinters off each other, let's nip next door. You put the kettle on. I'll listen.' As Maxwell waddled out, Smith turned to his two hopefuls. 'You know,' he said, 'that one of my many talents is being able to hear through walls. I shall be listening to every word.'

The Drama office was a shambles, which said a lot about Geoffrey Smith's mind. Rumour had it that he'd been in Nottingham Rep once and certainly he had all the affectations of an actor manqué. Staff went in slight fear of him, especially when they left, because his take-offs were legendary and the farewell speech parodies hilarious — unless it was you he was parodying. And many was the colleague who had turned up after an urgent summons over the phone from the Headmaster, only to find that the Headmaster was out of school on a course somewhere.

'There's that instant tea under the table, Max,' Smith said. 'Can you see the kettle?'

'That's it, isn't it?' Maxwell pointed. 'Silver thing, black handle? Mind you, I'm clutching at straws. They didn't have Home Economics in the school I went to.'

Smith picked the kettle up and shook it. There was water there somewhere and he plugged it in. 'Well,' he beamed, 'what news on the Rialto?'

1 found the tramp.' Maxwell moved a pile of exercise books and sat down.

'Oh . . . Guthsomething.'

'Guthrie. Yes. You remembered it perfectly well at Dr Astley's the other day.'

'Remembered what?'

'Oh, ha!'

'Helpful, was he? Guthrie? Oh, shit!' A rogue spoonful of instant tea sprinkled itself over Smith's hand.

'Yes and no.'

'Christ, you're cryptic this morning. Would you care to elucidate?'

'With these teeth?' Maxwell clasped his hands across his waistcoat. 'He was in one of the downstairs rooms at the Red House. Didn't go upstairs.'

'Or so he says.'

Maxwell looked at his old oppo. 'Why should he lie?'

Smith chuckled. 'Maxie, Maxie,' he said, 'why should Bill Clinton be President of the United States? Why haven't I been shortlisted for the Booker again this year?'

'Because you never write anything, Geoffrey,' Maxwell told him.

'That's never stopped Salman Rushdie. There are just some things in life that have no rhyme or reason. You shouldn't be so trusting.'

'Perhaps not,' Maxwell said, 'but I've been around people a long time now, Geoff. You get a nose for these things.'

'So you believe him?'

'Yes,' Maxwell told him, 'yes, I do.'

'Good for you. So Guthrie is downstairs at the Red House. And upstairs?'

'Upstairs,' Maxwell's face was dark in the darkened office, 'was the body of Jenny Hyde.'

The kettle clicked as the cut-out mechanism came into play, punctuating the silence.

'Did he see anything?' Smith asked.

'A car.'

'A car? Did he get the number?'

Maxwell shook his head. 'Didn't even know what colour it was.'

Smith snorted. 'Don't tell me,' he said. 'Test drive green or perhaps vomit yellow with just a hint of metallic flesh.'

Maxwell twisted his nose. 'Something tells me you aren't taking this sighting very seriously, Mr Smith.'

'I'm sorry, Max,' Smith poured them both a cup, 'but you know as well as I do how unreliable eyewitnesses are. You're a historian, for God's sake. Didn't you tell me once how many people claimed to have put the pennies on the eyelids of Abraham Lincoln?'

'Four,' Maxwell nodded.

'So unless the man had eight eyes, which is unlikely, three of the buggers are lying. Is that a fair assumption?'

'It is,' Maxwell agreed.

'Well, there you are, then. And this bloke Guthrie. What's he on?'

'What?'

'Well, out in all weathers with only the road for company. Cider? Meths? Boot polish? He probably wouldn't know a car if it drove right through him. I don't suppose he knows what day it is.'

'Well, thank you, Geoffrey, for that magnificent expression of support.'

Smith laughed. 'I'm sorry, Max. I don't want to belittle your efforts. Christ, you seem to be getting further than the police have.'

'No,' Maxwell said, 'I'm aeons behind them. At the moment. But I'm ahead in one sense.'

'Oh? What's that?'

'Jenny's diary.'

'Diary?'

'Betty Martin found it stuffed behind some lockers.'

'Get away. What did it say?'

'Cryptic stuff. I've got to decipher it yet.'

'What did the police say about it?'

'I haven't shown it to them.'

Smith paused before the cup reached his lips. 'Is that wise, Maxie?' he asked. It was the first time Smith had been serious all morning.

Maxwell shambled to his feet. 'Probably not,' he said. 'But the other day you were telling me to stay away from them.'

'The other day I didn't know you'd got Jenny's diary.'

'Thanks for the tea, Geoffrey,' Maxwell said. 'Please don't get up. I'll find my own way out.' He jerked his head towards the partition, where the actors moaned their lines. 'Coming on, that Hamlet.'

* * *

Peter Maxwell remembered Tim Grey from his first week at Leighford High. He was one of those natural targets in life, a small, unprepossessing, thin-shouldered kid you naturally want to hit. Unfair, really. But then life was full of little unfairnesses, wasn't it? Like some people being asthmatic or blind or poor or stupid or murdered.

And Tim Grey hadn't changed very much really. He was taller, his face harder, leaner, but he still had the scrawny shoulders and he still didn't quite look people in the face. Peter Maxwell had him in the soft chair in his office, his fingers curled around the mug of an Arsenal supporter. He didn't pretend it was his. He'd rather support a hernia any day. Oblique. That was the way forward. He'd been too abrupt with Anne Spencer. Too direct. What was the old adage? 'Softly, softly catchee monkey'? Or was that a line from Hiawatha?

'How's the term going, Tim?'

'OK.'

Maxwell reached over to rummage in some papers on his desk. Every time he saw it his heart sank with the sheer weight of paper and he wandered off to do something else. 'Let's see, you're applying for . . . civil engineering. Fine. Fine. Of these colleges here on your UCAS form, which is the one you really want to go to? Your first choice?'

'Don't mind.'

Maxwell found himself taking refuge in another swig of his coffee. It was that or drive his fist down the lad's throat.

'Tim . . . I need to talk to you . . .' and the phone rang. Damn. Maxwell picked it up. 'Yes?'

A disembodied voice Maxwell recognised as the school secretary wheedled at him over the internal wires. 'The Headmaster wants to see you, Mr Maxwell.'

'Joy!' said Max, but his face remained stony. 'And when will this meeting of like minds take place, Margaret? It is Margaret, isn't it? Not Geoffrey Smith being incredibly witty?'

'Of course it is,' the humourless secretary snapped. 'The Headmaster wants to see you now.'

'Ah. Now as in immediately?'

There was a pause. 'Yes, of course.'

'No can do, I'm afraid. I've got a bit of a crisis over here. I'll be along when I can.'

She began to say something but he'd already put the receiver down and he carefully hooked his foot under the wire to pull the plug out of the wall. 'Oops,' he said and sat down again.

'Tim, I have to go.' He looked the boy in the face, trying to catch his eye. 'So I'll have to come to the point. You know what the point is, don't you?'

Tim Grey nodded. 'Jenny,' he said.

Maxwell leaned back, cradling his knee with both hands. 'That's right. Look, Tim, it's not my place to pry,' he told the boy, 'but I have to know. I have to know some things about her.'

'Such as?'

'Were you . . . in love with her?' It was a strange question for a teacher to put to a pupil. Maxwell certainly felt uncomfortable with it.

1 don't know,' Tim said. 'I miss her.'

That was a breakthrough at least. Anne Spencer had lost her cool and told Maxwell nothing. Tim Grey was perfectly friendly and was still telling Maxwell nothing. Until now. Now there was a glimmer of hope. 'Of course,' he nodded. 'Of course you do. Tell me, when did you start going out together?'

The boy gazed into the middle distance, trying to remember. Maxwell remembered his lamentable performance in GCSE History. Tim Grey was not good on dates. 'About Easter time,' he said. 'April, last year.'

'Did you see a lot of each other? Outside school, I mean?'

'We used to go out at weekends,' he said. 'I got this part-time job.'

Maxwell knew that and he didn't approve. He'd never approved of part-time jobs. They detracted from the main thrust of a sixth-former's life — academe. But that was a heresy these days. Increasingly, Maxwell was a dodo, out of line with '90s educational thinking. As it was he was the last of that line. 'Where did you go?' he asked. 'What did you do?'

The boy shrugged. His eyes never for a moment met Maxwell's. 'Bowling,' he said. 'You know, the King Pin Club.'

Maxwell nodded. He didn't know it, of course. He'd never set foot inside the place, but he knew of it. People held birthday parties there and tournaments. He was more cerebral. A dominoes man to his fingertips.

'Cinema sometimes.'

'Ah.' This was home territory for Maxwell. 'What was the last thing you saw?' He could have kicked himself. He hadn't realised how final that innocent question sounded. He needn't have worried. Apparently, Tim Grey hadn't realised it either.

'*Beauty and the Beast*,' he said.

Maxwell smiled. 'Back to the old Disney, I thought,' he said, 'the ones I remember. The classics. Before your time, of course. Did the police talk to you Tim?'

'Yes.' The boy looked down. Maxwell was suddenly aware that Tim's fingers, cradled in his lap, were knotted together. It reminded him of Jenny's scarf in the hands of Marianne Hyde. 'Yes, they talked to me when she went missing.'

Maxwell allowed the silence to stand between them. Then he said, 'Where was she, Tim? Those days she went missing? What was it; from the Sunday to the Friday, the last week of term? Where was she? Was she with you?'

For the first time he could remember, Peter Maxwell saw Tim Grey look him in the face. It was for a fleeting moment only, then he looked away. 'No,' he said, 'she wasn't with me.'

'Do you know where she was? Did you look for her?'

There was a sharp rap at the door. Tim's eyelids flickered. He ran a nervous tongue over his dry lips.

'Not now!' Maxwell bellowed. 'Tim, if you knew where Jenny was that week, I have to know.'

Nothing. The knock came again. Maxwell ignored it. 'Did you tell the police?'

Tim shook his head quickly. 'I wasn't sure,' he said. 'I'm still not sure.'

This time the door burst open and a red-faced Roger Garrett stood there, eyes flashing. 'Mr Maxwell, the Headmaster would like to see you in his office, please. Right away.'

Maxwell ignored him. 'However unsure you are, Tim,' he said, 'try me.'

The boy sat in an agony of indecision.

'Will you leave us . . . um . . . Timothy?' Garrett said.

Grateful for the way out, Tim Grey leapt to his feet, but he wasn't fast enough for Mad Max with his hackles up. 'Tim!' he all but pressed his nose against the boy's, gripping his shirt firmly.

'Maz,' he said. 'They call him Maz. He hangs out round the Dam. That's all I know.' And he brushed past Roger Garrett into the corridor and was gone.

'Well, thanks, Roger.' Maxwell rounded on the First Deputy. 'Timing immaculate as ever.'

'You were asked to come to Mr Diamond's office ten minutes ago.' Garrett's glasses were bouncing up and down on his nose.

'Well, fan my flies!' Maxwell said. 'Sometimes, Roger, just sometimes, there are more important things in life.' It was now that Maxwell began to take in the oddity of the situation. Legs Diamond wasn't normally so insistent. Matters weren't usually that urgent. And he'd never sent his Deputy in person before. To fetch Maxwell to the presence. 'Well, well,' he said, 'and what does Himself want that's so important?'

'I can't tell you.' Garrett was tighter-lipped than Maxwell had seen the man in his five years in post.

'I see.' Maxwell snatched up a biro he'd left on the desk and considered finishing his coffee, only it had gone cold and he really couldn't face it. 'Well, then.' He beamed his most acid beam at Garrett. 'Let's go and see the Organ Grinder, shall we?'

* * *

The Organ Grinder looked terse, embarrassed. Maxwell had just seen the Senior Mattress leaving the Head's office as he arrived, so he knew there was something in the wind. It wasn't just that he and Deirdre Lessing didn't see eye to eye; it was that they weren't even standing on the same ground.

But there was somebody else in the Head's office. Another suit of an altogether darker grey. And Maxwell recognised the charcoal man from the odd sally into the bowels of County Hall. It was Dr Jenkins, the Chief Education Officer, who had last seen the inside of a school from the angle of the chalk face nearly thirty years ago. And beyond him the unprepossessing features and leather jacket of John Graham, contract builder and Chairman of Governors.

'Max,' Diamond was the only one on his feet, 'won't you sit down? Thanks, Roger.'

The First Deputy nodded in Maxwell's wake and closed the door on his way out. There was only one chair free, on its own in the centre of the opulent office — well, opulent by the standards of that of the Head of Sixth Form. Ah, he thought to himself, the siege perilous, but he sat in it anyway.

'Max.' The Headmaster leaned forward, having resumed his seat. Words appeared to fail him.

'There's been an accusation,' Graham cut in with all the directness of a contract builder. God alone knew how he'd got the job as Chair. It could only be that no one else wanted it.

'Oh?' Maxwell raised an eyebrow. He'd never suffered contract builders gladly. 'Against whom?'

'You,' all the men chorused.

'Jim.' Dr Jenkins flashed an order-by-Christian-name to the Headmaster. His school. His territory. His job.

'Yes, of course.' Diamond cleared his throat. 'There has been an accusation, Max, that you . . . behaved improperly with a girl in your charge.'

'Improperly?' Maxwell repeated.

'You touched her up.' Graham crossed the 't's for him.

Maxwell sighed. 'Anne Spencer,' he said.

'So you admit it?' The Chairman of the Governors leaned towards him.

'On the contrary,' said Maxwell. 'I deny it.'

'You were quick enough to name the girl,' Graham challenged him. 'None of us did.'

'That points rather to my powers of judgement of human nature than to my capacity for perversion.' He knew he'd lost Graham already.

Jim Diamond did his best to pour oil on the waters. 'Max, I'm sure there's nothing in it,' he said.

'Thank you, Headmaster. Then why . . . ?'

'Sexual abuse is in the headlines, Mr Maxwell,' Dr Jenkins said quietly. 'You know as well as I do that gross moral turpitude is one of the few things we can still dismiss teachers for.'

'Interesting word, turpitude,' Maxwell commented. 'It means depravity, Mr Graham, baseness. Can you manage either of those?'

The contract builder's face was a picture. 'I wouldn't be so fucking flippant if I were you, son.'

Bearing in mind that Maxwell could easily give John Graham ten years, the threat did seem a little idle. It also made Jim Diamond wonder anew what Chairmen of Governors were coming to these days.

'I am here,' Dr Jenkins thought it necessary to justify himself, 'because the parents of the child in question wrote to me personally. As they did to Mr Diamond . . . and to Mr Graham.'

'I'm afraid, Max,' Diamond folded his arms, then thought the mannerism too smug and unfolded them again, 'I'm afraid I'll have to suspend you. On full pay, of course. Just until this thing is settled.'

Maxwell stood up. He dug his hand into his pocket and threw a piece of chalk on to the Head's desk. 'That's how they do it in the movies, isn't it? Clint Eastwood or somebody hands over their gun and their shield? Well, that's my gun, Headmaster. And my shield.'

'Max . . .'

But John Graham cut the Head short. 'I'll make no secret of it, Maxwell,' he growled, 'I've never liked you. Too cocksure by half. Well, we'll see. There'll be a full enquiry. The police will be wanting to talk to you.'

'No one said anything about the police.' Diamond stood up.

'I bloody did,' Graham told him, 'just then. And you,' he jabbed a finger at Maxwell, 'you stay wide of that girl and her parents, you dirty bastard.'

'Thank you, Mr Graham,' Dr Jenkins cut in. 'I feel we all understand your concern.'

'We do,' smiled Maxwell. 'It's quite touching in a Neanderthal sort of way. I assume, Headmaster, that you'd like my departure to be immediate and that my lessons for the rest of the day will be covered?'

'Yes, Max,' the Head said. 'Paul Moss is in the picture. At least, as far as he knows, you're not well. Please don't discuss this with anyone. You're entitled to have your professional association rep to speak for you, but I'm afraid it's rather gone beyond that now. You need a solicitor.'

'No,' Maxwell shook his head. 'What I need is some backbone,' he said. 'In those about me, I mean.' He turned in the doorway. 'And while you . . . gentlemen . . . are eagerly pursuing the allegations of Miss Anne Spencer, you might also ask her what she knows about the murder of Jenny Hyde.'

* * *

They'd scaled down the incident room and Jacquie Carpenter was on her own when the call came through. 'It was from Mr Hyde,' she told Chief Inspector Hall later.

'We've nothing new for him,' Hall said.

'No, it wasn't that.' The girl shook her head. 'He just thought you ought to know. His wife is being pestered. By that Mr Maxwell, from up at the school.'

CHAPTER 10

The mist lay like a spider's web carpet in the hollows and lent a fairy light to the evening. Peter Maxwell left White Surrey at home that night, still saddled under the stars, the dew forming on crossbar and mudguard. He took the way that Jenny Hyde had taken that last afternoon, as if walking in her footsteps might bring a flash of light, a solution to the riddle. But this was no Damascus Road and the age of miracles, it seemed, was past.

He'd never known why they called it the Dam, that three acres or so of copse where, in the twilight, lovers walked, hand in hand and heart on heart. When he'd first come to Leighford, all those years ago, he'd done some local research. Found that in Domesday it had three mills and land in demesne for ten teams. But the river meandered to the east, as it always had, give or take a curve or two, and there was never a dam on the site where the trees darkened and the last of the dog owners whistled their animals home under the creeping September night.

Maxwell eased himself down on the seat the Council had thoughtfully placed there in memory of Ethel Hazelrigg who, according to the inscription, had loved this place. The ground swept into the sea of mist before him and the bushes rose like dark islands dotted here and there. He saw the lights of Lower Harton twinkle and the little road winding up to join those of Harton-on-the-Hill.

It had been a while since he had been here. He'd forgotten how lovely it was. And how easy to forget that two miles away the M27 thundered and that this was 1993 and that a girl was dead. He couldn't place it precisely, that spot on the *Crimewatch* programme where the Jenny Hyde lookalike had been filmed talking to that lad, the tall one with the spots. He remembered that they had been arguing; a woman had heard her say 'No' several times.

Then she'd walked along the old railway line where the locomotives of the South-Western rattled and snorted before Beeching, the mad axeman, had struck. Less than a mile in that direction lay the little village of Moorfields, where Alison Miller lived with one of the biggest shits it had ever been Peter Maxwell's misfortune to meet. Beyond that, the Shingle and the Red House and the sea.

But where did she go then? Straight to the Red House? Why? Mr Arnold, whose dog had ducked in there, had said it was too derelict for courting couples. And Maxwell agreed. The night that he and Smith had gone sleuthing, that was obvious. Unless she didn't know it was derelict. Didn't know the Red House. But then, surely, all kids knew the Red House. Didn't they?

He stood up. Sitting on that hard old bequest of Ethel Hazelrigg wasn't going to get him very far, watching the mist wreathe the meadow and the stars come out one by one. Orion, he thought to himself. There's Orion's belt, Orion's club and ah, there they are, Orion's trousers. He smiled in the dim light and trudged on down the slope. It was cold now. An early autumn. Soon, it would be fires and cocoa and draughts at every corner of Leighford High . . . but what if for him there was no more Leighford High? He'd shut the events of the day out of his mind. They were a bad dream and he'd wake up shortly.

But Peter Maxwell was awake and he heard some kids calling to each other in the deeper woods, scaring each other in a dummy run for Hallowe'en. He tried to see his watch, but it was hopeless. Time, certainly, that those kids were in bed. Listen to me, he chuckled to himself, sounding just like a geriatric schoolmaster. What would he miss most about Leighford High, he wondered, and turned for home. The kids? No. The staff? Christ, no. After all, he knew his collective nouns; an arsehole of teachers. No, he realised as he reached the road and his scarf and his suit and his hat all turned a vicious orange under the street lights; he'd miss the graffiti. He ran through it in his mind. In the gents' loo on the first floor of the Arts block — 'No graffiti please,' to which some wag had appended 'Mine do.' He suspected Geoffrey Smith of that one. And next to the hot air button in the ladies (he'd been told), 'Please press for a message from the Secretary of State for Education.' He suspected Geoffrey Smith of that one, too.

'Go home, Maxwell,' he said out loud. 'Your mind's beginning to wander.'

* * *

It was a little after eleven that the door bell rang. Maxwell was up in the loft he'd spent months converting for his own peculiar purposes. Shit! Who the hell was this, at this time of night? If only he had the technical expertise to install the intercom gizmo the Kleeneze man was talking about, all he need do was flick a switch, ascertain who his caller was and let him in. As it was, he had to hurtle down three flights of stairs only to find it was Paul Moss.

'Max.' The young man looked dishevelled without a tie, he who was usually so precise. 'I know it's late.'

'It is, oh wise Head of Department.' Maxwell bowed. 'But you'd better come in. Look at those stars.'

Moss didn't. He was too busy climbing to have time. Here was a man of thirty-two, already Head of History, but the sands of time were running out. He more than most knew the historical precedents he was up against — William

Pitt, Prime Minister at twenty-four; Napoleon Bonaparte, General at twenty-five. By their standards, Paul Moss was an old man. He followed Maxwell up to the lounge.

'I'd offer you that one,' his host said, pointing at a chair, 'but it's Metternich's by day and you might catch something. Scotch?'

'Why not?' Moss sank into the sofa. 'Jesus, Max, how are people supposed to get up from this again?'

'Do you mind?' Maxwell feigned outrage. 'I really had to rummage down at the tip for that. You young fellas have no sense of the past.'

He poured them both a stiff one and handed the glass to Paul Moss. 'Here's looking at you, kid!' he snarled in a passable Bogart. In his heart of hearts he knew it wasn't as good as Geoffrey Smith's.

'It's all over the school, Max,' Moss told him raising his glass in a silent toast.

'Gross moral turpitude,' Maxwell chuckled. 'Yes, I expect it is.'

Moss studied the Great Man's features for a moment — the mutton chop whiskers, the broad, long face, the gap in the teeth. 'You're taking this very lightly,' he said.

Maxwell shrugged. 'What do you want me to do, Paul?' he asked. 'Sob? Tear my shirt? Stick my head in the oven? For a start, I haven't got gas; there again shirts cost an arm and a leg and as for sobbing . . . well . . .' and he smiled at some distant memory, a long, long time ago. 'Been there,' he said, 'done that.' But he saw the grim face of the Boy Wonder. 'Well, Paul. What are they saying?'

Moss sighed. 'The bottom line is that you shouldn't have been alone in your office with Anne Spencer.'

Maxwell threw his hands in the air. 'And I shouldn't have stirred my coffee clockwise or blown my nose or scratched my arse. Come on, Paul, life's too short.'

'You're too trusting, Max,' Moss told him. 'There's no way I'd put myself in that situation. Not with the likes of Anne Spencer.'

'I suppose you're right,' Maxwell nodded. 'But she's not the worst by a long way.'

'Garrett's going around with a look of smug satisfaction on his face, like the cat who's got the cream. I heard two or three colleagues ask him about you and he said he couldn't actually say anything. Then he proceeded to blab it all out. I should have punched him on the nose.'

'Keep out of it, Paul,' Maxwell advised him. 'It's not your fight. The Senior Mattress was enjoying it all, too, no doubt?'

Moss snorted. 'She certainly had a craftier-than-thou air about her. There's somebody the bloody Chairman of Governors ought to be gunning for. She put the turpitude in that quaint old phrase.'

Both men fell silent. Neither of them had been in this situation before. They'd both read, as you do, about teachers who abuse their authority by abusing their children. But that was usually some hole-in-corner private school you'd never heard of in a county far away.

'Presumably . . .' Paul Moss was placing a toe into dangerous waters, 'presumably, nothing actually went on?'

Maxwell looked at the younger man. Was this the time to jab him in both eyes with his fingers? Kick him in the crotch and throw him downstairs? Or just take away his rusks and refuse to change his nappy? In the event, he practised as though before any enquiry that might be set up.

'I just asked the girl questions about her friend Jenny Hyde.'

'I see.' Moss had got off lightly and he knew it. 'And what did she say?'

'Nothing.' Maxwell shook his head. 'She took umbrage and ran out. Over-reaction, if you ask me.'

'To what?' Moss badgered him. 'What had you asked that upset her?'

'Damned if I remember now,' Maxwell said. 'I know I asked her if the police had been to see her. Whether that question specifically triggered it or whether my asking her things at all was the cause, I don't know. Either way, she did a runner. And ran, of all places, to Deirdre Lessing.'

Moss rolled his eyes upward. 'Yes, she's that sort of girl. I remember . . .' and his voice trailed away.

'Mmm?' Maxwell looked up.

'Oh, nothing. Look.' Moss checked his watch. 'I've really got to be going, Max.' He downed his drink and stood up. 'Are you going to be all right?'

Maxwell chuckled. 'I expect so,' he said.

'What will you do?'

'The Charge.'

'What?'

Maxwell looked at his man. 'It's not everybody I show this to,' he said, 'if you've got a minute . . .'

'Yes, of course.'

The older man led his guest up the open plan stairs to the bedroom level and then up into the space under the eaves. Paul Moss was still surprised after two years to find that Peter Maxwell lived in a new town house. Where there should have been oak beams and open fires and flagstones, were breeze-blocks and radiators and Habitat-by-way-of-Oxfam.

'Good God!' Moss stood open-mouthed as Maxwell pinged on the light. In the triangular room in front of him stood a huge trestle-table and on it a diorama with sand and a scattering of bushes. Regiments of 54-millimetre horsemen, hand-painted in Humbrol, sat their horses patiently, as though waiting for the word of command. 'What's this?'

'Oh, Philistine,' chided Maxwell. 'If you hadn't specialised in the impact of the enclosure movement on existential nihilism or whatever crap you did at Cirencester Tech . . .'

'Keele University,' Moss corrected him.

'That's what I said,' Maxwell chuckled. 'If you hadn't done that, you might have done some real history — like the Charge of the Light Brigade, for instance.'

'Bloody brilliant.' Moss moved closer, crouching to examine the figures from eye level. 'Can I touch?'

'Well,' Maxwell whined, 'normally, you touch, you die, but seeing as 'ow you're almost a historian, well, OK, but gently, mind. Polystyrene only goes so far, you know.'

'God,' Moss replied, 'they're all different.'

'Of course they are,' Maxwell said. 'You've got Captain Oldham of the 13th Light Dragoons in your hand there. His boss, Doherty, was sick on 25th October 1854, so Oldham led the regiment. He was last seen in the Charge, unhorsed, pistol in one hand, sword in the other. They never found his body.'

'Well, I'll be buggered.'

'Very possibly,' Maxwell took the diminutive figure from his colleague, 'but not by me, however nicely you ask. My moral turpitude isn't as gross as all that.'

'Is this all of them?' Moss asked him.

'God, no. My researches have turned up 678 men who rode the Charge. So far I've got 308. Number 309,' he crossed to a side table, full of plastic bits, paints and a fixed magnifying glass, and picked up an unfinished bugler, 'is trumpeter John Brown of the 17th Lancers. He was field trumpeter to William Morris who led the regiment. Survived the Charge and lived on till 1905, by which time he was honorary Lieutenant-Colonel.'

Moss shook his head. 'This must take for ever,' he said.

'Well, you know how it is,' Maxwell said. 'Single man and so on. How is Denise by the way?'

He saw the younger man's face darken as he picked up — and put down again — the figure, of Jack Vahey.

'He was the butcher of the 17th,' Maxwell explained, puzzled by Moss's look. 'The reason he's wearing his butcher's apron is that he was late for the line-up that morning. He just buckled on his sword, grabbed a horse of the Scots Greys and rode the Charge in his shirtsleeves.'

'What's all this?' Moss asked, pointing to the figure's chest.

'Blood.' Maxwell thought it was obvious. 'He'd been chopping meat minutes before. I said,' he repeated, 'how is Denise?'

'Fine.' Moss was already on the stairs. 'She's fine, Max. Now, I really must be going.' And within a minute, he had, glancing back once at the suspended Head of Sixth Form, framed by his own doorway. A dog barked across the estate as Moss's light blue metro coughed away into the night.

* * *

The next morning, Maxwell looked on things as positively as he could. He skipped breakfast, fed Metternich before he had his arm off and saddled White Surrey for the field. Contrary to all expectation, he didn't start to slaver, a la Pavlov, when his clock chimed nine. But perhaps that was because he couldn't hear the Leighford bell. He had seen a few Leighford kids, though, creeping out of the estate — his country estate as he called it, legitimately as it was backed by fields — and crawling, unwillingly, to school.

He pedalled to the High Street, bought a paper, mooched in Second Read, his favourite antiquarian bookshop, considered again the leather-bound Boswell and again thought it too pricey, and had a coffee. He had his back to the wall — an increasingly common position for Peter Maxwell these days — and could watch the world go by outside the window. The coffee was an all-time low, but the iced bun was very edible for all it was probably hardening his arteries to a tungsten-like consistency. Then he saw her — Mrs Grey, the mother of Tim, wandering past the window with a distant expression. On an impulse, he left his table, gesturing at the surprised floozie that he wasn't really doing a runner without paying, and caught up with Mrs Grey, outside Woollies.

'Mrs Grey?' He tipped his hat.

'Yes?'

'Peter Maxwell, Leighford High.'

'Oh, yes.' She smiled uneasily at him. 'Yes, of course, Mr Maxwell.'

'Look,' he took her elbow, 'could we have a chat? I was just having a cup of coffee. Perhaps you'd like to join me?'

'Well, I . . .'

But Peter Maxwell's grip was firm and Peter Maxwell's step was sure. He, public school boy that he was, held out her chair for her and she was his. The floozie, no doubt delighted to see him back, hovered at the Great Man's elbow.

'Er . . . Mrs Grey?' he said.

'Oh, I'll just have a cup of tea, please.'

'They do a particularly pleasing line in iced buns,' he assured her.

'No,' she smiled awkwardly. 'Just tea, thanks.'

The floozie wrote it down. 'Is this goin' on the one bill?' she asked.

'Oh, yes,' Maxwell told her and waited until she was out of earshot. 'Mrs Grey, I'm glad I bumped into you. I wanted to have a word about Tim.'

'Tim?' He saw the woman's colour drain until she was the same shade as the tablecloth. 'What's happened? Is he all right?'

'Yes, of course,' he reassured her and placed his hat on the table. 'It's just the business with poor Jenny Hyde.'

'I know,' Mrs Grey said. 'It's terrible, isn't it? I feel so sorry for her parents. Not that we've ever had anything to do with them.'

'I talked to Tim yesterday,' he told her.

'Did you? He never tells us anything, Mr Maxwell. He never has. He's ashamed of us, y'see.'

'Oh, no,' Maxwell frowned. 'I'm sure he's not.'

The floozie brought the tea.

'Oh, yes.' Mrs Grey poured for herself. 'Yes, I've realised it for some time now. Will — that's his father — Will works at Leonards. He's a finisher. He's always worked in a factory, has Will. Me, I'm just a housewife.'

'Now, then.' Maxwell put on his schoolmaster voice. 'I won't have you saying that,' he said.

'What?' Mrs Grey was one of those working-class women who had never shone at anything. She was forty-four years old and she was still afraid of teachers. It was surprising how many people were.

'I'm a housewife too, you know,' Maxwell confided in her.

'You?' She didn't believe him.

'Needs must when the Devil drives,' he told her. 'We crusty old bachelors have to do it all. See that?' He pointed to his shirt.

'Yes.'

'All my own work.'

Mrs Grey was astounded. 'You made it?'

'No,' he explained. 'I ironed it.'

'Ooh, yes.' She peered closer. 'That's good, that is. My Will never does a hand's turn. He did of course when we was first married, but they go off, don't they?'

'They'. That was a good start. Maxwell had only been talking to this lady for five minutes and already she'd welcomed him to her bosom as an honorary woman. The old Maxwell charm had done it again. There was no doubt about it, if Ian McShane didn't make another Lovejoy, he knew who the studios would ask.

'Did Jenny come to your house?' he asked her.

'Once or twice,' she remembered. 'Always had a bit of a smell under her nose, if you ask me.'

Maxwell was picking up the vibes. 'You didn't like her?'

'Well . . .' Mrs Grey shifted in her seat, 'I don't want to speak ill of the dead. My boy . . . well, he's changed.'

'Changed?' Maxwell leaned towards her, gently so as not to frighten her off. 'How, changed?'

'Well . . .' She was making little ruts in the tablecloth with her spoon. 'Tim started going out with her . . . when would it have been? Last May time, I think. 'Course his father started taking the . . . you know, making fun of him. But he got all stuck up after that. Sort of la-de-da. It was her what put this university idea into his head.'

'You don't want him to go to university, Mrs Grey?' Maxwell asked.

'Oh, I don't know,' she said. 'You hear such things, don't you? Such stories. All these drugs and things. I remember once, me and my Will went to Oxford for the day and there was these students there, you know, by the river. And one of them came up to the others and said,' her voice dropped to a whisper, '"Where have you bastards been?" Just like that.'

Maxwell clicked his tongue and shook his head. It was almost impossible not to condescend to Mrs Grey. He could understand the problem Jenny Hyde must have had.

'Well, I ask you.' She was nattering on. 'Will and I don't want our boy mixing with people what talk like that.'

'There is more to university, though,' the honorary housewife told her.

'Oh, I know,' she said, 'but there's no guarantee of jobs, is there? No, I think his father would like him to get a job at Leonards, you know. They seem to have survived the recession all right.'

'Tell me, Mrs Grey,' Maxwell re-stirred his coffee, 'was there another change in Tim?'

'Another one?' The woman looked confused. 'How do you mean?'

'Recently, say . . . oh, about a week before Jenny was murdered. Did he seem . . . well, different?'

She struggled to remember. 'He was in a bad mood,' she said, 'that last week of school. Slamming about the place. Look at him funny and he'd bite your head off.'

That wasn't the Tim Grey Peter Maxwell knew. He'd long entertained the idea that 'Tim' was short for timid. But he also knew from his long years of experience that most kids were mildly schizophrenic. By day, particularly boring members of the Silent Majority; by night, Offspring from Hell.

'We put it down to his exams,' Mrs Grey explained.

'Exams?' Maxwell prodded.

''Cos he'd done bad in his exams.'

'Oh, yes,' Maxwell nodded. 'Well, I shouldn't worry about that.'

There was no need to worry the Greys about it. Not now. Not after all this time. The fact was that Tim Grey had done well — surprisingly well — in the end-of-terms exams.

And Maxwell noted ruefully that yet another end-of-term report had not got home.

'Good Lord,' Maxwell checked his Rotary, 'is that the time? Mrs Grey, would you excuse me? I have an appointment.'

'Oh, yes.' She downed the last of her tea. 'Is that why you aren't at school, then?'

'That's right.' He winced and held his cheek. 'I've had a bitch of a toothache for the past few days. By the way, does the name Maz mean anything to you?'

She frowned. 'Maz?' she repeated. 'No, I don't think so. Why?'

'Not a friend of Tim's?' He jogged her memory.

'No. No, I've never heard that name. I'm sure I'd remember it. Why do you want to know?'

'Oh, nothing.' Maxwell beamed and slung his hat on his head, fumbling for change to pay the floozie. 'Nothing at all. It's been very nice, having this chat. 'Bye.'

'Cheerio.' She smiled at him and padded out to resume her vague sortie through Woollies.

So; Peter Maxwell checked his watch again. The Nag would be open by now. Quite a novelty to drink during the day, in September, in the middle of a week. He'd have a quick one just for the hell of it. He had to talk to Tim Grey again. All right, so he didn't talk much at home. But he lied there. Why? Why should he tell his parents that he'd done badly in his exams when he hadn't? Why didn't he show them his report? And more importantly, what made him change about a week before Jenny Hyde was found dead? It would be about the time she'd gone missing. Would that explain it? Was that all it was? Did he know where she'd gone? What had happened to her? And who was the Maz he'd mentioned? The Maz his mother didn't know, had never heard of. Still, it was going to be a bitch, Maxwell realised as he wandered into the pub and ordered his pint, to get hold of Tim Grey now. In the confines of his office, it was easy. Consult the lad's timetable, find the room, oik him out, grill him. Now, he'd either have to lurk outside school, with all the delicious ammunition that would give John Graham and the vigilantes at County Hall, or he'd have to visit the Greys. Either way, he'd be at a disadvantage. How could he get hold of Tim Grey now?

* * *

Four policemen got hold of Tim Grey. They lifted him on to a stretcher from the place under the bushes where he'd been lying. He was wrapped in a black plastic bag like so much rubbish and there was a livid purple mark where someone had choked the life out of him. How could he get hold of Tim Grey now?

CHAPTER 11

Jim Astley's wife had gone to dry out again. Jim Astley himself was back in the mortuary, in his dark green apron and cap, probing and prodding what had once been Timothy William Grey.

Chief Inspector Henry Hall had left his dwindling team back at the incident room and was propping up the wall behind Astley's back.

'What have we got, then, Jim?' he asked.

Astley grunted, apparently wrestling with something gristly. 'As far as I can tell,' he said, 'it seems to be a carbon copy of the Jenny Hyde business. Minus the potential sexual interference, of course.' Hall forced himself to go closer. He never relished moments like this, the remains of a human being picked over by a vulture in green. But he knew it had to be. It was the only way to get results. And he had precious few of those at the moment.

It had got so he hated going into work of a morning. The smell of the incident room was enough. He'd nod curtly to his staff, down now to six men and two women, and disappear inside his inner sanctum, emerging only for the weekly pep talk. It had got less convincing each time and he knew it. He knew too that they knew it. The noise was less, the hubbub over. Eight people just didn't fill the space of thirty and one of the eight was only part-time. One by one, the leads ran out, the options closed. Avenue after avenue proved to be yet another cul-de-sac. And now everybody avoided everybody's gaze. 'Scaling down', it was called in the force. You couldn't keep X officers together on one case for long. There wasn't the manpower and there wasn't the cash. First he'd lost five to a spate of burglaries, then an armed robbery took three of his best lads. By the beginning of September his little force was decimated and the successful arrest of a rapist the week before had only diminished it still further because of the mountain of paperwork. It proved to have nothing to do with Jennifer Antonia Hyde. They pulled the plug on that one too.

And now? God knew certainly. And Dr James Astley knew a bit. As for Chief Inspector Henry Hall, he felt he didn't know diddly any more.

'Strangulation,' Astley was saying, pulling the mask away so that Hall could hear his pearls of wisdom, 'by ligature. Look here, to the left of the cartilage, a distinct knot.' He was right. A large blue area discoloured the dead boy's neck up to his jawline. Hall looked down at the face. Tim Grey was the colour of old parchment, his lips peeled back from his teeth, his eyes sunken in. The dark hair, never tidy in life, lay like a black thatch above the pale forehead.

'But this time,' Astley held up the boy's right hand, 'he went down fighting.' Grey's knuckles were cut and scraped. 'It's my guess he hit a tooth,' he said. 'There's a particularly jagged cut in the index finger . . . just . . . here.'

Hall peered closer, nodding.

'Did he die where he was found?'

'That's a fair bet,' Astley said. 'His clothes were covered in grass and burrs, not to mention cobwebs. Of course, I'll have to wait for the soil specimens.'

'When?' Hall was a middle-aged man in a hurry.

Astley screwed up his face. 'Friday?' was the best he could do.

Hall nodded. 'Now for the sixty-four thousand one, Jim,' he said. 'Am I looking for the same man?'

Astley straightened up, feeling his back click. 'Come on, now, Henry,' he said. 'The impossible I can do at once. Miracles take a little longer.'

'Your best shot, then,' Hall shrugged.

'Deep down,' Astley said, looking at the corpse, 'and off the record,' looking at Hall, 'I smell copy cat.'

'But we didn't give details to the press,' Hall reminded him. 'Nothing about the ligature, with the knot to the left.'

'No.' Astley shifted his weight from foot to foot. His own indiscretion hit him in the pit of the stomach and he felt uncomfortable. 'No, that's true. But I hear that teacher's been snooping around.'

'What teacher?' Hall frowned.

'From Leighford High. Whatsisface? Maxwell? Maxforth? Something.'

'Peter Maxwell,' Hall nodded. 'Where's he been snooping?'

'Here, there and everywhere, from what I hear. Does the family know?'

'The Greys? No,' Hall said, sighing, 'I was on my way over there now. Friday then, Jim,' he said, grabbing his raincoat and making for the door. 'Soil samples. Oh, by the way, I'd kill for a time of death.'

'Eightish,' he said. 'Perhaps nearer nine.'

'This morning?'

'No, no,' Astley corrected his man. 'Last night. All you've got to do is find out who was on the Dam last night and you've got him.'

Hall's smile was cold, empty. 'Thanks, Jim,' he said. 'I'll be in touch.'

* * *

DI Dave Johnson had gone to Leonards to winkle out William Grey from the Finishing Shop. DC Jacquie Carpenter sat with Mrs Grey, patting her hands as she cradled the photograph of her only son, the one they were telling her was dead. She couldn't understand. Would never understand. Not as long as she lived. She just sat with tears trickling silently down her cheeks and when Will and the other policeman arrived, she just looked at him and went into the kitchen to make them all a cup of tea.

The detectives left the couple alone for a while, mentally noting anything in the little terraced house that might be of significance later. Then the couple came out, Will Grey putting on his donkey jacket again. He'd go with the policeman to the place. No need for his wife to come. He was the boy's father. He'd identify him.

'Mrs Grey?' Jacquie Carpenter had said softly. 'Can I see Tim's room?' She was dying for a ciggie and dying to be anywhere but where she was. It didn't seem long ago that she'd been saying the same thing to Mrs Hyde and feeling the same way she felt now; bloody awful.

The dead boy's room was bleaker than the dead girl's. He had no telly, no video games, precious few books. A disused pair of football boots hung in a wardrobe, with his school clothes and a pack of playing cards. A battered hi-fi system filled a corner and a handful of tapes lay scattered on the bed.

'I thought he'd gone to school,' Mrs Grey was saying. 'I don't work, y'see. Not at the moment. But I had to go out on an errand. Mavis — that's the girl next door — her eldest has just started school; y'know, in the Infants. And Mavis has got two more, both under three, so I offered to take the other one to school. I thought he'd gone.'

'Where did he go last night, Mrs Grey?' Jacquie Carpenter asked, still carrying her mug of tea.

'Ooh.' The woman looked vague. 'I don't rightly know,' she muttered. 'I think he was going to a teacher's house.'

'A teacher?' The policewoman looked at her. 'Do you remember who?'

'No.' Mrs Grey shook her head. 'He didn't say. Are there any teachers, then, who live on the Dam?'

'The Dam, Mrs Grey?'

'That's where they found him, isn't it? My Will said the Inspector had told him that's where Tim was. Did he suffer, miss?' she asked suddenly, all in the same breath as her last sentence. 'Would he have suffered, my Tim? Only I don't mind him being gone, but I couldn't have stood it if he'd suffered.'

Jacquie Carpenter just held the woman's hand with the one that was free. This time she hadn't seen the body. Hadn't been at the scene of the crime. But she knew what her colleagues knew. She knew about the ligature and the dead boy's throat and the bulging tongue and the mottled skin. People suffered in a death like that. Just how much only two people knew — the victim and his murderer.

'No,' she lied. 'No, Mrs Grey, he didn't suffer.'

'Oh.' Mrs Grey raised a shaking hand to her lips. Jacquie Carpenter put her mug down quickly, ready to handle the collapse that was near. But Mrs Grey wasn't collapsing. She was remembering. 'I've got to get a message to someone,' she said.

'Who?' Jacquie asked. 'Is it Tim's granny or someone?'

'No,' Mrs Grey said. 'It's that nice Mr Maxwell from up at the school. He was asking after Tim only this morning.'

* * *

If you haven't been in a school staff room, the chances are you haven't been in a police incident room either. Chief Inspector Hall's at Tottingleigh was the old library. Some decrepit old biddy, whose grandfather was a Major-General or something, had died and left a bob or two to the local library services. It was probably her intention to tart up the old place where she sat hour after hour poring over Barbara Cartland or Catherine Cookson in the rather maudlin way that women will. But the local Cultural Services had different ideas and they built a spanking new library, with electronic anti-theft devices and computers all over the place; about as close to culture as Australia is.

So it was that the old Tottingleigh Lending Library was currently vacant — and West Sussex CID had moved in. Henry Hall had got the call by midday and his heart leapt as he heard the news. Still, he didn't believe it until he saw it and when he climbed the well-worn steps that afternoon, he did see it — the hushed room full again, busy and bustling. Manpower? No problem. Cash? Well, put in for overtime and we'll see what happens. Another kid was dead. Let's get the bastard who did it.

Some faces he recognised. Others not. But they all knew him, and by the time the old library clock struck three, the team had come to order and he was faced with fifty-eight coppers, draped on chairs or leaning against filing cabinets, shirtsleeves rolled and ties loosened. Hall sat alone to one side of the front desk. DI Johnson had the chair.

'Timothy William Grey,' he began and the light went out and the beam of a carousel hit the screen behind him, cigarette smoke swirling and recoiling in the shaft of light. 'You'll have to bear with us on some of these slides — some of 'em are still wet.' A school photograph flashed in front of the watching detectives of a thin, plain-looking schoolboy of about fourteen. 'This is an old photograph,' Johnson told them.

The same face appeared again. Older. Unsmiling. Dead. 'This is a new one.' Johnson had been this way before. 'Taken at seven thirty hours this morning. His body was found under a clump of bushes at the Dam. For those of you drafted in from the sticks . . .' he waited for the snigger to die down, 'this is a beauty spot a mile and a half from the sea. Open parkland, bushes, trees.'

'There's talk of a golf course,' Hall added. The next slide swept the area, but the natural beauty of it was scarred by the blue and white police cordon ribbon fluttering to the left. A closer view showed the bushes and the next eight were devoted to the body from different angles. Everybody respected DS Davis, the photographer. Dedicated. Thorough. No job for the squeamish, police photographer, recording for all time nature's saddest handiwork. But somebody had to do it. And Davis had.

'He was found on his back,' Johnson said, 'knees drawn up and left leg flat on the ground. The cause of death was strangulation. A ligature of some kind drawn and knotted to the left of his Adam's apple.'

Davis's mortuary photographs flicked on to the screen, exactly as Hall had seen the body on Astley's slab.

'Approximate time of death,' Johnson checked the sheaf of paper on his clipboard, 'twenty-thirty to twenty-one hundred hours last night. No witnesses so far.'

'Who found the body, Dave?' a voice called from the back.

'Kids, Er . . .' Johnson flicked through his pages. 'Two paper boys taking a short-cut on their round. They saw his trainers and feet sticking out from under the bush. Ran back home and the parents rang us.'

'So the dead lad had been there all night?' Biros slid across notebooks as the team's specialists selected their information from Johnson and wrote it down.

'All night,' Johnson nodded. 'His knuckles were cut and the pathologist thinks he may have got a decent one in on his attacker before he died. Our man may have a loose or missing tooth.'

'Footprints?' someone asked.

'Ground's too dry,' Johnson said to the mass of silhouetted heads in front of him. It didn't sound likely to him either. Ever since the Jenny Hyde murder it seemed to have done nothing but rain. But the Dam was high above sea level and the short grass left few secrets.

'Tyres?' somebody else tried.

'You can't get a vehicle up there,' the Inspector told them. 'We had to cart the body by stretcher to the ambulance, what . . . quarter of a mile. We've got some bike tracks though.'

'The paper boys?' a faceless voice suggested.

'They were on foot,' Johnson told the team. 'Even so, it doesn't help at the moment.'

'Was he actually killed where he was found?' Jacquie Carpenter's voice was clear to the right.

'We don't know,' Johnson said, still subconsciously wondering what business it was of hers. 'Soil samples due Friday.'

There was a series of guffaws and hoots. 'I thought it was vicars worked a one-day week, not pathologists.'

'All right.' Johnson felt it was time to keep the lid on things. 'Sir?'

The room fell quiet again as Henry Hall took Johnson's place. It was a quiet not exactly born of respect. Those who knew Hall knew he was a lacklustre bastard. Those who didn't know him had heard he was. No, it was just the norm. When the guv'nor stood up, you shut up. Because this was an incident room. And this was a murder enquiry. Miss something, however small, however irrelevant and you'd miss your man. Forever.

'Similarities,' Hall said quietly, his eyes wandering over his team. His suit. His accent. It reeked of university. He spoke fluent graduate. One or two of the younger lads who had followed in his wake from Bramshill were impressed. The older ones were quietly contemptuous. Somebody else lit up. 'I won't bore you with the slides again, ladies and gentlemen. The photographs are all around the walls. But for those of you drafted in from . . .' he smiled at Johnson sitting beside him, 'elsewhere . . .' no one sniggered this time, 'I suggest you familiarise yourselves with them and with the details of the Jennifer Hyde case.'

The fierce light of the projector still dazzled in his face, giving his eyes an eerie white blankness. 'Could we have that off, Reg?'

Reg killed the light. 'Similarity one.' Hall moved slowly along the front row, like a general reviewing his troops. 'Both victims died by strangulation. Strangulation caused by a ligature with a knot to the left.' He let that one sink in before he went on. 'Similarity two, both victims were aged seventeen. Similarity three,' he paused, 'and I'm not sure similarity is the right word, these victims knew each other. Not only that.

They were going out together. For a time,' he cleared his throat, 'we had our eye on Timothy Grey for the murder of Jenny Hyde.'

There was a murmur. 'Which is still,' he accurately read their minds, 'a possibility. Grey had no effective alibi for the time of the girl's murder. And he may have had any one of the usual run of motives.'

'Are we talking about revenge, then, guv?' a particularly scruffy detective constable asked.

'Mr . . . er . . .'

'Halsey.' The detective instinctively straightened in the chair. 'George Halsey. Stationed at Chichester.'

'It's possible, George,' he said. 'The girl's father has a short fuse, we believe, and a powerful build. But we mustn't let our hypotheses run away with us.'

For all the silent social revolution of the twentieth century and for all the rigours of modern police examinations, there were still one or two in front of him who wouldn't know a hypothesis if it got up and bit them. He knew who they were. Their heads were down and they suddenly found their shoelaces absolutely fascinating.

'Jacquie, you've been working with the mother. What have we got?'

The girl stood up and smoothed down her skirt. George Halsey turned his wolf whistle in the nick of time into a click of his teeth. The new boy couldn't afford to antagonise anybody yet. He'd noticed no ring on the policewoman's hand. And he liked the curve of her bum. He'd give her a day or two, then chance his arm.

'Mrs Grey is a simple, working-class woman,' Jacquie said, her voice trembling a little as it always did in moments like these, which she hated, when the guv'nor asked her to hold forth. 'She's bearing up quite well, really, everything considered. She left home before her son this morning and assumed he'd already gone to school. She knows he went out last night to see a teacher, but we don't know who.'

'Dave?' Hall cut in.

Johnson jerked back to his feet. 'Mr Hall and I will be paying another call to Leighford High tomorrow morning,' he said. 'The bastards do no work after four o'clock.'

Guffaws and snarls all round. 'Bit like pathologists,' somebody sneered. Whistles and applause. Then the team fell silent again.

'We don't know,' Jacquie Carpenter hated the sudden silence she stood in the centre of, 'if Tim had any enemies. The mother didn't know anything about that, but she didn't seem to know much at all. Bit out of her depth, really.'

'Is there a dad?' Halsey asked.

'Joe Grierson's on that now,' Johnson told him. 'Bloke works shifts at Leonards. Meek sort of bloke from my conversation with him. Less so, I understand, with the gentlemen of the press. But then I had just told him his only kid was dead. Wonder how we'd react.'

There were nods and murmurs. These men had kids too. It was hard. Bloody hard. Best not to think about it. But you had to think about it. Divorce it, then, from reality. It's all pretend. A game. Like that *Prime Suspect*. Except it wasn't a game. And it wasn't raunchy Helen Mirren up there but the sullen, sour face of DI Dave Johnson, a man you didn't cross.

Hall was on his feet again. 'We've got to restart,' he said. 'Everything. From the beginning. Jenny Hyde. Her friends. Her enemies. Her acquaintances. Everybody she ever talked to. Everybody she bought her sweets from. Everybody she sat by on the school bus. The same for Timothy Grey. She went missing the week before she died. Why? Where was she from the Sunday to the Friday we found her body? What was Grey's involvement in it all? What was he doing on the Dam last night? And who was this teacher he went to see?'

Questions. Questions. And not an answer in it. But there was a new urgency in his voice. A new fire down below. The lights came up and the team hauled itself into action, filing cabinets grating open, VDUs flashing on, telephones ringing. An incident room back, like Lazarus, from the dead.

‘Jacquie,’ Hall said as he swept into his office, ‘get me the BBC. I want Nick Ross to do a follow-up.’

George Halsey, the new boy, shook his head. He wasn’t fooled for a minute. For all the clash and hurry, he saw right through it.

‘What a lacklustre bastard,’ he muttered.

And everybody knew he wasn’t talking about Nick Ross.

* * *

They just sat there, Peter Maxwell and Sylvia Matthews, staring disbelieving at the set. Sylvia had called round to see how he was. She’d put it off for two days, not quite knowing what to say, how he’d react. She’d been married for seven years, before her husband got the itch, and she knew the last thing men wanted was sympathy. So she’d stayed away. Then her maternalism had got the better of her and she’d gone round there, all concern and cocoa. She’d just finished patting him, asking him how he was, probing, when they both heard it simultaneously. The Meridian newscaster, whose name neither of them could remember, just sat there, as newscasters will, reading his autocue.

‘The body of seventeen-year-old Timothy Grey from Leighford was found this morning on the Dam, a well-known beauty spot in the area. Chief Inspector Henry Hall heading the enquiry said that there may be a link with the so far unsolved killing of teenager Jennifer Hyde who attended Timothy’s school last July.’

Sylvia was on her feet first. ‘Max,’ she said, blinking as the south’s unemployment figures replaced the smiling school photograph of Tim Grey. ‘Oh, Max.’

He was beside her, patting her shoulder. She turned to him and he saw the tears start. He cradled her head against his chest, running his fingers through her hair. ‘I don’t know,’ he smiled, ‘you come over to comfort me and I end up comforting you. Women!’ and he tossed his head in mock disgust.

She pretended to kick him in the shins and ended up laughing into his solid, warm chest. 'I'm sorry,' she sniffed. 'Carrying on like this. It's just. . . well, I can't believe it.'

'Neither can I.' Maxwell rummaged in his pocket. 'Here,' and he gave her his handkerchief. 'Now, then, big blow for the Queen.'

'Shan't.' She smiled up at him though the tears. 'Bellowing into someone else's handkerchief is not very ladylike, Max,' she said.

'You're right.' He held her at arm's length. 'Remember the old Hancock sketch? The blood donor? Where he's walking around singing "Coughs and sneezes spread diseases" to the tune of "Deutschland, Deutschland"? Ah, they don't make 'em like that any more.'

There was a sharp, brittle ring of his door bell. 'Christ,' he muttered.

'I'll go,' she said.

'But you've been crying,' he told her. 'Aren't women supposed to go away and fix there faces or something? Bette Davis always did.'

She swiped him with his own hanky. 'You're a fraud, Peter Maxwell,' she said. 'On the surface, you're a chauvinist git, but deep down you're just a chauvinist git . . . Unless you mind me answering the door? It's not going to ruin your reputation, is it?'

He sprawled on the settee. 'Ah, well,' he said, 'that little ol' thing is going through rather a bad patch at the moment, but I suppose I'll have to live with it.' And he watched her pad off down the stairs.

He wasn't ready for the raised voices. Or the crash of his own front door. And he wasn't even on his feet by the time two burly strangers stood in his living-room. At least, one was a stranger. The other he'd met before. Once. And he hadn't enjoyed the experience.

'Peter Maxwell.'

'Detective Inspector Johnson, isn't it?' Maxwell stood up slowly.

'This is Detective Constable Halsey.' The stranger nodded curtly.

'We'd like you to accompany us to Leighford police station.'

'My God,' Maxwell smiled, 'you really do say that sort of thing, then, you policemen. Well, well.'

He wasn't really ready for what followed either, Johnson squared up to him, his face inches from Maxwell's. 'Look, you fucking shit, I've just come from helping a father identify his dead kid. I've not had a lot of sleep in the past few weeks and I've got a feeling you know something about the cause of that. If you want a coat, get it.'

'You can't talk to him like that.' Sylvia Matthews spun the man round.

'Can't I? Mrs Maxwell, is it?' Johnson asked, knowing perfectly well it wasn't, 'well, let me tell you something about your husband . . .'

'He's not my husband,' she corrected him. 'Not that that's any of your business. You don't have to go, Max. You've already told them about the diary . . .'

'Diary?' Johnson turned back to his man.

Maxwell closed his eyes. 'I'll get my coat,' he said.

'Right. You don't mind if DC Halsey has a look round?'

'Yes.' Maxwell was level with his man now, his eyes burning into Johnson's. 'As a matter of fact I do. And you won't mind dropping Mrs Matthews off at her home? She came on the bus.'

'No.' Sylvia said, almost deafened by the thump of her own heart. 'No, Max, I'm coming with you.'

'I'm afraid not.' Johnson looked at her coldly.

'No.' Maxwell held her shoulder gently. 'No, Sylv, I'll be all right. After all, Criminal Procedure Act, FACE, the Sheehy Report. The days of people falling downstairs while in police stations are over, aren't they, Inspector?'

'Let's go,' Johnson sneered at him. 'Miss?'

'Thanks,' Sylvia Matthews snapped. 'But I'll catch the bus.'

CHAPTER 12

They left him alone for a while. Made him sweat. But Peter Maxwell had been a couch potato for longer than he could remember. *No Hiding Place*, *Gideon*, *The Sweeney*. He knew all the moves. He sat as relaxed as he could be on the hard, tubular steel chair, his hands clasped across his chest, his eyes closed, and he recalled to himself as much as he could of Palmerston's foreign policy.

He'd just reached the Don Pacifico affair, when the terrible milord had despatched the British fleet to the harbour of Piraeus in defence of one rather dubious Portuguese-Jewish-Englishman, when the door crashed back. Clearly, Detective Inspector Johnson was fond of the grand entrance. The solid, averagely good-looking George Halsey was with him.

'Right.' Johnson sat on the chair opposite Maxwell. 'We've done the introductions,' he said, calmer than when they'd taken their leave in the yard outside. 'Let's get down to business.' He nodded to Halsey who flicked a switch on a machine stacked in the corner of the bare room.

'Interview commencing,' Johnson leaned forward to talk into a microphone on the table, checking his watch simultaneously, 'at ten thirty-eight. DI Johnson and DC Halsey in the interview room with Peter Maxwell. Speak into that, please.'

Maxwell glanced at the microphone, then chewed his little finger. 'The day war broke out, my missus said to me . . .'

'Your own voice,' Johnson growled.

Pity really. It was the best Rob Wilton Peter Maxwell had ever done.

'Aren't I allowed a phone call?' Maxwell removed the finger from his mouth, but his body hadn't moved.

'Who you gonna call?' Johnson sneered. 'Ghostbusters?'

Halsey sniggered and pulled up a second chair. The policemen now faced Maxwell, they on one side of the table, he on the other, like strangers obliged to share in a restaurant. No one was comfortable. No one intended to show it.

'You are here under your own free will?' Johnson put the formalities forward for the benefit of the tape. 'No one has forced you?'

'No,' said Maxwell. 'No one.'

'I have to advise you,' Johnson was glancing over a sheaf of notes, 'that Mr Hall and I were not entirely happy about the answers you gave us in connection with the murder of Jennifer Hyde.'

'Really?' Maxwell allowed his left eyebrow to crawl upward. 'In what way?'

'I've read the file too,' Halsey butted in. 'It sucks, mate.' He fixed Maxwell with his steely, dark eyes. 'From beginning to end.'

'Take this bit, Peter . . .' Johnson said.

'If you don't mind, Detective Inspector,' Maxwell broke his clasp for the first time and all six legs, his and the chair's were on the floor, 'I'd rather you called me Mr Maxwell.'

Johnson's grin was a sneer. 'Well, now, Peter,' he said, 'I was hoping to keep this friendly.'

'So was I,' said Maxwell, 'and your rather feeble attempt to patronise me is not the way to go about it.'

Johnson straightened up, stacking his papers with a thump that made the tape's needle bounce to the far side of its arc. Maxwell leaned back again. For all Johnson seemed to be a graduate of the school of body language, Maxwell had founded it.

'Very well,' the senior policeman said. 'When you . . . broke up, I believe is the phrase you teachers use . . . when you broke up at the end of last term, where did you go?'

'To Cornwall,' Maxwell told him. 'On holiday.'

'Bit unusual, that, isn't it?' Halsey frowned.

'To go to Cornwall?' Maxwell smiled. 'I think you'll find thousands of people do it. I couldn't get into Mevagissey on the Thursday morning for the queue of traffic.'

'No,' Johnson grinned, 'no, Peter . . . er . . . Mr Maxwell. See, you're missing the point. What my colleague means is that you left school rather precipitately.'

Maxwell was impressed. This wasn't bad for a man with three O levels to his name. He must have been to night school. 'Did I?' he asked.

'We made some enquiries,' Johnson told him, 'up at the school. Seems you're the life and soul of the end-of-term party usually. Knees-ups in the staff room, presentations to leaving teachers, that sort of thing. Some of your colleagues claimed you're usually one of the last to leave.'

'Nothing to go home to, I guess.' Halsey lit a cigarette. 'Bachelor like you. Must be a lonely life. Empty. Desolate, even.'

Maxwell leaned forward and his eyes burned back into Halsey's. 'I'm not the type,' he said, 'to kill for company.'

Johnson's mouth fell open. 'Now,' he said, his voice stunned with mock exasperation, 'whoever said anything about killing? Did you, George? Did you say anything about killing?'

'Not a word, Inspector.' Halsey hadn't taken his eyes off Maxwell's. 'Not one blessed word.'

'So you see our dilemma.' Johnson wasn't at all bad at playing the nice policeman, considering he'd had so little practice. 'Here we've got half a dozen of your colleagues — your friends — who have told us you usually hang about in the staff room at the end of term and here you're telling us you buggered off to Cornwall.'

'So I broke the habit of a lifetime,' Maxwell shrugged. He could tell the police weren't impressed. 'Look,' he said, 'there was a deal with Hamilton's Coaches, here in Leighford. If you caught the coach that left Tottingleigh at four thirty, you'd be in Exeter by seven and Penzance by two in the morning. Cheap excursion rates because of the weird timing. Check with the company.'

'We did, Mr Maxwell,' Johnson said, still smiling with his thin, smug lips. 'You see, they don't have a record of you travelling on any of their coaches that weekend.'

'What?' Maxwell sat upright again.

Johnson flashed a look at Halsey. He sensed his man's composure about to crack. 'Oh, I'm sure it's all just a mistake,' he went on. 'You know how it is, computer error or something. It's just that all records from that Friday to the Monday have been wiped. Almost as if . . . Are you familiar with Apple Macintosh, Mr Maxwell?'

The pending Head of Sixth Form looked his man in the face. 'As far as I am concerned,' he said, 'one of those is a fruit, the other is a type of raincoat.'

'Oh, very droll,' Halsey scoffed. 'I'm glad you're still laughing, sunshine.'

'One of those little coincidences, I expect.' Johnson was getting into his stride now.

'The driver,' Maxwell snapped his fingers. 'I gave the driver my ticket.'

'Of course you did.' Johnson frowned and nodded in mock-earnest support. 'But unfortunately Hamilton's drivers don't keep their stubs once they've collected them. Normally, you see, the computer records all bookings, so there'd be no need.'

'Cheque stubs,' Maxwell said. 'Look at my cheque book. My bank statement.'

'Oh, we have no doubt that you booked on that coach,' Johnson said. 'Or a coach, certainly. You probably even paid the fare.' He rested his elbows on his papers and jutted his jaw forward so that he and Maxwell were eyeball to eyeball.

'But the fact is, you don't have the first bloody bit of corroborative evidence to prove you caught the four thirty from Tottingleigh, do you? None whatsoever.'

For the second time in his life, Peter Maxwell couldn't think of a damn thing to say. And he'd been wrong. The nightmare he thought had begun when he'd seen Nick Ross reporting Jenny Hyde's murder on the television had not started then. It was starting now.

'Well,' Johnson leaned back, thoroughly enjoying Maxwell's predicament. 'We'll leave that for now, shall we? So you left the school at what time?'

'Er . . . I don't know. Just before three, I think.'

'The kids went home at two,' Halsey reminded him.

'That's right. Last day of term is always short. Assembly followed by a bash in the staff room — a "knees-up", as you put it.'

'Anybody retiring this time?'

'No.' Maxwell shook his head. 'The odd supply bod, that's all. They come and go.'

Johnson nodded, peering at Maxwell through Halsey's cigarette haze. 'How far would you say it was from Leighford High to the Red House?'

'Oh, I don't know.' Maxwell weighed it up in his mind. 'About a mile and a half, I suppose.'

'How long would it take? For you to do the journey, I mean?'

'Why would I want to do the journey?' Maxwell was careful enough to ask.

'Ah,' Johnson beamed, 'that's the sixty-four thousand dollar question, isn't it? Why indeed? Just humour me, Mr Maxwell. How long would it take?'

'Well, by car . . .'

'No, not by car,' the Detective Inspector was quick to cut in. 'You don't drive, do you?'

He saw Maxwell's eyelids flicker. 'No,' he said, 'not any more.'

'By bike,' Johnson narrowed it down. 'Say you were travelling by bike.'

'I don't know,' Maxwell shrugged. 'Let's see. It's uphill towards the house, isn't it? About twenty minutes; perhaps more if you hit traffic at the flyover.'

'That's what I thought,' Johnson said. 'So if you left the school at three o'clock, you'd be there by half-past.'

'Assuming that's what I did.'

'Yes,' Johnson nodded acidly, 'assuming that. And of course, Jennifer Hyde didn't die until about four o'clock. That means that you had half an hour with her.'

'Long enough,' Halsey pointed out, 'long enough to rip the poor kid's blouse and bra . . .'

'Long enough for me to run seven miles if I was Superman.' Maxwell refused to be ruffled. 'I wasn't there.'

'Your bike was,' Johnson countered.

'What?'

'Or one very like it. Seen leaning up against the wall of the Red House on the afternoon in question.'

'If Jenny died at four o'clock,' Maxwell said, 'I was already in the waiting-room at the coach station.'

Johnson slid his chair away from the table and crossed purposefully to the window. The blinds were down, but he parted the slats and looked out. The rain trickled like tears down the glass with the cold, hungry darkness beyond. 'How did you get there?' he asked.

'Where?' Maxwell had lost his thread. For all his outward coolness, he was a mass of jangled nerves inside.

'The coach station.' Johnson turned to him, wide-eyed. 'Isn't that where you said you were?'

'I walked.'

'Where was your bike?' Halsey asked.

'At home,' Maxwell said.

'How did you get to school that morning?' Johnson worried his man like a terrier.

'I walked.'

'Who saw you?'

'On which journey?'

'Either.'

'I don't know,' Maxwell flustered. 'In the morning, kids. In the afternoon . . .'

'The kids had all gone home,' Halsey blurted at him.

'Nobody. Somebody. I don't remember.'

There was a pause. A mocking silence that hung on Maxwell like a stone. Johnson wandered back to his seat as if it was the last place he actually wanted to be. 'You know,' he said, grinning broadly at Maxwell, 'there's one line in the course of our enquiries which is always music to my ears.'

'Really?' Maxwell couldn't quite see what was coming.

'Yes.' Johnson nodded, as though to the village idiot. 'That line "I don't remember."'

'Why?'

'Because,' Johnson put his face close to Maxwell's, 'when I hear it, it usually means someone's lying.'

Maxwell said nothing. Just sat there and looked at his adversary.

'Questioning paused at ten fifty-eight,' Johnson said and switched off the microphone. 'I expect Mr Maxwell could do with a cup of tea, George,' he said, genially. 'I know I could.'

'Right, guv.' The beefy detective hauled up his chair and slid it against the wall, a smirk hovering around his lips. Then he was gone and the world was full of David Johnson.

'Right, you self-satisfied bastard,' the policeman loomed over Maxwell, 'I'm going to tell you a story.'

Maxwell looked levelly at him. 'Not the best Max Bygraves I've heard,' he said.

'Cut the crap!' Johnson ordered. 'If you think a double murder is anything to laugh at, you pervert, I'll soon change your mind about that.' He slapped a buff envelope down on the table between them. 'Have a look,' he snarled. 'A bloody good look.'

Maxwell hesitated. 'What is it?' he asked.

'There's only one way to find out, isn't there?' Johnson's eyes were bright under the strip light.

Maxwell fumbled with the manilla and half a dozen glossy black and white photographs fell out. They showed the twisted body of Jenny Hyde, her lips drawn back from her teeth, her hair splayed wide, her eyes staring. And cold. And dead.

Maxwell shut his eyes. Just because he still could. They snapped open again when he felt Johnson's hand on his shoulder. 'Take a good look, I said,' the Inspector was shaking him, 'because that's what you did to her. That's how you left her, all alone in the house. Wouldn't play, would she?'

Maxwell's hand clasped over Johnson's and wrenched it from his jacket.

'Wouldn't let you touch her? What did you do, get her tits out? Put your hand up her skirt?'

The door clicked open with a sharpness that made Maxwell jump.

'Not now, George.' Johnson hadn't turned, hadn't taken his eyes off his man.

'Dave,' a soft voice said.

The look on Johnson's face said it all. The lacklustre bastard had arrived with that impeccable bloody timing of his. Just when he'd got his man on the ropes. In another minute, he'd have got a confession out of him. Either that or he'd have rammed that bloody college scarf down his perverted throat.

'Your shift finished twenty minutes ago, Dave,' Hall said, patting his man on the shoulder. 'You get off home, now. I'll finish up here.'

'Guv . . .' Johnson straightened.

'Now, Dave.' Hall's jaw was firmer than Johnson had ever remembered it. He knew an exit cue when he heard one and took it.

Hall closed the door in the Inspector's wake, then turned to Maxwell, still sitting in his chair. 'We're all a bit on edge,' he said, by way of explanation. It was not an apology.

'You can say that again,' Maxwell nodded.

'You had a right to call your solicitor,' Hall told him.

'I haven't got one,' Maxwell said. 'Nor an accountant. Nor a dentist and not much of a doctor.'

Hall sat down and opened the file, then he saw the photographs still scattered on the desk. He gathered them up. 'If you feel there have been any irregularities here . . .' He looked over his glasses at Maxwell and watched the Head of Sixth Form shake his head.

'No, no,' Maxwell sighed. 'As you say, we're all a bit on edge.'

'Mr Maxwell,' Hall said, 'you're an intelligent man. Informed. You have a right to have a lawyer present and you need not speak to me at all. You know that.'

Maxwell nodded. 'The right of silence. Yes.'

'You also know that any statement you make to me must be heard by at least two police officers and recorded with time and place. You know that?'

Maxwell nodded again.

Hall chewed his lower lip. Then his gaze fell on the last photograph as it disappeared into the envelope. '"And Lancelot mused a little space,"' he murmured. 'He said "She hath a lovely face" . . .'

'"God in his mercy, lend her grace . . ."' Maxwell continued for him.

Hall smiled. 'I expect you think I'm something of a cliché,' he said. 'A detective spouting poetry. All rather Dalgleish and Morse.'

It was Maxwell's turn to smile. 'Let's just say after the last half an hour, it comes as a pleasant relief.'

The door clicked open again. It was DC Halsey with a tray of tea. 'Oh,' he pulled up short, 'I thought . . .'

'Very thoughtful . . . er . . . George.' Hall was always at pains to remember new men. It gave them a sense of belonging to a team. 'Sadly, you've forgotten to bring a cup for me. Mr Maxwell?' and he passed the solitary mug to the Head of Sixth Form.

'Er . . . DI Johnson . . . ?' Halsey probed.

'Went off duty five minutes ago,' Hall told him. 'Working too hard, that man,' he said. 'We all are.'

'Right, sir.' Halsey hovered in the doorway.

'No sugar, thanks, George.' Hall turned to the constable, who saw the cold reflection in the Chief Inspector's glasses in a new light for the first time. He let the plastic tray drop to his side and ducked out.

Maxwell had never been so grateful for a cuppa in his life. It was hot, sweet and irrepressibly wet. He gulped at it.

'Mr Maxwell.' Hall leaned forward again, his elbows on the table, his face supported on his hands. 'I'd like to have an off the record chat with you,' he said. 'No heavies. No microphones. Just you and me.'

'Fine,' Maxwell shrugged.

'You see . . .' Hall struggled for the right words. 'I wonder if you can appreciate my predicament. Here I am with a murdered girl. What do you think we look for in situations like that?'

Maxwell shook his head, scanning the clinical white wall in search of an answer. 'I don't know,' he said. 'A sex maniac.'

Hall smiled. 'Well, that's right,' he nodded. 'That's what the public expects us to look for. Some dribbling lunatic with eyes rolling in his head leaping out of the shrubbery with his mac open.'

Maxwell chuckled.

'But that's not how it is.'

'No?'

'No,' Hall shook his head. 'No. Most cases of rape, assault, murder, they're committed by someone known to the victim. Oh, the random maniac exists, certainly, and he's bloody hard to catch. But I think . . . well, I know, really . . . that Jenny knew her killer. She went willingly with him to the Red House. What I don't know is why.'

'I thought . . .' Maxwell spoke for them both. 'I thought Tim Grey.'

'So did I.' Hall nodded as Maxwell cradled the hot mug in both hands. 'Until this morning.'

Maxwell nodded. 'I haven't really had time to take all this in,' he said. 'I only heard about it tonight. On the news. It said Tim was strangled.'

'Yes.' Hall sounded distant, detached. 'Yes, that's right. He was killed in the same way Jenny was.'

'With a ligature?'

'No, not with a ligature,' Hall lied. 'Bare hands.'

'But I thought . . .'

'What?' Hall edged closer. 'What did you think, Mr Maxwell?' It was a crude trick, but it had worked before. It might work again.

'I thought the papers — and *Crimewatch* — said it was a ligature.'

'In the case of Jenny Hyde, yes,' Hall told him, 'with a knot here,' he tapped his neck, 'on the right.'

Maxwell frowned. 'The left, surely,' he said and could have bitten his tongue off.

A strange look came into Hall's eyes, one that Maxwell certainly had never seen before, one that only ever came into his eyes when he smelled the satisfactory conclusion of a case. 'Do you know,' he said softly, 'I do believe you're right.'

There was a knock and Halsey appeared with Hall's tea. 'Thank you, George. Has DI Johnson gone home yet?'

'No, sir. He's in the ward room.'

'Tell him I'd like a word, would you?' Hall got up and smiled at Maxwell. 'Won't keep you a minute,' he said.

* * *

But he did. He kept Maxwell waiting several minutes. And a little before midnight, he came back.

'The Dam,' he said, without introduction and without apology, scraping back the chair as he sat down. Automatically he switched on the tape again. 'How well do you know the Dam?'

'Tolerably,' Maxwell shrugged. 'Look, Chief Inspector, I really think it's time . . .'

'You were seen there,' Hall told him.

'What?'

'Last night. You were seen on the Dam.'

'Was I?'

Hall sighed and leaned forward. 'Mr Maxwell,' he said, 'let me just scratch the surface of the case against you. One of your pupils, Jennifer Hyde, is found murdered at a house known to you . . .'

'And thousands of others,' Maxwell reminded him.

'As things stand you have no effective alibi for the time of her death. We only have your word that you caught the four thirty coach from Leighford to Exeter and even if you did, you would still have had time to get to the coach station from the Red House in fifteen to twenty minutes.'

'But . . .'

'Another of your pupils, Timothy Grey, is found murdered in a secluded beauty spot not only known to you, but on which you have been identified at the time of the murder . . .'

'Who?' Maxwell wanted to know. 'Who identified me?'

Hall leaned back. 'That doesn't matter. For now. Do you deny being there?'

'No,' Maxwell said. 'I was there last night.'

'Why?'

'I was . . . I was looking for the boy; the one you talked about on *Crimewatch*, the tall blond lad seen talking to Jenny on the Dam.'

'And why would you be doing that?' Hall asked.

'Because, like you, I want this wretched business cleared up,' Maxwell told him.

'Like me?' Hall repeated. 'I wonder if our goals are really the same?'

'Believe me,' Maxwell said, 'they are.'

Hall nodded, his mouth twisted with the irony of it. 'That's the rub,' he said. 'Can I believe you, Mr Maxwell?'

'That's up to you.'

'Tell me about the diary.' The Chief Inspector tried a new tack.

‘What diary?’

‘When DI Johnson came to collect you earlier this evening, a Mrs Sylvia Matthews — the school nurse, I understand — mentioned a diary. What was she talking about?’

‘Oh, you know women,’ Maxwell bluffed. ‘I expect Sylvia had got the wrong end . . .’

‘Mr Maxwell,’ Hall reminded him, ‘there are laws against withholding evidence from the police.’

‘Yes,’ sighed Maxwell, ‘I suppose there are. All right. Sylvia was talking about Jenny Hyde’s diary.’

Hall frowned. ‘We didn’t know there was one.’

‘Neither did I,’ Maxwell said. ‘The caretaker found it in school and gave it to me.’

‘To you, Mr Maxwell?’

‘I was her Year Head,’ Maxwell said. ‘Jenny was my responsibility.’

‘And Tim,’ Hall threw at him. It wasn’t necessary. Maxwell felt deadly enough as it was.

‘And Tim,’ he repeated.

‘And where is this diary now?’ Hall asked him. ‘It’s at home,’ he said. ‘In my study.’

‘Well then.’ Hall stood up and passed Maxwell his battered tweed hat from the wall hook. ‘Let’s go and get it, shall we? And on the way, we’ll talk about how you know so much about ligatures and knots and right and left.’

CHAPTER 13

In a jam though he was, Peter Maxwell was a public schoolboy. To confess the source of his knowledge about details of Jenny Hyde's death would have been to shop Dr Astley and he couldn't do that. So he played the lucky beginner bit, the inspired amateur. And all the way in the car, he felt that Chief Inspector Hall didn't believe a word of it.

'Jesus Christ.' The unlikely epithet had slipped from the thin, wary lips of DCI Hall. He'd rarely seen a place so thoroughly done over.

'You should have seen it before I tidied up,' Maxwell said and instinctively moved forward to pick something up.

'Don't,' Hall warned him. 'Just leave it. Where's the phone?'

'Well it was over there,' Maxwell told him. 'On the wall.'

Hall was there first, his feet crunching on glass. He found the receiver, wrapped it in his handkerchief and pressed the buttons. The random succession of notes that always reminded Maxwell of that bit from *Close Encounters of the Third Kind* hit his eardrums.

Maxwell didn't know where to sit. Where to stand.

'Saltmarsh? Hall. Get scenes of crime round here straight away. Thirty-eight, Columbine. Suspected break-in.' And he dropped the receiver on to its cradle, somewhere between the upturned lampshade and the horizontal radiator.

'Suspected?' Maxwell gave up trying and flopped heavily down on to his sofa.

Hall didn't say anything. He just surveyed the wreck of the lounge.

'Where was the diary?' he asked.

'Oh, no!' Maxwell made for the stairs, kicking cushions and books in all directions as he went.

Hall was on his heels.

'It was up here.' He flicked on lights as he hurtled through the bedroom. The pillows had been thrown into a corner, the mattress wrenched on to the floor. He dodged left and stared up into the blackness of the attic. Then he was clattering his way up, the soles of his shoes pounding on the pine of the treads. He floundered for the cord pull in the darkness and sat down heavily on the top stair.

Hall pushed his head up over the edge of the trap door. It was a bare room, except for a large table in the centre and hundreds of hand-painted soldiers sitting their horses patiently in the swinging light. 'Good God,' the Chief Inspector muttered. 'What's this?'

'A little hobby of mine.' Maxwell crawled to the diorama and squinted along it at ground level. Nothing was out of place. At the head of the Light Brigade, the last of the Brudenells sat his charger, Ronald, staring imperiously at Captain Nolan whose arm was thrown back to point suicidally to the guns at the end of the wrong valley somewhere beyond Maxwell's south-facing wall.

'You kept the diary up here?'

'That's right.' Maxwell straightened up, sensing Hall standing above and behind him. He checked his model-making desk, it was here,' he said, switching on the powerful desk lamp. 'Just here.'

Hall took in the attic room now it was fully lit. He couldn't quite stand up under the sharp angles of the beams, but that didn't matter. He'd seen enough.

'What we have here,' he said, 'is a very interesting situation.'

'Really?' Maxwell only now thought of tugging off his hat and scarf.

'I don't suppose you've seen as many break-ins as I have, Mr Maxwell.' The Chief Inspector leaned against the far wall.

'This is my first,' Maxwell told him. 'I hope you'll be gentle with me.'

'You see,' Hall folded his arms, not taking his eyes off the older man for a moment, 'what usually happens is that stuff is taken — usually money, jewellery . . . if it's a slightly more specialised job, hi-fi, computers, antiques.'

'So?'

'So I noticed a midi system in the lounge,' Hall said. 'It seemed intact. And that teapot in the middle of the floor . . .'

'What passes for the family silver,' Maxwell nodded.

'Valuable?'

'I don't know. A couple of hundred, I suppose.'

'I've a very shrewd suspicion, Mr Maxwell, that when my lads have done their bit and you make an inventory, you'll find only one thing is missing from this house.'

Maxwell looked at his man, the light shining in his glasses, hiding, as always, his eyes. 'The diary,' he said.

'The diary,' Hall nodded. 'And another thing.' He crossed to the plastic soldiers waiting to ride into the Jaws of Death. 'Except in the very professional jobs, it's usually kids out for kicks and they usually go on the rampage. Urine in the flower pots, faeces in the bed and daubed half-way up a wall.'

'Nice.' Maxwell grimaced.

'Very,' Hall agreed. 'This lot,' he waved across the models, 'wouldn't last five minutes. With a couple of kids — or even one working on his own — you'd never find all the pieces.'

'From which you conclude?'

'Either you've been done over by the most considerate burglar since Raffles or . . .' 'Or?'

'Or you did it yourself.'

Maxwell looked at his man. 'Oh, come on!' he bellowed. He refrained from doing his John McEnroe. Henry Hall didn't look the type to appreciate it. Besides, he was always conscious that his take-offs weren't as good as Geoffrey Smith's.

'Consider,' Hall said, smiling. 'You are asked to accompany DI Johnson to the police station. You do so. Inadvertently a friend of yours mentions a diary. The diary belonged to a murdered girl. You knew what it was. You knew all about its contents — and how damning those contents may be. It was a bit of hard luck that Mrs Matthews landed you in it like that, but landed you were. It was only a matter of time before DI Johnson or I asked you about it. And then you'd have to produce it. Or at least, you would have done if . . .'

'But Johnson was here,' Maxwell spread his arms at the ridiculousness of Hall's hypothesis. 'Did he find the place wrecked? No, of course not.'

'But the place isn't wrecked, Mr Maxwell. We've just been through that. Oh, yes, everything is strewn about, I'll grant you, but I'll lay you odds the only damage is what I did to your picture downstairs. Send me a bill and I'll put it right, by the way.'

'What are you saying? That unbeknown to Johnson and that ape he works with, I nipped out of the interrogation room, got a taxi back here, rearranged the place to make it look as if I'd been burgled and then caught another taxi back to the nick, where said DI and his monkey found me coolly blowing on my nails? You'll forgive me if I wonder what level of attainment is required for a Chief Inspector nowadays.'

'But none of that was necessary, was it, Mr Maxwell?' Hall had never lost his cool in his life. He wasn't about to start now. 'Because you had an accomplice.'

'An . . .' Hall should have had a camera. He may have been the first person in the world to witness Peter Maxwell utterly lost for words.

'DI Johnson tells me that Mrs Matthews did not leave precisely when you did, but was still in the house as his car took you to the station.'

'So?'

'So, she could have doubled back. It all hinges on whether she closed the front door or not.'

'That's very good, Chief Inspector,' Maxwell nodded, acknowledging a good one-liner when he heard one. But neither of them was smiling.

'That's why the place looks convincing,' Hall said, 'because Mrs Matthews genuinely didn't know where the diary was. She knew it was somewhere in the house, because you'd told her about it. And she didn't want to break anything because I understand she is a . . . friend . . . of yours.'

'Correction,' Maxwell speared the air with his finger. 'I do know what level of attainment is required for a Chief Inspector. He has to have a bloody degree in the ancient art of Innuendo. What's the scenario here? Are Sylvia Matthews and I some sort of latter-day Bonnie and Clyde?'

'I was thinking more of Hindley and Brady,' Hall said coldly.

There was a pause. 'I think that's slander, Chief Inspector,' Maxwell pursued.

For once, Henry Hall actually smiled. 'Forget I said it,' he said. 'Now, to cases. My lads will be here in a minute. In fact,' he checked his watch, 'there'll be some balls on a plate as it is. I promise you, their size elevens will be everywhere. Before that chaos ensues, why don't you tell me what's in the diary — wherever it is by now.'

Maxwell sighed. It had been a bitch of a night already and would very probably get worse. 'I'd better see where Sylvia Matthews stashed the kettle,' he said. 'I feel a cup of tea coming on.'

Beyond that, his memory was curiously poor that night.

* * *

It was raining by three o'clock. And the late September nights were turning unseasonably cold. It was difficult to say who looked the greater apparition, Peter Maxwell, dripping wet and clutching the handlebars of White Surrey, or Geoffrey

Smith, shaking the sleep out of his soul and peering out into the night.

'Don't tell me you've come for your boy,' Smith grimaced, in his finest John Wayne, hauling his dressing-gown around him. 'Or,' he squinted at Maxwell's face, 'are you after my body?'

'As a matter of fact I am.' Maxwell barged past him into the hall. 'On account of how I don't think I've got one any more. I'd kill for a large Scotch, Geoffrey.'

'Er . . . Max.' Smith followed his guest into the lounge. 'I don't want to sound boorish or anything, but it is three in the morning.'

'"It's quarter to three,"' Maxwell crooned, '"there's no one in the place, except you and me . . ." Oh, and Hilda, presumably.'

'Hilda is in bed, Maxie,' Smith told him, 'where I was but moments ago.'

'Oh, God, Geoff, sorry.' Maxwell dripped on to the hearthrug. 'I hope I didn't interrupt anything nuptial.'

'Anything nuptial?' There was real scorn in Smith's tone. 'I've been married for twenty-four years, man. Besides, Hilda's menopausal.'

'Oh, I'm sorry.'

'That's all right. Interesting word, menopausal. From the Greek meaning "stopped to have it sewn up". Plato would have sympathised.'

'Yes.' Maxwell eased the wet scarf from around his neck. It felt like a trawler's net. Or how he imagined a trawler's net would feel if he was in the habit of wearing one around his neck. 'Yes, I knew the Greeks would have a word for it. Well, apologise to Hilda for me.'

'"What's it all about, Maxie?"' It was Smith's turn to croon, a near-perfect Cilla Black.

Maxwell looked at him oddly. 'You know I wouldn't hurt you for the world, *mon vieux*, but that Michael Caine needs work. Shall I tell you about my night?'

'Why not?' Smith's eyes rolled heavenwards and he padded in his carpet slippers to the drinks cabinet.

'First, I was picked up by the fuzz.'

'Literally?' Smith raised an eyebrow.

'Literally.' Maxwell positively squelched as he landed on the settee. 'Then Sylvia landed me in it about the diary.'

'What diary's that?' Smith passed his friend a triple Scotch and switched the fire back on.

'Jenny's diary. Didn't I tell you about it?'

'Oh, yes, you slippery old bastard, you did. How come you knew about it and the police didn't, again?'

'Luck, I guess.' Maxwell relished the rush of the Scotch to his tonsils. 'Betty Martin found it — thought I might like it.'

'And did you?'

'Well, I hadn't deciphered it fully,' Maxwell held his hands out to the electric coal glow.

'I wouldn't have put Jenny Hyde down as the cryptic sort,' Smith said.

'Perhaps not,' Maxwell nodded. 'Anyway, as I say, Sylvia had popped round, visiting the condemned man and so on . . .'

'She's a brick, that woman,' Smith commented. 'You know she's in love with you, don't you?'

'In . . . ? Don't be ludicrous, Geoffrey.'

'I know,' Smith chuckled. 'Cantankerous old duffer like you. Defies belief, doesn't it? But you just remember where you heard it first.'

'When the law arrived,' Maxwell dismissed him with a wave, 'Sylv mentioned the diary.'

'I take it all back,' Smith said, 'She obviously hates your guts. That would make sense. After all, everybody else does.'

'She didn't mean it,' Maxwell defended her. 'She no doubt assumed that I'd told them all about it.'

'Which you hadn't?'

Maxwell looked like a kid with his hand in the cookie jar. 'Well, I was going to,' he explained.

'Ah, the way to hell . . .' Smith shook his head.

'. . . is paved with good intentions; yes, I know. Anyway, I had the misfortune to fall into the hands of Robocop whose twin personality is Attila the Hun.'

'The third degree?'

'DI Johnson wouldn't know a degree if it bit him on the ankle, which is what I damn nearly did.'

'They've got to be careful nowadays.' Smith was serious, his endless hairline glowing in the firelight. 'It's got to be done by the book.'

'So it was until he sent his Number Two out of the room and switched off the tape recorder.'

'Did he now?' Smith nodded. 'The cheeky little sod. Didn't you have the famous phone call? To a lawyer, I mean?'

'I haven't got a lawyer, Geoff. This is me, Maxie. Lone Crusader; remember? I haven't even got a milkman.'

'Bit off, though, Maxie.' Smith frowned. 'God knows what that officious bastard could have winkled out of you . . . Not that you've got anything to hide, of course.'

'Thank you for that.'

'Still,' Smith peered into the amber recesses of his glass, 'I think I'd have handed the diary over, personally.'

'No. I was all right with Johnson. I went to a public school. I'm used to prefects.'

'What was the problem, then?'

'Hall,' Maxwell said. 'Chief Inspector Hall.'

'Oh, yes,' Smith remarked. 'The band-leader.'

'The nice policeman,' Maxwell corrected him. 'I misjudged that man. When I first met him — at school — I had him down for a Diamond clone. All suit and no bottle. Now, I think I'll watch my back.'

'What did he do? Call you Peter and give you a fag? It's a very old ploy, Maxie.'

'I'm a very old suspect, Geoffrey,' Maxwell told him. 'No, it was more subtle than that. I don't know, I just get the impression . . . Oh, I don't know.'

'What?'

Maxwell made an indefinable snarl and dismissed the notion as preposterous.

'No. Go on,' Smith insisted.

'Well, I got the impression that there are those in Leighford CID who think that I did it.'

'You?' Smith blinked. 'Kill Jenny Hyde? Come on, Maxie. This is galloping paranoia even by your standards.'

'No.' Maxwell was serious. 'See it from the point of view of the police. Two young people are dead. I knew them both . . .'

'So did fifty other members of staff,' Smith said. 'Not to mention kids.'

'A bike is seen propped up against the Red House on the night in question. I ride a bike.'

'So do five thousand million Chinamen,' Smith pointed out.

'I've got no alibi for the night Jenny Hyde was killed.'

'Yes, you have. You were in Cornwall. Or at least en route.'

'Who says so?'

'Er . . . you do.'

Maxwell shrugged with I-told-you-so sort of shoulders. 'Maxie . . .'

'No, Geoffrey,' the damp man shook his head, 'you're not being objective, man. You're looking at good ol' Maxie whom you've worked with man and boy for . . . what is it . . . nearly twenty years. We've sat in staff meetings, we've caught smokers, we've gone on strike, we've trod the boards. Christ, we've even peed together, although that's not something I'm proud of. Shall I tell you what the police are looking at? Peter Maxwell. An arrogant old shit of fifty-two — a funny age. A bachelor — one of those inexplicable people who are probably martyrs to self-abuse and have an inflatable woman in every room. And above all, an arrogant, peculiar old bachelor who has a diary belonging to a dead girl and doesn't tell the police he's got it.'

'Yes.' Smith's face was darker. 'I see what you mean. Still, I wouldn't adjust the white hood just yet.'

'That's because you haven't heard the bottom line.'

'Oh?'

'The diary's gone.'

'Gone?'

'There seems to be an echo in here, Geoffrey.'

Smith looked confused. 'What do you mean, gone?'

'Nicked. Taken. Lifted. I don't want to have to condescend to a literatus of your stamp, Geoffrey, by using the word "purloined". Oh!' Maxwell slapped his leg, 'there, I've been and gone and done it.'

'Where was it?'

'The diary? In my loft.'

'And now it isn't?'

'Hall insisted I show it to him so he accompanied me out of the police station.' He clicked to attention.

Smith smiled. 'That Jack Warner of yours is really coming on, you know. Just a little straighter with the finger for the salute.'

'My place had been ransacked.'

'Bugger me!'

'Nothing else had gone. I had to wait while some copper who looked about six dusted everything down.'

'Any prints?'

Maxwell shook his head. 'Clean as a whistle, apparently. Chummie wore gloves.'

'Is your cat all right?' Smith suddenly remembered the beast.

'Bless you for that, my darling.' Maxwell's Julie-Walters-doing-the-woman-who-played-Mrs-Overall-in-Acorn-Antiques was pretty convincing, all things considered. 'The Count was asleep in his basket in the bathroom, no harm done.'

'Now if he'd been a dog, Maxie . . .'

'The poor sod might well be dead. As it is, a cat's no threat to a burglar.'

'So how did you part, then?' Smith asked. 'You and the police?'

'Let's just say I'm not yet under arrest.'

'Oh, Maxie.' Smith took the man's glass. 'It won't come to that.' He crossed to get a refill.

'It might, Geoffrey,' he said. 'You see, there's a sort of PS below the bottom line.'

Smith hesitated half-way across the carpet. 'It must be my tonsure,' he ran a hand over his polished head, 'that I can play the Father Confessor so convincingly.'

'I was there,' Maxwell told him, 'at the Dam. At the time when Tim Grey died. I was actually there.'

'Shit a brick, boss.' Smith nearly missed the glass with the bottle's mouth. 'Why, for Christ's sake?'

Maxwell got up and squelched across Smith's rug, the steam rising from his trousers. 'Because I'm a stupid, interfering old bastard, I suppose,' he said. 'I know it's laughable, but I was looking for that tall kid, the spotty one on *Crimewatch* that Jenny was seen talking to on the day she died.'

'Did you see anything? At the Dam, I mean?' Smith pressed a refill into Maxwell's hand.

'The odd bloke walking his dog. I heard a couple of kids.'

'Kids?'

'Yes. You know, those things their parents leave with us for the day.'

'You . . . er . . . you didn't see Tim, I suppose?'

Maxwell didn't like the look in Smith's eyes. Was even his Old Contemptible beginning to doubt him now?

'No,' he said, 'no, of course not.' He caught sight of the time on the wall clock. 'I've got to go, Geoff.' He downed his Scotch, though it burned his mouth. 'I've taken up too much of your time already.'

'Maxie.' The Head of English gripped his man by both shoulders. 'This is me; Geoff. What does it matter? Right now, I think you could use a friend or two.'

Maxwell looked him in the face. 'Yes,' he nodded. 'Yes, I could.' And he retrieved his scarf from the floor. 'Keep me posted, Geoff,' he said. 'About school, I mean. Keep your ear to the ground.'

'You're still going on with this, aren't you?' Smith said. 'Still sleuthing.'

'It's what your right arm's for,' Maxwell smiled. 'Give my love to Hilda,' and he wandered into the night.

* * *

'All right, Count.' Peter Maxwell lay in his bath, his arms crossed over his chest like something out of Tutankhamun. The cat lay curled tightly on top of the wicker linen-basket and twitched an ear at him. 'Let's talk diary.' He closed his eyes. 'No, it's not Sam Pepys this time, off to the Cheap for a quick one. It's not even the Hitler diaries or Jack the Ripper's, so I know that whoever stole the thing, it can't be a *Times* journalist. Jenny's diary. You know. Jenny Hyde's. You must have seen it lying about. It was blue. A blue exercise book. Odd that, don't you think? I mean, the sixth form use file paper. A4. Only the main school use exercise books. Oh God!' He splashed through the suds suddenly and the cat quietly lashed his tail. 'Listen to me. If somebody said "Good morning" to me now, I'd find it sinister; look for the hidden meaning. It's funny. I never really believed in the conspiracy theory of History. Not until now, anyway. What did it say? Did you read it? I say,' he called louder, 'wake up. Look at me when I'm talking to you.' He pretended to slide his glasses sideways in memory of the late, great Eric Morecambe. 'Yes, yes, I know,' he chuckled softly to the cat. 'As Geoffrey Smith would say, "Not your best Ernie Wise." No, I distinctly remember. When I was reading the diary, you were looking over my shoulder. Yes, you were. Don't deny it. Now, think. Think, damn you.' He closed his eyes again.

'She'd quarrelled with Tim. Well, it's too late to ask him about that now, isn't it? Then, she'd gone somewhere. Gone to K.'s. That was it.' He began to see her writing in the steam. 'Now, she found him lovely and K. loved her. K. Who's K?' He let his mind wander over the layabouts in the sixth form. 'Ken Byfield,' he said, then shook his head. 'No, he's sixteen stone and prey to nervous disorders. She wouldn't have found him 'lovely', would she? Still, she saw something in Tim Grey, when all's said and done. K? Oh, bugger!' and he slapped the flat of his hand on to the water's surface.

There was a pause. Beyond the wobbly glass of Maxwell's bathroom window the first fingers of dawn were reaching out tentatively to push back the night. 'If I hadn't had you bricked, Count, you'd be out there now, wouldn't you, rogering the entire neighbourhood. Life's a bitch, all right. "P.",' he suddenly remembered. '"What shall I do about P?" the diary said. "Why do I always fancy the married ones?"' He chewed his lip. 'So Jenny was playing fast and loose with a married man, eh?' He reached for the soap, 'Not the sort of behaviour Mumsy would approve of. Maybe the sort of behaviour Anne Spencer knew all about, though? What d'you think, Count? How's your female psychology? Was Anne so uptight because Jenny was playing around with the same bloke she fancied? The same married man? Oh, Count, what a tangled web we weave.'

He stood up suddenly and the noise of the Kraken waking caused the cat to lift his head. 'It's all right,' Maxwell said, 'I'll get the towel myself,' and he dripped all over the place as he wandered through into his bedroom. 'I'll say this for being burgled, Count,' he called back through, 'it rearranges the dust nicely. You should have seen old Geoffrey Smith's place tonight. I could have written my name on the coffee table. Old Hilda's not pulling her not-inconsiderable weight these days. Mind you, she's older than he is, isn't she? And a bit of a dog on the quiet. Oh, sorry,' he whispered. 'Didn't mean to upset you. D-O-G.'

Metternich the cat looked up as Maxwell came storming back into the bathroom, one towel round his waist and another on his head. He looked like a bit player in Ali Baba. 'That's another thing the diary said,' he told the animal. 'Mad Max had a go at me over deadlines.' He blinked at his pet. 'What's wrong with that? I'll tell you what's wrong with that. I never had a go at Jenny Hyde in my life, over deadlines or anything else.'

CHAPTER 14

The next day a letter arrived for Peter Maxwell. A buff envelope stamped with a reminder that the Local Education Authority had offered ninety years of service. Odd year to celebrate, but in John Major's England no one expected the Local Education Authority to see its hundredth out. Perhaps they were quitting while they were ahead.

'Black tie, do you think, Count?' he consulted the cat. 'Or hood and gown? What does one wear when one is on the carpet accused of gross moral turpitude? Well,' he checked the date of the hearing again, 'I've got a few days to decide, I suppose.'

He wasn't ready for his visitor that night at all. It was a little after eight and he'd settled down to watch the video he'd treated himself to earlier in the day. Dame May Whitty was just writing her name — 'Froy' — in the dust of the train window prior to vanishing, when the door bell rang. It was a tall kid with blond frizzy hair and hideous, striped leggings.

'Sally Greenhow,' Maxwell said, 'and I claim my five pounds.'

'How are you, Max, you old shit?' Never one to stand on delicacy was Sally Greenhow. She'd spent her entire career — all nine years of it — in the Special Needs Department. They didn't just call spades down there, they ate with them.

'All the better for seeing you, Sally, you ravishing creature.'

She looked at him through her owlish specs. 'Well, if you're going to talk dirty, I'm leaving.'

'No, no.' He opened the door fully. 'There could be a drink in it for you.'

'Southern Comfort,' she ordered, brushing past him. 'No ice.'

'A woman after my own heart,' he smiled.

And he followed her up the stairs. 'And you can keep your eyes off my bum,' she said without turning round.

'Without wishing to be rude,' he riposted, 'that's a little easier said than done.'

She stopped abruptly. 'If I thought you were implying that my derriere fills your stairway . . .' she scolded.

'Oh, but it's so delightful,' he purred. 'Metternich, get up and give the lady your seat.' Maxwell threw the affronted animal off the settee. 'He normally has the one by the fire,' he said and poured them both a drink.

She patted the seat beside her and pulled out a packet of cigarettes. 'Do you mind, Max? It's been a bitch of a day and Alan's out at the squash club. Or so he says.'

'Oh.'

She caught sight of his face. 'No,' she laughed, blowing smoke to the ceiling, 'it's not like that. He's no Keith Miller.'

'How is Alison?' Maxwell asked her.

Sally Greenhow shrugged. 'Near the edge, I'd say.'

'What is it, Sally? With Alison, I mean?'

'Maxie, Maxie,' she laughed, shaking her head. 'For a middle-aged roué you're bloody naive, you know.'

'Oh,' he nodded. 'Woman's trouble.'

'If by that you mean a man, yes. It's Alison's misfortune to be between a rock and a hard place. She doesn't like her job very much and she likes her home situation even less. She's married to a shit and she hasn't got the bottle to get out of it. Got an ashtray? Or can I throw caution to the winds and flick over your Berber?'

He rummaged in a drawer under the coffee table. She read the legend on the ashtray he found there — 'Joe's Bordello — Where the customer always comes first'. She looked at him with steady blue eyes. 'Are you really a pervert, Peter Maxwell?' she asked.

He burst out laughing. 'But of course,' he said. 'Come and sit on my mac, little girl.'

She sighed. 'Unfortunately, Max, it's not something either of us can afford to joke about any more.'

'Either of us?' he frowned. 'Don't tell me you're under suspension accused of gross moral turpitude too? Bloody school's going to the dogs.'

'It's my lot in life to sink or swim with you, Maxie, as your professional association representative.'

'Oh, I see.' Maxwell clicked his fingers. 'You're here as my union rep. Yes, it all fits now. A sort of soldier's friend for my court martial. The question is, will my sword-hilt be pointing towards me at the end or not?'

'That's up to you,' she said. 'I'm offering you my help, Max. I'm not a solicitor. I'm a colleague. And I hope a friend. But I'm far enough away to see you as you are. Sylvia Matthews is too close. So's Geoffrey Smith. I can see you, warts and all. The fact is that Diamond played a bit of a blinder confronting you like he did, with Graham and the CEO. He ought to have wheeled me in as well. It's not exactly wrongful arrest, but it puts them in a bad light.'

He looked at her. 'What's a bright young thing like you doing in Special Needs, Sally?' he asked her.

'Now, look . . .' and he felt her hackles rise.

'No, no,' he laughed, holding his hands in the air. 'Spare me the lecture! I know what Special Needs kids mean to you.'

'Yes,' she said levelly, 'I know you do. And if you weren't several miles to the right of Genghis Khan, you might be able to see it too — but tonight, this Pinko-Liberal has just galloped to your rescue. Take me or leave me.'

'About now,' he said solemnly, 'I'll take you, Sally; in the narrowest sense of the word, of course.'

'Good.' She slammed down the glass and stood up. 'How long have you worked at Leighford High School, Mr Maxwell?'

He'd been doing role play, though they didn't call it that then, when this kid was in nappies. 'Who are you?' he wanted to know first. 'That Neanderthal Graham, that slime Jenkins or that dickless wonder, Diamond?'

She stood behind him and leaned over his shoulder. She felt his whiskers tickle her cheek. 'Ve vill ask ze questions,' she breathed.

'All right,' he said, smiling. 'This is my twentieth year.'

'And before that?' She'd whirled away to the window.

'Greylands Comprehensive.'

'What is your present post?'

'Head of Sixth Form . . . er . . . Years 12 and 13.'

'Are you married, Mr Maxwell?'

'No.'

'You live alone?'

'Apart from my cat, yes.'

'Have you ever had sex with a minor?'

'No,' Maxwell said solemnly, 'it's the coal dust — I find it something of a deterrent. Plays merry hell with my asthma.'

'Max.' The voice was different, seductive.

He found himself turning round. The shapeless jumper had gone. The blouse was open to the navel. It was obvious that Sally Greenhow wore no bra. Maxwell could see her nipples in the half-light, jutting against the white material. Only now did he realise how short her skirt was and that she was standing with her legs apart.

'Do you want to take me to bed, Max?' she asked.

He turned away, slowly, sadly. 'No, Sally,' he said, 'I want you to leave now.'

'Good!' The voice was crisp again, business-like.

'What?' He'd turned back again.

'I'm sorry,' she said, 'teasing you like that,' and the blouse was quickly buttoned again and the jumper was back on. 'But I had to know.'

'Know what?'

'If that come-on was going to work. Not exactly conventional union rep stuff, is it? I'm not sure Doug McAvoy would approve.'

'Wait until he's asked, that's what I say.'

She sat next to him again and took his hand. 'Of course,' she said, staring into his eyes, 'it might just be that you're a better actor than I give you credit for. That you turned me down just now because you saw through it.'

'It might be,' Maxwell nodded.

'The point is, Max,' she said, staring him in the face, 'you could have had me.'

'I could?' His eyebrows lifted.

She nodded, closed her eyes and kissed him. It was a long, lingering kiss, the type that Barbara Cartland writes about. And it was a long time since anyone had kissed Mad Max like that. 'But you didn't,' she said brightly.

'So that means I'm not a child molester?' he asked.

She laughed. 'No, but it does mean you're a decent man who won't take advantage of an available girl when she's offered to you on a plate.'

'That's encouraging.'

'Oh, I don't suppose it'd impress anybody else — not Diamond or Jenkins et al. But it convinces me, if I needed convincing.'

'I don't like the sound of that if, Sally,' he scolded.

'Then there's your basic intelligence,' she said, returning to her drink.

'Oh.' He looked down at the carpet and hugged himself, swaying from side to side. 'That little ol' thing.'

'If you won't play along with me in the privacy of your own home, you're certainly not going to risk all by trying to grope a girl in your office in the middle of Leighford High with the best part of fifteen hundred kids and staff dashing hither and yon.'

'Ah,' Maxwell wagged a finger at her, 'but what if I was overcome with lust?' he asked her. 'If the sight of her little cleavage and daring hemline didn't drive me into a frenzy? Sorry, do I sound a little Mills and Boon?'

'Just a tad,' she nodded. 'Of course, it's possible. But in that case I can't help wondering why you haven't been driven into a frenzy before, say at any time over the last twenty years?'

'Compliant girls,' Maxwell shrugged, 'who kept their mouths shut.'

'You're not making this easy, Max,' Sally told him.

'And I don't suppose my Inquisitors at the hearing will either, Sally,' he said.

'What actually happened in your office when you talked to Anne Spencer?'

He got up and wandered to the window. In the darkened street below he saw the arc light shine on the polished roof of Sally's car. 'I didn't know you drove one of those,' he said.

'I don't.' She quaffed her Southern Comfort, 'it's Alan's. He jogs to the club these evenings. Stop changing the subject.'

'The subject?' He frowned to help him remember it. 'Oh, yes. I was asking Anne if she knew where Jenny Hyde had got to in the days she'd gone missing — the days before she died. She got snotty and ran out screaming. As God is my judge, I didn't lay a finger on that girl.'

'Just as well,' she said, 'I don't suppose her old man's very likely to believe it, mind. Nor Maz.'

It was as though someone had just dropped an icicle down Peter Maxwell's back. 'What?' he asked.

'I said, "It's just as well . . ."'

'No, no.' He'd crossed to the girl. 'Maz. You said Maz.'

'That's right.'

'Who the hell's that?'

'I don't know. He's just Maz. All the kids know him — the sirens of Years 10 and 11. He hangs out at the Dam.'

'Is he tall? Fair-haired?' Maxwell bellowed. 'Acne?'

'I don't know, Max,' she shouted back. 'What's the matter, all of a sudden?'

He broke away, confused, bewildered. 'I don't know,' he said. 'It's a name that Tim Grey mentioned.'

'Tim?' Sally frowned. 'I wouldn't have thought that was Tim's scene at all.'

'A tall, fair-haired boy who hangs out at the Dam,' Maxwell was pacing the floor, talking to himself, to the furniture, to the cat, 'is the boy they're looking for. On *Crimewatch*.'

'"Sleep well,"' Sally quoted Nick Ross. '"Don't have nightmares."'

'But that's exactly what this is, Sally.' Maxwell was facing her again, his eyes bright. 'How do you know about this Maz?'

'Special Needs,' she said proudly. 'You know the sort of kids we get down there. I'm going to write a book one day.'

'What do they say about him? Your kids?'

'About Maz? Well, he's not one of ours. That's for certain. He's in a squat somewhere, Barlichway way . . . that's not easy to say, by the way.'

'Sally,' he was gripping her arms, shaking her, 'this is important.'

'OK, Max.' She shook herself free. 'I get the message. It's all right. He's . . .' She scratched her frizzy head, searching for the words, summoning up all the jumble of gossip the kids threw at her. 'He's a sort of Svengali figure, or Rasputin; I don't know. If this was London — or Brighton, even — he'd be a pimp or a pusher — I don't know which.'

'So the police must know him?'

She shrugged. 'I suppose so,' she said. 'Except that the sort of kids he goes with aren't likely to be into Neighbourhood Watch.'

'Let's get this straight.' Maxwell blinked, trying to think it through. 'This Maz shacks up with under-age girls.'

'Under-age. Over-age. I don't think he's all that choosy.'

'And he's running around the place like bloody Chanticleer with his brood of hens and I'm out of a job because I raised my voice to a girl?'

Sally nodded. 'Welcome to teaching, Max,' she said sadly.

'Bollocks,' he growled. 'I'm not taking any of this lying down.'

'Of course you're not,' she smiled, eyes shining. 'You're Mad Max — Beyond the Hippodrome!' and she brandished an invisible something in the air.

'Where can I find him?'

'Maz? I dunno.'

'Oh, come on, Sally,' he pleaded. 'Do I have to stuff fivers down your brassiere?'

'Maybe I was wrong about you,' she said wistfully. 'Maybe you are an old pervert.'

'Well?'

'I really don't know,' she assured him. 'Why not try Humphrey's or Little Willie's? That's where most of our riff-raff end up.'

'Right.' He had to concentrate to remember where these places were. 'Right.' And he kissed her hard on the forehead. 'Thank you, Sally Greenhow,' he said, wrapping his scarf around his neck and hunting for his jacket. 'Thank you for what you've been.'

'Max, you're not going there? Not now?'

'Why not?' He frowned at her. Then he crouched and swivelled his hips. 'I can still do the Twist, you know.' He suddenly winced and straightened. 'Just.'

'Oh, God.' Sally closed her eyes.

'And,' he plopped his hat on his head and trailed her down the stairs to the newly repaired front door, 'they say the late Rudolph Nureyev had never seen a Mashed Potato like mine.'

And he waltzed her into the night.

'Give me a lift in your husband's automobile, you vixen. And I'll see you in court next week.'

* * *

Big Willie's it had been called in the '80s, when Margaret Thatcher was Prime Minister and people still wore open-necked shirts and medallions bounced on hairy chests. In the rather more self-effacing '90s, what with the culmination of the AIDs scare and the arrival, from nowhere, of John Major at Number Ten, they'd changed the name to Little Willie's. Well, size wasn't everything.

Peter Maxwell had only ever crossed those hallowed portals once. One of the 'characters' of the sixth form you never seemed to get any more had held a 'Vicars and Tarts' party there a few years back. Maxwell, in his quaint and schizophrenic way, had gone as a Tarty Vicar, that being a slightly more likely persona than the other way around. The place was darker than he remembered, more claustrophobic.

'Be careful,' Sally Greenhow had warned him as he tumbled out of the Peugeot. He'd kissed her hand and gone inside. On his last visit the haunting 'Bohemian Rhapsody' had filled the night. Now it all seemed to be no tune known to man. He ordered a double Southern Comfort from the spotty lad who ran the bar and found a seat in the corner.

How long he stayed there, he didn't know. People came and went, girls with bums encased in tight, short skirts, lads in trainers or Doc Martens. Some he recognised from Leighford High, all of them looking rather older than they actually were and most of them under the legal age for drinking. The lad on the bar didn't give a damn. If they showed him folding stuff, he served them.

A few of them recognised Mad Max too and veered away. Only some thick shit he'd taught in Year 11, perhaps three years ago, hailed him.

'All right, sir?' and he raised his pint in Maxwell's direction.

Maxwell raised his third Southern Comfort in retaliation. It was usually the way. They couldn't stand you in school, made your life one long hell, but outside, on the street, in the pub, in the dark of Little Willie's, it was all mates together. Maxwell couldn't even remember the thick shit's name.

He'd been watching all night for a tall, fair-haired youth who attracted girls. He'd asked the barman, on his second drink, if Maz ever came in. 'Who wants to know?' had been the response. When Maxwell told him he did, the barman didn't know any Maz. He knew a Baz. But Baz was doing three years in Maidstone. He wouldn't be in tonight.

Maxwell had had enough Southern Comfort. The room was beyond that vague wobble — it was positively swimming. He'd had enough of the noise too. It was hammering through his head like a pneumatic drill. He downed the last of his glass and grabbed his hat. A totally pointless evening.

'Oi, watch it, Grandad.' He collided with a blonde girl in a mock-leather jacket, almost as passé as he was.

'Sorry,' he said.

''Ere, it's Mr Maxwell, ain't it?'

'Um?' For the life of him, Maxwell couldn't place the name. The face he knew certainly, the full mouth, the rows of ear-rings glittering in both lobes. He'd never seen the cleavage before, either, but that would have developed after she'd left school. She'd never joined the sixth form; that much was certain.

'It's Janice,' she jogged his memory. 'Janice Dodds. I've got a kid now.'

'Well, well.' Glancing at her frontage, Maxwell was surprised she didn't have several. 'Congratulations.'

'Wot you doin' 'ere, then?' she asked him, hauling him down beside her. 'After a bit of skirt?' and she winked and drove her elbow into his ribs. She crossed her legs without an inch of suavity and he couldn't help glancing down as men will. Perhaps that was the bit of skirt Janice had in mind? There certainly didn't seem to be much of it.

'No,' he smiled, 'I was just having a quiet drink.'

'That's a laugh round 'ere,' she bellowed over the din. The lights flashed red and blue and green, casting lurid shadows on the dancers who gyrated in the centre of the floor. 'I thought you was after a bit. Old blokes come in 'ere all the time.'

'Do they?'

'Oh, yeah. One the other night had his tadger out under the table. Laugh!' and she did, rather like a donkey in labour. Not that Maxwell had ever heard a donkey in labour.

'Are you here with your husband?' he asked the girl.

She snorted and blew bubbles in her drink. 'You must be jokin',' she told him. 'Nah, I'm 'ere wiv Kay.'

'Kay's your friend?'

'Yeah.' She looked at him oddly. 'Yeah, that's right. 'E's just 'avin' a slash. 'E'll be 'ere in a minute.'

'Oh, I see,' Maxwell said. 'Kay's a man.'

'Of course he's a man. I ain't come 'ere wiv another girl since I was fourteen. 'E's a proper gent is Kay.'

'Oh, yes.' Maxwell's eyes focused on the figure who suddenly stood before them, beer in hand, staring at him. 'Yes, indeed. Keith Miller is a proper gent.'

'We're going.' Miller was talking to the girl.

'They call you K?' Maxwell was with them, batting people aside as all three of them made for the exit.

'Piss off, Max,' he heard Miller grunt and Maxwell collided with a column, his concentration broken, his quarry gone. Frantically he looked around him. There. On the steps. By the door. Janice was being dragged by the wrist, teetering on her ludicrous platform soles, glancing back to see where Maxwell was. He launched himself at the steps, bounding up two at a time, jostling past a couple necking at the top. Then he was out in the night and the tarmac glistened at his feet.

'Keith!' He could see them running across the car-park, could hear the girl's heels clattering like some demented typewriter. It had been a long time since Peter Maxwell had run like this, a long time since his sprinting days at Jesus. Still, some things you didn't forget. Like falling off a bike really. His hand gripped Miller's sleeve and he spun him round. 'Just a word, Keith,' Maxwell gasped.

'Let go of me, Max.' Miller's eyes flashed in the darkness. 'I don't want to hurt you.'

'Hurt me?' Maxwell watched his breath snake out on the damp air. 'Why would you want to do that, Keith?'

'Just leave well alone!' Miller barked and fumbled with his keys in the lock.

'How well did you know Jenny Hyde?' Maxwell asked him.

'Shit!' Miller's key had slipped from the lock.

'Keith,' Maxwell spun him round, 'I have to know.'

It had been a long time since Peter Maxwell had had a fist fight too. In his day there were vague rules and some misguided knight-errantry within him had told him never to throw the first punch. So it was now. He felt the breath leave his body as Miller's fist came from nowhere and caught him in the pit of his stomach. He felt his knees hit the tarmac and his lungs hit his chin. His reaction was faster, however, than Miller had expected and Maxwell threw himself forward so that his head thudded into Miller's groin.

'Bastard!' the younger man hissed, reeling away from the car and clutching his crotch.

Maxwell was back on his feet by the time Miller was able to straighten.

'What's the matter, Keith?' he rasped, fighting to regain his breath, through the shock and the winding he had received. 'Guilty conscience?'

'Come on, you two!' Janice Dodds's shrill tones tried to break the tension of the moment.

There were shouts from the neon-lit forecourt of Little Willie's as punters realised a punch-up had started and hurried over to watch or join in, as they saw fit. Maxwell was ready for the next one. Clearly, Keith Miller had been misjudged by Janice Dodds. He wasn't a proper gent, after all, and he proved it by lashing out with his right boot. Maxwell caught it with his left hand and wrenched to the right, throwing the younger man heavily against his car. Then he broke all the rules he'd ever lived by and drove his elbow into the man's kidneys. Miller slumped forward over the bonnet.

'Bloody right!' someone shouted. 'Good on yer, granddad.'

Janice was reaching down, trying to peel Keith Miller off the car, to see how badly he was hurt. She was knocked sideways as he hauled himself up and caught Maxwell high in the ribs with both fists clasped together. Then the boot came up again, once, twice, three times in quick succession and Maxwell went down. He felt Miller's boot hit his head, his back, his head again. Then there was a scraping of boots on tarmac and he heard Janice screaming at her proper gent, 'Fuckin' leave 'im alone. You're fuckin' killin' 'im.'

Miller pushed her away and scrabbled for his keys again. Then he was in the car and was gone. A pair of hands cradled Maxwell's head. He felt cold, old, finished. 'Well, then,' he coughed in the wake of the car's rear lights, 'we'll call it a draw, shall we?' He could just make out the contorted face of Janice Dodds peering into his own. 'It's a line,' he managed, 'from Monty Python and the Holy Grail.' He didn't remember any more.

CHAPTER 15

'Do you give your cat milk or what?'

Peter Maxwell recognised the words but the voice was alien at first.

'Can you hear me?' It got louder.

He realised he was lying on his own settee, blinking up at the over-made-up face of Janice Dodds. 'Yes. Yes,' he replied to her questions.

'Do you give your cat milk?' she asked again.

'Yes,' Maxwell repeated.

'Wassisname?' she asked.

'Metternich.' He tried to straighten.

'Now, come on,' she steadied him, 'you've got a great big lump on your 'ead. You don't wanna to be jumping about for a while.'

'Janice.' Maxwell felt his temple. She was right. A great big lump. And his jaw wasn't working too chipperly either. 'How did I get here?'

'In a taxi, darlin',' she said. 'The fare was two pound twenty-five. I found it in your pocket. 'Ope you don't mind.'

'Er . . . no.' Maxwell couldn't even focus on his living-room, much less the small change that may or may not have been in his jacket pocket. 'The cab-driver didn't think it odd, my bleeding over his plastic?'

'Nah, 'e thought you was pissed. Anyhow 'e was too busy coppin' the view up my skirt to notice you.'

Maxwell groaned as the pain hit him in the side.

'Oh,' she put her arm around his neck, 'an' I reckon Kay broke one or two o' your ribs an' all.'

'I reckon you're right,' Maxwell winced.

'Why?' She looked him in the eyes. 'Why did you 'ave a go at 'im?'

'I thought you said he was a proper gent.'

'Did I?' She dropped her arm and shrugged. 'Well, nobody's perfect. 'E's got a bloody terrible temper, 'as Kay. An' 'e's gotta be twenty years younger than you.'

'Well, perhaps ten.' Maxwell had a bruised ego somewhere, as well as a bruised body. 'How did you know where I lived?'

She reached to her left and wagged his wallet at him. 'I may not have done very good in GCSEs but I can fuckin' read like the next one.' She pulled out a card. 'Peter Maxwell, Thirty-eight, Columbine Avenue, Leighford, West Sussex, Haitch Ell One Five, Two Eff Oh. Who's this?'

Maxwell forced his eyes to focus on the faded, crumpled photograph in the girl's hand. For an instant, he wanted to reach out, snatch it from her. But he didn't have the strength. And he didn't have the will.

'My wife,' he said. 'My wife and daughter.'

'I didn't know you was married,' she said. 'At school we all thought you was gay.'

'Thanks,' and even to smile cost him dearly. 'I'm a widower,' he told her. 'My wife and daughter . . . They were killed in a car crash before I came to Leighford. By a police patrol car chasing some tearaways. If she were alive today, my little girl would be twenty-two.'

'Oh, that's ever so sad,' Janice said, her bright eyes like saucers. 'What was 'er name? Your little kid?'

'Jenny,' he said. 'It was Jenny.'

'Mine's Tracey,' Janice beamed. 'She's two an' a 'alf.'

'Of course it is,' Maxwell smiled. 'Lovely name. God . . .' and the pain caught him again.

'Look, Mr Maxwell, you oughter be in hospital. You could die, y'know.'

'I could,' he nodded. Secretly he thought he already had. 'What time is it, Janice?'

'Half-past two.'

'Christ. Look, shouldn't you be getting back? I mean, your baby . . .'

'Me muvver's looking after Trace. She didn't expect me back for ages anyhow.'

'What if someone saw you?' Maxwell asked her, bringing his lolling head forward as quickly as he dared. 'Coming here, I mean?'

'Nah, it's a nice place,' she assured him. 'Oh, I see. You mean, seen wiv you? I ain't proud,' and she was about to dig him in the ribs when she remembered his predicament. 'Look,' she said, 'I'm worried about you. Mean, you're bloody knockin' on, aintchya? Lie down.'

'What?' But even as he said it, she'd tucked his feet up on the sofa and had hauled up his shirt tails. 'Bloody 'ellfire. You're all black and blue.'

'Thanks,' he said. 'It goes with being a colourful character.'

'No wonder they used to call you Mad Max. 'Ere, you got any cocoa?'

'In the kitchen.' He pointed vaguely to it. 'The cupboard on the left.'

'D'ya want anything in it? Brandy or somefink?'

'What?' Maxwell coughed. 'And ruin a perfectly good cup of cocoa? No thanks. What I would like, Janice, are some answers.'

'Oh yeah?' She peered oddly at him. 'Like what?'

'Like what Keith Miller's got to do with girls like Jenny Hyde?'

She got up and he heard her rattling the kettle, running the tap.

'I'm not asking too much, am I?' he called, but the pain was too much and he had to lie back, thinking of England the while, of course.

She filled the doorway, leaning against the frame, hand on hip, the eternal piece of chewing gum rotating slowly around her mouth. Languidly she blew a bubble. 'Nah,' she said finally, 'I was wrong about 'im. 'E ain't a proper gent, 'e's a proper shit.'

Well, Maxwell thought; that at least was progress.

'Mind you . . .' She'd gone again, rummaging in his cupboards for cups. Metternich the cat had loped off upstairs to sulk. 'I don't know all the details.'

'You must know some.' Maxwell managed to raise his voice again. The beads of perspiration stood out on his forehead.

'You're runnin' a temperature.' She was next to him again, wiping his face with a tea towel. 'Poor little bleeder. You know,' she peered closely at him, 'you're smaller than I remember.'

'Size isn't everything,' Maxwell reminded her.

'That's just as bloody well,' Janice giggled. ''E's 'ad a lot of girls.'

'Who?'

'Kay. Look, I'm not proud. It's not easy, y'know, bein' a single parent family. Especially with what them bastards in the government are tryin' to do. So I took up wiv Kay cos 'e's a meal ticket. Y'know, the odd nosh, a few drinks at the bar. An' if that means a knee-trembler now and then, well . . .'

'I hope I haven't spoiled all that for you,' Maxwell said.

'Nah.' She patted his knee, probably the only part of his body that didn't feel it had been squeezed through a mangle. 'There's plenty more where 'e come from.'

'About the girls . . .' Maxwell couldn't leave it there.

In a moment, Janice had gone away and come back again with two steaming mugs of cocoa. 'Like I say,' she flounced down again, smoothing her leather skirt over her solid thighs, 'I don't know all the details.' She saw his crest fall and took pity on him. 'But, yeah, I do know some of 'em,' and she winked. 'But first,' and she clasped her hands on her knees, 'I got to know why you want to know.'

'Because I have to,' Maxwell told her. 'You've heard about Tim Grey?'

'That lad what was murdered?'

'One of my sixth form. At Leighford High. Before that, Jenny Hyde.'

'She was done in months ago. Some maniac raped her.'

'Well, not exactly, Janice.' He sipped the cocoa but it hurt going down. 'A maniac killed her, certainly, but she wasn't raped.'

She squinted at him over her nose. 'How do you know?'

He never remembered her arguing with him at school. But then she'd been five years younger and Maxwell had been on his own turf — the intellectual rigours of GCSE History. Now it was a different story.

'I spoke to the doctor on the case. It was made to look like rape; that's not quite the same thing.'

'Why should anybody want to make it look like rape?'

'I don't know,' he said. 'I was hoping Kay could tell me.'

'Nah,' she dismissed it. ''E's' not a killer. Oh, 'e's got a foul temper, yeah — well, you saw that tonight. But 'e's never knocked me around.'

'How long have you been going with him, Janice?'

'Ooh, about three months. Before that 'e used to 'ang around wiv a Chichester girl and then there was Lucy Somefink-or-other from Tottingleigh. You wouldn't know her — she didn't go to Leighford High. 'E just fancied 'isself, that's all. His wife was always up the spout and didn't come across. Always the headaches, y'know.'

Maxwell knew as he forced his lips to the mug again. Maxwell knew.

'I never heard 'e was with that Jenny Hyde. But I'm not sayin' 'e wasn't. I just don't know. 'Ow's your 'ead now?'

'I'll let you know when I've found it again,' he said and flopped back on the settee.

'I bet Maz'd know, though. 'E knows everyfink, does Maz. He's a fuckin' shit, mind. You gotta watch 'im.'

'Maz?' His head snapped forward again and he instantly regretted it.

'Malcolm, then.' She spelt it out. 'Malcolm Whatsit . . . oh, I forget his other name. If it wears a skirt, Maz'd know all about it.'

'Where do I find him?' he asked.

'Over at Barlichway. In a squat. I dunno the address. But it's down by the railway. I could take you there.'

'You've done more than enough,' he said.

'Nah. But look,' she gulped down the last of her cocoa, 'you're all in. You need a bit of shuteye. D'you want me to put you to bed or are you all right down 'ere?'

'Here will be fine,' he said.

'I'm on the social at the moment,' she told him, 'so I'm free in the mornin', but I gotta take Tracey to the clinic. She's got the squits somethin' awful. What time d'you want me round? I'll take you to Maz. You won't be goin' into school wiv ribs like that.'

'No,' he tried to chuckle, but soon regretted it. 'I won't be going into school tomorrow. Janice . . .'

'What?' She paused on his sheepskin.

He reached out a hand. 'Thanks,' he said. 'You've made an old man tolerably happy.'

She reached down and patted his crotch. 'Yeah, well, I'd make you even 'appier, but I'm not sure you're up to it. I'll see myself out. Good-night.'

* * *

The only sound at first was the clack of her platforms on the glistening pavement. Then, the growl of the car engine, snarling behind her, drowned out her footsteps. She walked faster, aware of the headlights, but it was too late.

He wound down the window and leaned out. 'You working, darling?'

'Not for you, wanker,' she sneered.

The car screeched and jolted alongside of her. Two men got out, one at the front, one at the back and Janice Dodds disappeared inside.

* * *

She did not come in the morning. She did not come at noon. Peter Maxwell had spent a horrendous night, of the sort you get once in a lifetime. He certainly hadn't slept and Metternich the cat, sensing that the alien presence had gone, ignored his shattered master's wounds and lay throughout the wee small hours on his chest. It felt like fifteen men, but Maxwell didn't have the strength to boot him off and put all his concentration into breathing with the minimum of pain.

'No pain, no gain,' he muttered to himself as he watched the September morning climb the walls. It would soon be half-term in the world and he was an old man in a hurry. Somehow he lifted Metternich off and sat up. It was only then that he realised how much better he'd felt lying down. Steadying himself on the coffee table, he hauled himself upright and crawled along the furniture. He knew he couldn't make the bathroom so he dabbed his burning face and bursting head with cold water from the kitchen tap and draped his jacket over one shoulder. He certainly couldn't manage the other.

'Very jaunty,' he said as he caught sight of himself in the mirror. 'Very gay hussar. Jesus, Maxie, is that you?' He daren't peer too close. He looked like Hurd Hatfield at the end of Dorian Grey, when the man's sins had caught up with him. There was a purple ridge running from his hairline to his eyebrow and both his eyes were black. He fumbled for his wallet and his scarf. The hat he would leave behind as he wasn't sure it would fit on his head. He would go to Barlichway. He'd catch a cab. Better still, ring for one. He'd knock on every damn door in the area if necessary, but he'd find Maz. But first he had to find the stairs.

* * *

Chief Inspector Henry Hall didn't like the way the wind was blowing. There were two men in front of him in his incident room office and he didn't like either of them. What was worse, and this was an altogether new sensation, he didn't trust them.

'Well then,' he said softly, his eyes cold behind the gold-rimmed specs, 'this surveillance that I didn't order; what fruit did it bear?'

'Fruit, guv?' DC Halsey chuckled, frowning at the same time.

Hall leaned forward, the relaxed pose gone, the fist quietly clenched on the desk. Only the face remained unchanged; immobile. 'I assume, Detective Constable, that you are an obnoxious shit by birth and inclination and not just putting it on for my benefit.'

Halsey blinked, clearly dumbfounded. He cleared his throat. 'I request a transfer, sir,' he said.

'Excellent.' Hall sat back again. 'That's four hours' paperwork before it even reaches Mr Johnson here. I ask again, Dave — the surveillance?'

'Maxwell was visited by a Mrs Sally Greenhow from Leighford High at twenty thirteen hours last night.'

'Do we know her?'

'She was interviewed by DC Carpenter earlier this month. Routine stuff. She'd taught Jenny Hyde at some time in the past, but had no known recent link.'

'What's her connection with Maxwell?' Hall wanted to know.

Johnson shook his head. 'Colleagues,' he said. 'Both in the History Department. But she doubles up in Special Needs, whatever that is.'

'A frequent visitor to his home?'

Johnson shrugged again. 'We don't know,' he said, and couldn't resist adding, 'Of course, if I'd been able to set up surveillance earlier . . .'

'. . . I'd have been two men short earlier,' Hall observed. 'You've yet to convince me, Dave.'

'It's my guess there's something going on between them.' Johnson put his cards on the table.

'Why?' Hall asked.

'How would you describe Sally Greenhow, George?' Johnson turned to the constable.

'Young, quite pretty. Quite . . . girlish, really.'

'Pubescent.' Johnson underlined it for his boss. 'Slim. Little tits.'

'So?' Hall scowled. Johnson certainly had a way with words.

'Well, don't you see the pattern, guv?' Johnson was exasperated, his hands outspread.

'Not yet.' Hall remained a wall of obstinacy.

'Little girls,' Johnson said. 'Jenny Hyde. Sally Greenhow. Others we don't know about.'

'You're reaching, Dave,' was Hall's comment.

'They went out,' Johnson continued, 'Maxwell and Greenhow, at . . .' he checked his notebook, 'twenty-one sixteen hours. They got into her car and drove to Little Willie's.'

'Little Willie's?'

'It's a night-club, sir,' Halsey told his ultimate guv'nor.

'I am aware of that,' Hall said, 'I'm just wondering what a middle-aged man and his teacher-colleague were doing there. Not exactly hokey-cokey country, I wouldn't have thought.'

'Ah, but she didn't go in,' Halsey beamed.

'No?'

'No.' Johnson took up the tale again. 'Sally Greenhow just dropped him at the entrance and drove off. He went in alone.'

'You followed?'

'No; he knew us both, remember.' Johnson had the humility to shift a little as he went on. 'As you point out, guv, I didn't have the green light on any surveillance, so I could hardly put in a new team. Halsey and I waited for him to come out.'

'And when he did?'

'When he did he was in a hurry. This was twenty-three thirty-eight hours. Little Willie's has an extension licence until the end of the month. He was chasing somebody.'

'Chasing somebody?' Hall frowned. This didn't sound like the Peter Maxwell he'd spent time with recently.

'A girl,' Halsey said. 'A young girl.'

'Anybody we know?' Hall asked.

'Janice Dodds,' Johnson told him. 'Twenty-one. Part-time prostitute. Works the Leigh vale area. Little Willie's is a bit off her patch.'

'What happened?'

'George?' Johnson passed the reins to the constable. 'You're more twenty-twenty than I am,' he said.

'This Dodds had a bloke in tow — boyfriend, pimp, we don't know. He and Maxwell had a go at each other in the car-park.'

'With what result?' Hall wanted to know.

'Maxwell got a smacking,' Halsey said. 'Had it coming, if you ask me.'

'I don't,' Hall told him flatly. 'Do you mean to tell me that you witnessed an affray and you just sat there?'

'Couldn't blow our cover, guv,' Johnson explained.

'You didn't have a cover to blow,' Hall reminded him. 'How badly was Maxwell hurt?'

'Oh, not bad,' Halsey said. 'Whoever the bloke was, he was pulling his punches, I'd say.'

'You got the vehicle registration?' Hall asked.

There was a silence.

'Tell me you got the registration,' the Chief Inspector said. But neither of them did, because neither of them could. Hall sighed. 'What about Maxwell?'

'The girl helped him into a cab,' Johnson told him. 'Took him home.'

'To Columbine?'

The Detective Inspector nodded.

'Then what?'

'They went inside.'

'And?'

Johnson shrugged. 'And they stayed there. We had to break off before three. She hadn't come out by then.'

Hall pushed his chair away from the desk. He crossed to the wall where the smiling schoolchildren faces of Jenny Hyde and Tim Grey looked down at him. Every morning they did the same. And every evening they were still there. Well, they seemed to say, what's the matter? Why haven't you caught him yet?

'Is there anybody on Maxwell now?' he asked.

'No, sir,' Johnson said, 'but it's easily managed. Just say the word.'

Hall turned to face his inferiors. He felt vulnerable, alone. It was the price of command and he paid it every day. 'A middle-aged man is visited by a colleague and he goes to a night-club where he gets involved in a fight over a scrubber. It may not be very edifying gentlemen, but it's not exactly criminal. And it's light years away from murder.'

Johnson got up too, leaving Halsey sitting by the desk, smiling, knowing the trump card Johnson had yet to play.

'We've got a woman in the nick, sir,' he said, 'making a statement to DS Gilbert as we speak. She's worth having a word with, I think.'

'Why?' Hall had a feeling he knew what was coming.

'Because her name is Janice Dodds and she says that Peter Maxwell took her to his home last night and he raped her. That's why.'

* * *

Peter Maxwell didn't remember much of that afternoon. He'd got into a cab, one of those roomy London types with the polished seats, and each corner saw him sliding about and groaning with pain. He didn't notice the disapproving eye of the taxi-driver in the rear mirror. The man was a lifelong teetotaller of the Methodist persuasion way back and here was this piss artist not remotely in control of himself. And it was only two o'clock.

The Barlichway estate was endless. It had grown like lichen over the brow of Barlichway Hill and the views were breathtaking. But the estate itself was a concrete jungle of flats and bungalows, with skate-boarding pavements and subway art daubed on every angle. People kept away from the badly lit underpasses, preferring to take their chances on the busy A31. At least if you were hit by an artic you wouldn't know much about it, but a mugger's knife . . . well, that was different.

You never saw a policeman on the Barlichway estate. Not that this was a no-go area exactly. The Chief Constable had said there was no such thing. Really it was a choose-not-to-go-area, which amounted to the same thing. Supermarket trolleys lay broken in unweeded corners and kids who should have been at school wrestled each other on the sort of rope and tyre thing they give to pandas in zoos to play with. No one noticed Peter Maxwell limping through the walkways, peering over fences into people's backyards. No one, that is, except the occupant of Patrol Car Bravo Delta Tango cruising the perimeter of the flyover area. The description over the radio had been clear enough. 'Suspect wanted in connection with a rape in Columbine Avenue early this morning or late last night. Suspect answering to the name of Peter Maxwell, male Caucasian, aged fifty-two. Greying hair, side-whiskers, otherwise clean-shaven. Apprehend and detain for questioning.'

True, there was no mention of the incongruous college scarf. Or the fact that his coat hung off his shoulder or that he walked like a dead man or that his face was one spreading bruise. But it was Peter Maxwell for all that. And Bravo Delta Tango picked up speed and slid past before cutting in sharply.

Maxwell brought his head up to the level, feeling that he knew what Joseph Meyrick, the elephant man, had gone through for all those years. It must have been bad enough for John Hurt wearing pounds of plastic padding. A boy in blue looking all of fourteen stood in front of him, pasty, thin, apparently in desperate need of a square meal.

'Peter Maxwell?' he asked.

Mad Max nodded as best he could.

'Would you come with us, sir?' Another uniformed kid had joined the first.

'Why?' Maxwell asked.

'Because I've asked you to, sir,' the lad said.

'Tell me,' Maxwell tried to smile, but ended up dribbling, 'have you ever thought of becoming a teacher? I like your style.'

And he'd never been so grateful to sit down in his life.

CHAPTER 16

This time they didn't keep Peter Maxwell waiting. Instead he was taken to hospital, whizzed on a stretcher through those ghastly yellowish-see-through plastic doors and into Casualty.

'What's this one done?' the big black Casualty nurse wanted to know.

'Nothing,' Maxwell growled at her, 'I assure you, madam.'

'I was talkin' to the policeman.' She flashed her eyes at him.

'Oh, he's innocent, Bella,' the constable grinned. 'At least he is until we prove him guilty,' and he winked at her.

'Of what exactly? Oh, Jesus!'

'Is that tender?' the nurse asked, pressing her none too subtle fingers into his left side.

'Just a threat,' he gasped, feeling not a little as though he was about to have an out-of-body experience.

'Well, we'll get you on to a bed. Come on, get this shirt off. The doctor will be along in a little while.'

The doctor made the boyish policeman look like Methuselah. It was all very depressing for Maxwell, founder member of the Over the Hill Mob as he was.

'Broken ribs,' the boy wonder diagnosed after a cursory prod. 'X-rays will confirm.'

'Thank you, Dr Mengele,' Maxwell scowled up at him.

The doctor coiled away his stethoscope and hooked his head around the screen that separated Maxwell from the outside world. 'What's this one done?' he asked the waiting constable.

Before he had a chance to answer, Maxwell shouted, 'I'm in here for my own protection. I might get beaten up by a policeman.'

* * *

'Miss Troubridge?' The ubiquitous DI Johnson had hammered on her door.

'Yes.' She was a whiskery old trout to whom the years had been less than kind. What was well preserved about her had been accomplished by liberal applications of neat gin.

'I'm Detective Inspector Johnson, West Sussex CID.' He flashed his warrant card. 'May I come in?'

'Very well,' she said, checking behind him that none of her neighbours along Columbine Avenue had seen him arrive.

'I'm making enquiries into an alleged incident,' he said, 'that took place next door during the early hours of the morning.'

'Next door?' she frowned. 'Do you mean Mr Maxwell?'

'I do, madam.'

'Good heavens. I feel the need for a drinky coming on. Can I corrupt you, Inspector?'

Looking at her, Johnson doubted it. 'It is a little early for me, madam,' he said.

'Well,' she sighed, 'it's a little late for me.' She caught a brief glimpse of her reflection in the cheval. 'Wouldn't think I was Miss Tottingleigh of 1940, would you? Still there was a war on, I suppose.' She poured herself rather a stiff one. 'Oh dear,' she tittered, 'there I go again. Overfilled the damn thing. Never mind.' She raised her glass. 'A bloody war and a sickly season!' she toasted. Her father, Colonel Troubridge, was an old Indian officer pre-war. Promotion was hard in his day and the toast had stuck with the family ever since.

'Er . . . may I sit down, Miss Troubridge?'

'Yes, of course.' She threw a pile of newspapers unceremoniously on the floor. 'And that's Mrs, by the way. I must be one of the very few women who didn't change her name on her wedding day. Charles was my cousin, so I stayed a Troubridge.'

'Fascinating. How well do you know Peter Maxwell?'

'We have the odd drinky,' she beamed. 'I feed his cat when he's away.'

'Well, I suggest you get the old tin opener out.' Johnson was smugger than he had any right to be. 'Mr Maxwell's going to be away for some time.'

'Oh dear,' the old girl frowned. 'Not in any trouble, is he? Only I noticed he hadn't been going into school recently.'

'Oh really?' Johnson sat up. 'Since when?'

'Since he was suspended on full pay last Tuesday.'

Johnson was incredulous. 'He was what?'

'Oh well.' Mrs Troubridge held up her spare hand. 'Now, all this is strictly hearsay, Inspector. But I got it from Nellie Barnstaple whose word is invariably her bond in these matters; and she got it from Jocasta Phillips, whose youngest is on the Board of Governors at Leighford High.'

'So you reckon it's kosher, then?'

'As a bagel,' she nodded solemnly.

'And do your sources tell you why Maxwell was suspended?'

'Ah, now,' she trilled, the triple gin already playing merry hell with her delivery, 'that would be tittle tattle and I'll have no truck with that. Mr Maxwell is a friend. A good friend.'

Dave Johnson leaned over and topped up the old girl's glass. 'I appreciate your loyalty, Mrs Troubridge . . . er . . . Jessica, isn't it?'

She fluttered her eyelashes at him. 'It is, Inspector, but I'm not sure I should allow you to use it.'

'Well, Jessica,' Johnson leered, 'it would be a personal favour to me. And, do you know, I think I'll break the habit of a lifetime and join you in a little snort . . . if you don't mind, of course.'

'Oh no.' She positively giggled, ferreting in a settee-side cabinet for a glass. 'Delighted. Delighted. Well,' she half filled the glass she found there, 'this is only what I've heard, you understand. And you understand, I was told it in the strictest of confidence.'

'Absolutely,' Johnson nodded solemnly. This was going to be a piece of piss.

'He was, I'm afraid, caught in flagrante, so to speak.'

'In . . . what way?' Johnson probed.

'Well,' she nodded closer, lest her walls had ears, 'I wasn't brought up to be too graphic, Inspector, but I believe he had this young girl pinned to a wall in his office. There was even talk of her being spreadeagled over a pile of mats in the gym, but that's nonsense. You see, Mr Maxwell is not now, nor has he ever been, a PT instructor. No, I think the office has a ring of truth, don't you?'

'When you say "pinned" . . .' Johnson wanted more.

'Well, let's just say that his clothing was disarranged and so was hers.' She fanned her crimson face with her hand.

'I see.' Johnson sat back. 'And do your sources give you the girl's name?'

'Spencer, I believe.' She sat frowning. 'Yes, that was it. Anne Spencer. Now, Inspector, what was this incident of last night to which you referred?'

But Johnson was already on his feet. 'More of the same, I'm afraid, Jessica. Thanks for the gin. I'll see myself out.'

'Where is Mr Maxwell now?' She suddenly asked him. 'I saw him go out at lunchtime. He didn't look at all well.'

'Where is he?' Johnson couldn't resist a smirk. 'You weren't brought up to be too graphic, Jessica, I know, but he's in deep shit; that's where he is.'

* * *

They kept Peter Maxwell in overnight, just to be sure. There's something about hospitals, isn't there? That indefinable smell, cabbage and cold comfort, wafting over the wards. Bad enough that the wards pre-dated Aneurin Bevan, that saviour of poorly pillocks to whom consultant surgeons raised two fingers every day of their working lives. In the case of Leighford General though, the oldest wing pre-dated Lord Salisbury and that, down among the dead men, is where they put Peter Maxwell.

What with geriatric snoring on one side and the whimpering of a twisted testicle on the other, Maxwell spent a second sleepless night. He was wearing somebody else's pyjamas and somebody else's pyjama cord bound itself around his productivity area more than once. Lying on his left side was out, on account of the pain, so he was forced to lie on his right and watch the toothless lips of the old boy in the next bed rise, flubber and fall on each outing of breath.

After that and what the NHS laughingly called breakfast, he'd settle for the solitude of a police cell any day.

'What's the damage?' Chief Inspector Hall sat before him across the spartan table, the tape recorder running.

'What's the charge?' Maxwell was in no mood to play games.

'No charge,' Hall assured him. 'I just wanted another little chat.' He riffled through some papers on the table. 'Two cracked ribs. Oedema to left side and forehead.'

'If you know these things,' Maxwell said, 'why do you have to ask?'

'Because, Mr Maxwell,' Hall was patience itself for a man whose feet had been firmly in the clay of an aimless murder enquiry for the best part of two months, 'it's all about corroboration. I know some things. You know some things. Let's put all our cards on the table, shall we?'

'All right,' Maxwell said.

'Why did you go to Little Willie's night before last?'

'I was looking for Maz.'

'Who?'

'Maz. The tall, spotty kid seen talking to Jenny Hyde on the Dam the day she died. I've been told his name is Maz.'

'His nickname, certainly. His name is actually Malcolm. Malcolm Sadler. He's twenty-two years old and he lives in a squat on the edge of the Barlichway estate. Is that why you also went to the Barlichway estate?'

'You . . . you know about Maz?'

'Of course,' Hall shrugged. 'Oh, I grant you we didn't when we contacted the BBC to make *Crimewatch*. Then he was just a nameless witness. But our enquiries turned him up the following week.'

'I don't remember that in the papers.' He'd started reading them ever since Tim Grey died.

'We are not in the habit of confiding every little twist and turn to the media, Mr Maxwell. For a start most of it is deadly dull — doesn't make for good copy, as they say. And secondly, I suspect that both you and I know it would be *carte blanche* for them to speculate wildly in the wrong direction. We've interviewed Sadler and I'm convinced he had nothing to do with Jenny Hyde's murder.'

'What was he asking her to do,' Maxwell wanted to know, 'when that woman saw them arguing and Jenny was saying "No"? What was that about?'

'It doesn't matter, really, Mr Maxwell,' Hall told him. 'What matters at the moment is what happened at Little Willie's. Perhaps you'd care to enlighten us?'

Was this the royal plural, Maxwell wondered? Cops R Us? Hall was the only policeman in the room, Maxwell the only suspect.

'In detail, please,' Hall urged him. 'Loud and clear for the tape.'

Maxwell leaned back, gingerly resting against the chair. 'Well,' he said, 'you'll really have to forgive me, Chief Inspector, while the irony of all this sinks in. I appear to have received a bloody nose for no reason at all.'

'Go on.'

'I went to Little Willie's because that's where I understood I'd be able to find this Maz.'

'But he wasn't there?'

'No. I asked around for him, had a few drinks and was about to leave when . . .'

'When?'

'I ran into . . . an old friend, shall we say.'

'Janice Dodds.'

Maxwell smiled. At least that hurt him less than it had yesterday. 'No, I wouldn't exactly put Janice in that category. No, I was referring to her gentleman friend.'

'Ah, yes,' Hall nodded. 'He took umbrage at your pestering Janice?'

'No,' Maxwell said, 'he took umbrage at my asking about Jenny Hyde.'

'Jenny . . . Who is this man, Mr Maxwell?'

'Tsk, tsk, Mr Hall,' Maxwell wagged a finger at his interrogator, 'and you so knowledgeable on the Jenny Hyde case. The man in question,' and he leaned forward with the air of a conspirator, 'is Keith Miller, Alison's husband.'

'I see,' Hall said, in such a way that made it perfectly obvious he didn't.

'Keith is known as Kay,' Maxwell explained. 'The diary. Jenny's diary.'

'The one that so mysteriously went missing from your house.'

'That's right.'

'I thought you couldn't remember its contents.' Hall narrowed his eyes at his man.

'All of them, no,' Maxwell confessed. 'Some of them came back to me later.'

'How convenient. What else did the diary say? The bit of it that "came back to you later"?'

'Do you mind if I walk about a bit?' Maxwell asked. 'Sitting still gives me quite a bit of gyp.'

'Be my guest.' Hall waved his hand.

'It's obvious from what I remember of the diary,' Maxwell paced the floor, 'that Jenny was having an affair with someone. A married man.'

'Keith Miller?'

'She used the initial K.; that was all. But as soon as Janice Dodds introduced him as Kay, alarm bells began to go off in my head.'

'And what did he tell you? About Jenny, I mean?'

'Nothing. He proceeded to try to kick my head off. If Janice hadn't been there, he would have done.'

'Why should Keith Miller know Jenny Hyde at all?' Hall asked him.

'Well, I don't want to be the one to put anybody in the frame, Chief Inspector. Alison's a nice kid. Oh, she takes her pregnancies a bit seriously. Overdoes the fainting wall-flower bit, but as someone who's never actually likely to be in her position, maybe I'm being a bit harsh. The tragedy is that her husband is a shit. The Victorians called them cads, the new Georgians lounge lizards or gigolos. His motto is "If it wears a skirt, get inside its knickers." It was common staff-room gossip at Leighford High. What I didn't realise was that it extended to kids.'

'Not exactly a kid, was she?' Hall said, the face, as always a mask of blankness. 'Seventeen. Perhaps she'd been around.'

'Perhaps a lot of things.' Maxwell looked at the opaque glass in the solitary window. 'Perhaps the moon's made of green cheese.' He sighed. 'I don't really know any more.'

'So Keith Miller didn't admit to any sort of relationship with Jenny?'

'No.' Maxwell shook his head, jerked out of his own thoughts. 'No, for all I know I was barking up the wrong tree entirely. But he clearly resented my asking. Over-reacted, wouldn't you say?'

'I don't know,' Hall said, 'I wasn't there.' The fact that two of his officers were would remain his little secret for the moment.

Maxwell was thinking aloud. 'All right, so I'd caught him out with a bimbo. All he need have done was come the jack-the-lad bit; nudge me in the ribs,' and he blanched at the thought of it. 'Said "Don't tell the missus" and passed the whole thing off as a joke.'

'Instead of which?'

'Instead of which, he actually pulled Janice out of the club and made a run for it. I caught up with him at the car and things got a little rough. Bloody silly, really. I suppose I should be grateful he wasn't carrying a knife.'

'What happened afterwards?' Hall had left the table with its attendant microphone and joined Maxwell, silhouetted by the window.

'I'm not really sure,' Maxwell said. 'I only really came to at home. Apparently Janice had got me into a cab, found my wallet to pay for it and got me upstairs. Enterprising, I call that.'

'What was she wearing?'

'Wearing?' Maxwell frowned. 'God, I don't know. I'm not very good with clothes.' Hall could tell that just by looking at him. 'Er . . . some kind of jacket, I think. Black. It had silver studs and black fringes. Sort of Western thing, you know. God, I can remember when they first became fashionable; back in the '60's, wasn't it?'

'What else?'

'Er . . . black leather skirt.'

'Short?' Hall checked.

'Up to her bum . . .' Maxwell's eyes flickered. There was a strange look on the face of Chief Inspector Henry Hall. 'Why are you asking me all these questions?' he asked.

Hall returned to the table and gestured for Maxwell to do the same. He did and when they were sitting comfortably, he began. 'Mr Maxwell, I have to tell you that a very serious allegation has been made against you.'

Maxwell snorted. 'If I could stand it,' he said, 'I'd laugh out loud. I understood that that would be a civil matter.'

'A civil matter?' Hall was lost. 'I'm afraid you'll have to pass that one by me again.'

'Anne Spencer,' Maxwell explained. 'That nonsense about my suspension.'

Maxwell had never seen Hall smile before. It was altogether an unnerving experience — rather like Daniel O'Connell's description of the smile of Robert Peel, 'like the silver plate on a coffin.'

'Mr Maxwell,' he said, 'you really are full of surprises this morning.'

Maxwell sat back, confused. He felt a little shiver run up his bandaged spine. 'Shall I come in again?' he asked. 'You're not talking about Anne Spencer, are you? You didn't know about it. Not a damn thing.'

'But I do now,' Hall told him. 'No, the serious allegation, Mr Maxwell, has been made against you by Miss Janice Dodds. She says you raped her.'

Maxwell tried to form the words, but his lips obstinately refused to move.

'Would you like to make a statement?' Hall asked. 'You are, of course, entitled to have your lawyer present.'

There was a thump on the door. DI Johnson's lugubrious face appeared round it. 'Can I have a word, sir?'

'Not now, Dave,' Hall hadn't taken his eyes off Maxwell.

'It is important, guv'nor,' Johnson persisted.

Maxwell saw the Chief Inspector's jaw flex. He snapped off the microphone and stood up, abruptly. 'I'll arrange to have some tea sent in, Mr Maxwell,' he said.

Outside in the corridor, it was a different story. 'Your timing is perfect as ever, Dave,' Hall said, brushing past him into his own office. 'Well? What's so important that it couldn't wait?'

'I've been checking up with Maxwell's neighbour, sir, a Mrs Troubridge. Nice old duck. Fond of her gin, but doesn't miss much. You'll never guess what.'

Hall looked at his Number Two. 'That Peter Maxwell has been suspended over an alleged incident with Anne Spencer.'

Johnson was deflated, but he'd rather die than show it. 'What did he say about it?' He jerked his head in the direction of the charge room.

'Said it was nonsense,' Hall told him, throwing himself down heavily into his swivel. His eyes burned with tiredness and he felt like a rag that had been wrung out.

'Well,' Johnson smirked, 'to quote Miss Mandy Rice-Davies, "He would, wouldn't he?" Didn't mention that he exposed himself to the girl, then?'

Hall looked up at the Inspector, pushy, arrogant, cocksure. He shook his head.

'That he'd got her knickers off?'

Hall shook his head again.

'The only thing I can't understand is why we weren't called in earlier. It'll be them bloody teachers,' Johnson rationalised it, 'covering up.'

'The conspiracy theory of History.' Hall was talking to himself.

'What, guv?'

'Nothing. All right, Dave. Give me your report on this Mrs Troubridge. DS Gilbert around?'

'Off duty, guv.'

'Right. Jacquie.' He pressed the intercom on his desk.

'Sir?' the voice crackled.

'Two teas, please. One for me and one for Mr Maxwell.'

'That's right,' Johnson grinned. 'I knew we'd find a use for WPCs one day.' He bent over the intercom. 'One sugar for the guv'nor and a hefty dose of strychnine for the murdering, raping bastard.'

Hall's hand had already cut the link. 'I think we'll dispense with the levity, Inspector,' he said and when Jacquie Carpenter came in, she could have cut the atmosphere with a knife.

The intercom crackled again. ''Scuse me, guv,' the desk man spoke to the Chief Inspector, 'there's a Mrs Miller to see you. Alison Miller. Says it's urgent.'

'That'll be all, Dave,' Hall said. 'Show her in,' to the machine on the desk. 'Jacquie, forget the tea. I'll want you in on this one.'

Dave Johnson pushed past Alison Miller on his way out without so much as a sideways glance. Chief Inspector Hall towered over her as she waddled into his office. Please God, he thought to himself, don't let her give birth right now. He'd escaped all that on the beat. What an irony if he had to lend a hand now he'd made it to Chief Inspector.

Alison Miller avoided his gaze at first, but she was grateful to see the round, smiling face of Jacquie Carpenter.

‘I’m DCI Hall,’ he said. ‘I believe we met briefly at Leighford High some weeks ago.’

‘That’s right.’ She struggled down on to a chair.

‘Are you all right there?’ he asked her. For all his Helen had gone through this palaver three times, he wasn’t at one with pregnant women. He still found the whole thing vaguely embarrassing.

‘Can I get you some tea, Mrs Miller?’ Jacquie asked.

‘No, thanks.’ For a woman on the verge of tears, Alison Miller tried to put on a smile.

‘Well, then, Mrs Miller.’ Hall leaned back, his hands clasped over his waistcoat. ‘How may we help you?’

She bit hard on her lower lip. This was the moment she’d dreaded. Not since three in the morning when it had all come out into the open. Not since five when she’d heard the door slam on a chapter of her life. Not since she’d got the kids up and taken them to her mother’s. This was what she had dreaded for all her married life. For eleven years of doubt and loneliness and fear.

‘My husband,’ she said, ‘he’s the man you want. He killed Jenny Hyde.’

CHAPTER 17

If you follow the coast road that loops along the Shingle; past the house where Janet Foster lived with her dog and her Art; dip down, away from Leighford Cross where they say a gibbet used to stand, clanking and creaking in the wind; down to the dunes and the sea, you'll come to that spot where they found her that morning towards the end of September.

It was a Sunday, looking back. That day when millions of Englishmen gave their lawns a final mow before consigning their hovers to their winter quarters, when they washed their cars and their wives caught up with the ironing and their mothers still staggered to church, summoned by bells.

The Sandersons had meant to go to the beach for weeks. Little Roger had been to see Spielberg's *Jurassic Park* in the summer and was hooked for life in his hunt for fossil remains. Well, it was cheaper than video games and safer than girls, so his mum and dad bought him a geologist's hammer and off they went.

'Keep to the cliff face,' the guidebook had advised, where the wealden beds showed the meanderings of ancient rivers, uptilted to the sky. Dad said Roger would be lucky if he found an ammonite. It was known that the Germans had come over here in droves in the summer that had gone, intent on ripping everything remotely interesting out of the earth. From Lyme Regis in the west, via the Isle of Wight, to Folkestone in the east, they'd barely left one stone upon another. 'Bastards' was Grandad Sanderson's comment. They'd flattened his East End home in the Blitz, now they were digging under his foundations. Little Roger didn't believe a word of it, however. At every crevice in the cliff, at every concentration of stones, he expected to find, just lying there, the complete skeleton of a raptor the Germans had unaccountably missed.

Sarah was totally bored. Why did they always have to do things that Roger wanted to do? She was going through that period in her life when she hated her little brother. He was cute at first, like a doll that moved and cried without having to have his arms and legs twisted into position or his tummy pressed. She'd noticed, though, at two as she was when he was born, that he cried more readily when he had those things done to him. She'd put up with the noise and the rough-housing and his smelly friends who came round and ruined her toys, pulling the tails of her Little Ponies and trying to flush her Barbies down the loo. But this latest nonsense with fossils was just too much. She walked apart from the others, from mum and dad going on and on about granddad and his incontinence and that idiot Roger racing ahead tapping everything with his little hammer.

She had her hands firmly in her anorak pockets, her head down, her feet splashing through the wet sand at low tide. She wasn't looking ahead, only at the way her trainers splashed in the shallow puddles the receding sea had left behind. She almost fell over it — whatever it was. It looked like an old rotting sofa the sea had thrown up. She stopped. Looked more closely. It wasn't a sofa, was it? It was rotting, certainly. And it stank. She felt her freckly nose wrinkle even before she realized what it was. She could still hear mum and dad rabbiting away to her left, Roger's hammer still tapping somewhere ahead, the surf booming to her right.

But in front of her, at her feet, was the black, bloated torso of a woman, the eye sockets empty, the jaw hanging open where fish had gnawed the muscle tissue. The hair lay plastered to the skull like matted seaweed and the rib cage protruded through the swollen thorax. There were no legs at all, only strips of skin dangling from the smashed pelvis, a livid white under the glare of the sun.

Sarah's hands flopped out of her anorak pockets. And she screamed. And screamed. And screamed.

* * *

The sun came out through the Venetian blinds of the incident room in time for Henry Hall to have his lunch. He'd forgotten when he'd last sat down to a Sunday roast with Helen and the kids. Henry Junior had had a story to write at school about mums and dads. Helen couldn't help mentioning to Henry Senior that it hadn't mentioned dad at all.

So he was about to tackle his lead and egg roll, the sort that lay for ever in the pit of your stomach, when Dave Johnson popped his head around the door. 'Call from DI Groves, guv,' he said. 'Got a body washed up in Leighford Bay. Thinks we should take a look.'

So the lead and egg roll was stashed away for later and Henry Hall downed as much of the coffee as he could manage before the plastic cup burned through his fingers and he grabbed his coat and made for the car-park.

'I'd welcome your views on Alison Miller's tale,' he said, clunking and clicking as he did every trip.

'Load of cobblers, guv.' Johnson checked his rear-view mirror and kicked the engine over.

'That seems a considered and balanced judgement.' Hall's cold eyes raked his man.

'You asked me,' Johnson said. 'I told you.'

'What do you put it down to, then?'

'Move it!' Johnson bellowed at the old codger trying to negotiate his way back from church. 'Plain, old-fashioned vindictiveness,' he said. 'You've seen it before, guv. We all have. Wife approaches middle age, figure's gone to shit with multiple childbirth. Old man's attention wanders — younger, slimmer stuff. Off he goes, chasing skirt. Bible's full of it.'

'So it's just a woman scorned, then?'

'That's right.' Johnson swung left to make for the coast road. 'This Keith Miller's giving his wife the run-around. He's seen in public with a few tarts and she gets to hear about it. She's miffed. No, let me amend that, she's bloody furious. She doesn't just get mad, though — she gets even. She knows about Jenny Hyde. She's Deputy Head of Sixth Form at the girl's school. What a chance to stitch the bastard up. She knows there's no truth in it. But she hopes we'll have a word, feel his collar. It's probably a more satisfying come-uppance than her throwing the saucepan at him.'

'They didn't have a row, though.' Hall watched the Shingle come into view and the sun gild the stunted trees that lay above the Red House, ever in its own darkness on the other side of the hill. 'She just tackled him about it. About the rumours and the innuendo. He admitted it. Just like that, muttering things about a fair cop and he felt better that it was all out in the open. He'd met Jenny Hyde at some Fayre or other at the school. He'd met her again, by accident, in town and taken her for a coffee. He'd asked her out and she'd said yes.'

'Well, there you are.' Johnson felt vindicated. 'He got his end away and Mrs got narked. Domestic stuff. Not our problem.'

'An accusation of murder is always our problem,' Hall reminded him.

'Maxwell,' Johnson reminded him as the car came to a halt among the police vehicles on the dunes. 'There's our boy, guv; you take it from me.'

Hall couldn't consciously remember having taken anything from DI Johnson and he didn't intend to start now.

DI Groves was pointing out to sea, doing his boyhood of Raleigh bit, when his guv'nor arrived. 'What have we got, Tom?' Hall asked.

'Ah, morning, guv,' Groves nodded. 'Dave.' He had a year to go before they put him out to grass. He'd never make

DCI now and he knew it. There was a time when he'd resented Hall like buggery, with his university degree and his three-piece suit and his smarter-than-thou attitude. Now, he was tired and looked older than his fifty-five. Colleagues of his had gone ten years younger, but he was still here, in an orange anorak, up to his bollocks in somebody else's problems.

'Dr Astley's with the body now. He reckons it's been in the water about two months.'

The three men plodded through the dry sand, kicking the spurge and the sea pinks while the gulls screamed and wheeled overhead. Above the roar of the surf, the occasional crackle of police radios and the wind whipping the blue and white tape that cordoned off the scene of death from the civilized world. And just beyond that tape, denizens of the civilised world pressed as close as they could, some with binoculars trained on the little knot of men at the water's edge. The ghouls looking for blood.

'Get those people away!' Hall shouted to a couple of uniformed men on the dunes and he felt the wind whip in under his flapping jacket like a knife.

'Did we get you from the river bank again, Jim?' he asked Astley.

'No, from the squash club,' the pathologist grunted. 'Can't say I'm sorry. Ever played with Bob Gordon?'

'No.'

'Well, don't. He's sixty-three and he's got a body like a whip. I'm not ashamed to say I was losing — losing heavily — when your chap's call came through.'

'God's teeth!' Johnson hissed as he witnessed the remains that Astley was kneeling over.

'Welcome to Dead Man's Cove,' Astley grinned. 'You're getting old, Dave. We've been this way before.'

'Two months in the water, Tom says.' Hall knelt as near to the corpse as his stomach would let him.

'Give or take,' Astley nodded. 'It's a woman. Dark hair. Mature. Look at the teeth. I wouldn't like to guess an age at this stage.'

'Any unusual bridgework?' Hall asked. Johnson had already turned away.

'Nothing special,' Astley told him, 'but I'll put out a detailed description later. If she's local, some dentist might recognise something.'

'What happened to the rest of her?' Groves asked. It was a question he'd been asking everybody else for the past hour.

Astley shook his head. 'It's my guess the body was caught up in a boat's propeller or something. Look here,' he lifted the shattered pelvis with a steel probe, 'a clean slice to the ileum. Whatever it was virtually cut her in half. Like a circular saw.'

'Bloody hellfire!' Johnson muttered. He wished he hadn't grabbed that Vindaloo in the canteen now.

'Did she go in around here?' Hall asked. 'Can you tell that?'

'Not my field,' it hurt Astley to admit.

'Tom,' Hall squinted up at the DI, 'this is your turf.'

'My surf too, guv,' Groves grinned. 'The tide does funny things around the Bay. She could have gone in . . . well, if you're talking two months, almost anywhere along the south coast as far west as Selsey Bill. Of course, if she's local, and if Dr Astley's right about the propeller . . .'

'Which I am,' Astley insisted.

'. . . she could have been held down by the bladderlock under Brampton Ledge for weeks.'

'Tom,' Hall was back on his feet, motioning his colleague aside for a word, 'why did you send for me on this? You know I'm up to my eyes in the incident room.'

Groves looked at the boy wonder who'd stolen his job. It was time to face up to a harsh reality. 'I've never handled a murder, guv,' he said, feeling like a little boy again, staring his first day at school in the face. 'Not on my own. I'd just welcome your input, that's all.'

'Who said anything about a murder, Tom?'

'I did.' Jim Astley was suddenly at his elbow, wiping his hands on the towel he always carried in the car to dry the dog. 'It may be that the lady fell overboard off Selsey Bill and a ship's propeller ripped her up. Or that she's been washing about under the ledge for weeks. But I'm bloody sure she didn't wrap herself in a black bin liner first. What would be the point?'

* * *

They kept Peter Maxwell for as long as they could. He'd got another eight hours left before they'd have to charge him or let him go. He still hadn't asked for a solicitor. But he had made a phone call. It was to his fellow Old Contemptible Geoffrey Smith, and DC Halsey made a point of listening in on the phone upstairs.

'Oh, shit!' Maxwell growled as heard the pre-recorded voice of the Head of English. After the long tone, he launched himself. 'Get back to me, indeed, Geoff,' he said. 'I'm at Leighford police station, facing Richard Burton in 1984 . . . Er . . . oh, bugger, I hate these things.'

'Hello?' a voice interrupted his wanderings.

'Hilda?' Maxwell said. 'Is that you?'

'Max?' Smith's other half said. 'I was in the bath. I thought I recognised your voice. What's the matter?'

'Well, I'm in a spot of bother, Hilda. At the police station.'

'Oh, my God, Max . . .'

'No, no, it's all right. Look, could you ask Mrs Troubridge, you know, my neighbour, to look after Metternich?'

'Of course, but . . .'

'Give my regards to Geoffrey, will you? Say to him, "I will consider my cat, Geoffrey." He'll like that.'

'Never mind the one-liners, Max. You need help. A solicitor . . .'

'Nah,' Maxwell sounded like Janice Dodds. 'The hassle. The expense.'

'Something, then. Shall I send Geoffrey?'

'No. Really. I'm fine. I'll come and see you and tell you all about it when they let me out . . . And they'll have to let me out, you know.' The sound of his laughter didn't convince her. And it didn't convince him. 'After all,' he said, 'we do have laws in this country — habeas corpus and all that. And I haven't raped anyone.'

'I'm glad to hear it,' she said.

'Hilda,' Maxwell had forgotten his manners in the fraughtness of the moment, 'I'm sorry. I didn't ask. Long time no see. How have you been?'

'Me?' he heard her say. 'I'm fine too, Max. Happier than I've been in a long, long time.'

And he rang off.

* * *

The lab excelled itself. Marjorie Astley was taking longer than usual this time to be wrung out and Dr Jim was in an unusually efficient — and obliging — turn of mind. He knew he shouldn't have shot his mouth off to Smith and Maxwell, and he knew from the casual conversation of a couple of uniformed lads on the beach that the said Maxwell was now in custody helping them with their enquiries. He didn't know, couldn't know, what Maxwell had told them. But if he had blabbed to Hall about Astley's unprofessionalism, the good doctor would have some explaining to do. If he gave Hall the answers he wanted quickly, accurately, without further prompting, perhaps the Chief Inspector would overlook it. For Jim Astley, like Dave Johnson, knew that Henry Hall played everything by the book. The cold, humourless, lacklustre bastard.

It was a little before midnight on the Monday that the lacklustre bastard was sitting in the incident room in his shirtsleeves, the table lamp reflecting harshly in his glasses, reading Astley's interim report. Using some technique Hall could not pronounce, Astley had worked out the dead woman's height to have been five foot eight. Age was more difficult because of the advanced state of the body's decomposition. Could be anything from twenty to forty-five, possibly even fifty.

Her hair had been dark and the bad news was that she had exceptionally good teeth. Only one filling of the upper third bicuspid, and that was an old one. Groves's team would have to knock on a lot of dentists' doors to pin-point that one.

His best guess was that she'd gone into the sea towards the end of July. And the appalling wounds to her pelvis that had carried off her legs were not the cause of her death. They were clearly post-mortem injuries, however horrific, and Astley clung to the probability that a ship's propeller had done the deed. She had not drowned either. There were tell-tale diatoms, those little creepy things that live in water, as Astley had condescendingly written for Hall's layman's benefit in the margin of the print-out. But they were confined to the air passages. There were none in the bloodstream and none in what was left of the internal organs. The deceased had been placed in a black plastic bin liner and dumped into the sea. Whatever had been used to truss the bag up, rope or wire, had long ago become separated from the corpse.

'Black bin liner,' Hall murmured to himself. Well, that narrowed it down to however many million citizens bought these things from however many supermarkets there were in the south of England.

The cause of death, Jim Astley believed, was a blow or blows to the back of the head. Those injuries, which had caused a collapse of the cranium and radial fissures from it, were certainly ante-mortem and would have caused immediate unconsciousness, followed rapidly by coma. Death would have ensued within minutes.

What am I doing this for? Hall wondered to himself. He didn't owe Tom Groves anything and whoever this woman was she'd been battered to death and her body thrown into the sea. There was obviously no link with Jenny Hyde or Tim Grey. He read to the bottom paragraph. The face was unrecognisable — but he knew that — and even the fingerprints were lost because the skin of the hands had peeled off like rubber gloves. Only the sea knew her secrets now.

There was a knock on the door.

'Jacquie?' Hall looked at her over his glasses. 'Come in.'

'I know it's late, sir,' she apologized.

'Is it?' He looked at his watch. 'Well another day tomorrow. You look like you could do with a smoke,' and he ferreted in his pocket and threw her a packet of ten.

'Sir.' She sat down opposite him.

'Hmm?' He was consigning Astley's report to the tray that said 'Out'. He'd have it passed to Tom Groves in the morning.

'Why do you carry ciggies when you don't smoke?'

'Just in case,' he said, 'in case I get the urge. I gave up four years, eight months, three weeks ago. But in this job, you never know when you're going to have to start again. Besides, what would you do without me?'

It was a rare moment in Jacquie Carpenter's life. She saw the Chief Inspector smile. 'Well, well,' he said. 'Time is money, so they tell me. What's up, Jacquie?'

'Can I talk to you about Peter Maxwell, sir?' Her face was lost momentarily behind a cloud of smoke.

'Everybody seems to be talking about Peter Maxwell,' he said. 'Everybody except Peter Maxwell.'

'I've just had the medical report on Janice Dodds.'

'Just?' Hall frowned.

'I stole it, sir.'

'Jacquie?' Hall didn't like the way this conversation was going.

'It was in the vehicle of one of my superior officers, sir.'

'And you broke into this vehicle?'

'Not exactly. It was open. But I broke into the briefcase inside it.'

Hall leaned forward, hands clasped on the desk. 'Why?' he asked.

'Let's just say I had my suspicions,' she said, swallowing hard. Her eyes were large and steady in the lamp's glow. But the mottling on her neck said it all. DC Jacquie Carpenter was walking a razor's edge and she knew it.

'What does the report say?' Hall asked.

The girl swallowed hard. 'That Janice Dodds was not raped, sir,' she said. 'There was no evidence of recent intercourse, nor rough penetration. No bruising on the genital area or thighs.'

'I've read DS Gilbert's report,' Hall told her. 'It talks about extensive bruising to the face.'

'Three teeth missing,' Jacquie nodded. 'That's what the medical report says too. It also says something else.'

'Oh? What?'

'Janice Dodds was attacked not by one man, but by two. There were distinct fingerprints on her wrists where one of them had held her down. The ones on her throat were different.'

'Are you telling me Maxwell had an accomplice?'

'No, sir.' She felt her nerve going. As though she'd explode.

'What then?' Hall wanted her to spell it out. Needed her to.

'I . . .' and the gaze faltered and her hands trembled on the unsmoked cigarette.

'Whose car was it, Jacquie? Whose briefcase?'

And her answer was barely audible. 'DI Johnson's, sir,' she said, it was DI Johnson.'

* * *

If there was a bigger estate than the Barlichway, it was the one below the railway, to the south of Leighvale. It wasn't the sort of place to be out and about in, not in the early hours of a Tuesday morning, not if you were a senior copper and a DWPC.

'Do you know what fuckin' time it is?' The sound of Janice Dodds, woken from her beauty sleep. Only she wasn't very beautiful just at the moment. There was a livid bruise around her left eye and a jagged purple line around her throat. She wrapped her housecoat tightly around her.

'May we come in?' Hall asked.

'Who the fuck are you?'

He showed her his warrant card. 'DCI Hall, West Sussex CID. I believe you've already met DC Carpenter.' And he pushed past the girl into the narrow hallway. A dilapidated buggy almost took off his kneecap, but he kept going. It was less than salubrious, the Dodds' home. A tiny four-roomed flat on the fourth floor of an anonymous tenement block, terraced with other tiny four-roomed flats just like it. It made Del Boy Trotter's studio mock-up on the telly look positively palatial.

'Who is it, Janice?' a scrawny, middle-aged woman in curlers asked.

'It's the fuzz, mum. You go back to bed. I can 'andle 'em.'

'Like you handled them before?' Hall turned to her.

She frowned up at him. 'Waddyou mean?' she pouted.

'Look,' Janice's mum had not gone back to bed, 'my Janice has been through enough, thanks to you bleeders. What do you want now?'

'The truth, . . . er . . . Mrs Dodds, is it?'

'It might be.' She squinted at him.

'You see, we didn't get that last time.'

'You ain't got no right. . .' Janice's mum protested.

'I'm afraid we have every right,' Hall told her. 'Now if you intend to stay, I must ask you to be quiet.'

'What about a nice cup of tea?' Jacquie Carpenter suggested.

'Janice . . . ?'

'It's all right, mum. Go on. I'll be all right.'

'May we sit down?' Hall asked as the woman clattered and clashed in the tiny kitchen.

'I can't stop ya, can I?' Janice flounced, her housecoat falling open to reveal her powerful thighs.

'You spoke to Detective Sergeant Gilbert and DC Carpenter here the day before yesterday in connection with an assault,' Hall said.

'That's right. Has he coughed? That Maxwell? What'll he get? A smack on the wrist, I bet.'

'Let's just see if I've got it right,' Hall said. 'Maxwell took you back to his house.'

'Nah,' Janice corrected him. 'I took him.'

'Oh, yes, he'd been in a fight. With Keith Miller.'

'That's right.'

'He's a shit, that bloke,' Janice's mum told the company from the kitchen.

'Put a cork in it, Mum,' Janie told her. 'I'm telling this story.'

Hall looked at Jacquie. 'So you got Maxwell home. That was a kind thing to do.'

'Yeah, well, he was all right. At first, I mean.'

'What did you talk about?' Hall asked.

'We ain't got no sugar,' Janice's mum shouted through.

Hall jerked his head to Jacquie Carpenter who joined the woman in the kitchen. 'Can I help, Mrs Dodds?' she asked.

'What did you talk about?' Hall asked the girl again.

'Oh, I dunno. This and that.'

'Such as?'

'Well, it was mostly about Kay — Keith Miller. Maxwell thought he had somefink to do with that girl what was murdered. That Jenny Hyde.'

'And did he?'

'I dunno. Oh, he liked 'em young, but I don't know 'e ever knocked 'em off. He might of done. I told Maxwell. I didn't know.'

'What did he do?'

'Well,' Janice's eyes flickered from left to right, 'It must of been all that talk about girls 'n' that. Or 'e'd got the 'ots for me all along . . .'

'I've told you about wearing them short skirts, ain't I, Janice?'

Janice's mum had escaped Jacquie Carpenter's help in the kitchen and was back in the living-room, four mugs of tea in her hands.

'Oh, come on, mum. You used to wear 'em an' all. I remember your weddin'.'

'What happened at Maxwell's?' Hall asked her.

'I told 'er,' Janice nodded at Jacquie, ''an' that ovver copper.'

'And now I'd like you to tell me,' Hall said.

''E raped me,' she said flatly, as if he'd asked her the time.

'How?'

Janice looked at him open-mouthed. 'You what?'

'I asked you how he raped you.' Hall showed no emotion whatsoever.

'Well . . .'e . . .' Janice looked at her mother, who was still staring at Hall. 'E 'eld me down an' put it in.'

'Held you down, how?' Hall asked.

'By me shoulders,' Janice blurted, her colour up, her eyes flashing.

Janice's mum slurped her tea loudly. 'Bastard,' she growled.

'Not by the wrists?' Hall asked.

'Oh, yeah.' Janice saw what Hall could see and slid the cuffs of her housecoat over her bruised arms. 'Later, yeah.'

'And while he was doing that,' Hall said, 'holding you by the wrist and shoulders, what was the other copper doing?'

'Oh, he was squeezin' me froat an' . . .' and Janice Dodds froze in mid-sentence.

'And hitting you across the face.' Hall finished it for her. 'You see, Miss Dodds, the medical report on you doesn't tally with an attack by one man. And it doesn't tally with a sexual assault at all. What kind of cab did you take to Maxwell's?'

'Er . . . I dunno . . . a black one.'

'A hackney carriage?' Hall pressed her. 'A London taxi?'

'Yeah, that's right.'

'With plastic seats?'

'Ow the fuck should I know?' Janice snapped. 'I can't remember.'

'You see, your coat, the one you were wearing when you came in to report the incident, it had fibres all over it. Fibres which we believe came from a car with grey seat covers. One of my colleagues drives a car like that.'

'Wass 'e talkin' abaht, Janice?' her mum wanted to know.

'Nothin'.' Janice was on her feet. 'Why didn't yer go to bed like I asked yer?'

'I want to know,' her mum said. 'You told me that teacher 'ad done it to yer. Who are you sayin' done it now?'

'No one, Mrs Dodds,' Hall told her, 'no one raped her, at least; did they, Janice?'

'Well, what of it?' Janice bellowed. There was a cry from the room next door. 'Oh, fuck. You've started 'er off now; my Trace.'

'So what really happened, Miss Dodds?' Hall stood in the girl's way, blocking her exit with his tall, grey-suited body.

For a moment the girl stood there, swaying, all five feet two of her, her fists clenched, her head sunk into her neck, like a gladiator in the ring. Then she melted. Her lip trembled, her eyes flickered, her hands relaxed. 'They said they'd kill me,' she mumbled, 'if I didn't say Maxwell done it. They 'eld me down in the back of their car an' one of 'em 'it me. Kept on 'itting me. I was to tell the coppers,' she said, 'that it was Maxwell. That 'e raped me.'

And she sat down heavily on the sofa, Jacquie Carpenter beside her, patting her as she sobbed into her hands.

'Who were they?' Hall didn't need to ask.

'They was filth,' Janice wheezed as the sobbing racked her. 'I seen one of 'em at the nick. Big bloke wiv black hair.'

'DC Halsey,' Hall nodded. 'And the other one?'

'I don't know,' the girl sniffed, wiping her nose on her sleeve. 'The black-'aired one called 'im guv.'

'DI Johnson,' Hall said softly. He should have felt elated. But he didn't. He just felt sick.

'Why?' Janice looked up at him with tears and mascara trickling down her face through the bruising. 'Why did they want me to say that? I felt ever so bad about it. That Mr Maxwell. 'E's a nice old boy, 'e is. But I was scared. They said they'd 'urt my baby, my Trace.'

The crying from the other room had stopped now.

'Bastards,' muttered Janice's mum.

CHAPTER 18

Peter Maxwell had never been so glad to see Geoffrey Smith in his life. The bald old bugger sat in his car at the back of the Leighford cop shop. Except it wasn't his car. It was Hilda's.

'Jesus Christ, Maxim.' Smith helped his old oppo in, with much heaving and shoving. '2CVs weren't built for elderly cripples like you. What the hell happened?'

'Broken ribs.' Maxwell winced and flapped his right hand uselessly until Geoffrey Smith passed him the seat belt.

'Don't tell me the law did that?' For all he'd seen Magnum Force, Geoffrey Smith's idea of the police was still essentially Jack Warner.

'No.' Maxwell let his head fall against the seat rest. 'Keith Miller did.'

'Keith Miller?' Smith was astonished. 'Hang on. I'll come round.'

He disappeared behind the vehicle and nipped into the driver's seat. 'I'm taking you home, Max,' he said.

If possible, Geoffrey Smith was a worse driver of his wife's 2CV than he was of his own Honda. You could argue that, in so confined a space, Maxwell didn't have so far to slide. Conversely of course it meant that his swollen side same into contact with hard objects like the door handle all the more frequently. Smith couldn't help noticing that Maxwell's eyes were shut tight throughout the whole journey, though whether through exhaustion, pain or just plain terror, he couldn't tell.

Metternich the cat peered down at the pair as they staggered together up to Maxwell's lounge. Then he turned his bum, raised his tail in the air and was gone.

'Great to see you too, Count,' Maxwell said and lowered himself, gingerly, to the sofa.

'Southern Comfort, Maxie?' Smith was already at the drinks cupboard.

'Comfort in all directions would be nice,' Maxwell said, 'but we'll start in the south, yes. And a small one for yourself.'

'Hilda told me about your call.' Smith poured for them both. 'What the hell happened — as I believe I've asked you before?'

Maxwell sighed. 'Damned if I know,' he said, 'I went to Little Willie's last night.'

'The night-club? Good God, Max, I should've thought an inflatable woman would have been preferable.'

'As things turned out, you're probably right.' His old oppo grimaced. 'I was looking for Maz.'

'Max looking for Maz. Go on. I'll buy it.'

'It turns out that every bugger and his dog knows who Maz is. Sally Greenhow's heard of him; the law have talked to him; Janice thinks he's a shit.'

'Maxim,' Smith peered into his friend's tired old eyes, 'how many fingers am I holding up?'

Maxwell drove his left pupil in hard against his nose. 'Two, as always,' he said.

'Thank God.' Smith leaned back. 'I thought for a minute you were talking absolute gibberish there. Not a bad Ben Turpin, by the way. Who's Janice?'

'Janice Dodds. Do you remember her? Always smoking out beyond the hedge at school? Blonde. Solid piece. Built like the Pontypool second row.'

'Lord, yes. Cadged a fag off old Farson on Mufti Day.'

'It was his last year.'

'Yes.' Smith remembered. 'Gaga as a Peer of the Realm. What of her, *mon vieux*?'

'I met her in Little Willie's. Guess who she was with?'

''Er . . . Woody Allen.'

'Keith Miller.'

'Aha. So I was close.' Smith wagged a triumphant finger.

'He's K.,' Maxwell said soberly through the glow of the Southern Comfort.

'What?'

'K. You know. In Jenny Hyde's diary. "K. told me he loved me." He is K.'

'You're sure?'

'Let's just say he was prepared to break my ribs rather than admit it.'

'So you went to the police?'

'No. I went in search of Maz.'

'And did you find him?'

'No. I found two of our boys in blue who were kind enough to escort me to the police station.'

'So have they felt Keith's collar?'

'I shouldn't think so. I didn't press any charges.'

'Max. On the phone to Hilda, you said — and I think I'm quoting correctly here — "I didn't rape anyone." She didn't know what you were talking about any more than I do.'

'Janice Dodds,' Maxwell said, 'took it into her head to accuse me of raping her.'

'Christ! Why?'

Maxwell shrugged. 'Perhaps it's her idea of the ultimate shakedown. Some women would rifle your wallet. Perhaps she gets a vicarious kick out of crying wolf. Damn near worked.'

'But it didn't?'

'Is the Pope a Seventh Day Adventist? It was all very odd, actually. Hall gave me a grilling in his own politically correct way and told me I'd be kept until the morning, at which time I'd be charged.'

'But?'

'But . . . I'd barely got my head down when the cell door opened and it was Hall. He told me I could go. That all charges had been dropped. Naturally, I thanked him for his hospitality and buggered off into the night. And lo, who should be waiting there, but Geoffrey, the landlord's daughter, plaiting a dark red love-knot into his non-existent hair. How long had you been waiting?'

'Don't flatter yourself, Max; I'd only just arrived. I'd gone to the Odeon. Then Hilda had dropped off and didn't give me the message for ages. Sorry, old man.'

'What did you see?'

'What?'

'At the Odeon.'

'Oh, *The Fugitive*. Harrison Ford. Not at all bad. Not a patch on his dad, John, of course.'

'Can't make cars like his granddad, Henry, either, I understand,' Maxwell winked. 'How does it compare with the telly series?'

'Oh, yes,' Smith mused. 'My ol' mum used to tell me about it.'

'Cobblers,' Maxwell growled.

'No,' Smith chuckled. 'Nobody mumbles like David Jansen, do they? Looked as if he carried the sins of the world on his shoulders.'

Maxwell smiled, nodding. 'Geoff,' he said, 'you're good to look after me like this . . .'

'I know I am,' Smith nodded, waiting for the next bit.

'You couldn't run me down to Barlichway, could you? I think I know where to find Maz now.'

'Time was,' Smith reminded him, 'you'd rather die than travel in a car with me.'

'Geoffrey!' Maxwell was outraged. 'How can you think it? I'm not sure I've got the balls to mount White Surrey tonight. Anyway, my dynamo's on the blink.'

Smith downed the last of his drink. 'Don't ask me why I'm doing this,' he said. 'Dying man's last wish, I suppose. Come on.'

* * *

DCI Hall didn't wait for DI Johnson and DC Halsey to come on duty. He sent for them. Two separate cars were despatched from the station. Tight-lipped uniformed men banged on their respective doors — Johnson at home; Halsey at the station house.

They stood in front of Hall in his office in the incident room.

'Put your warrant cards on the desk.' He looked up at them.

'You what?' Halsey grinned.

'Don't ask me to repeat myself, Detective Constable. As of now you . . . gentlemen . . . have no powers of arrest or detention. You will go to your homes — you, Halsey, to your own division. You will talk to no one, on the force or off it. You will not discuss this matter with your families or friends. You will report on Wednesday morning at nine sharp; you, Detective Inspector, at Leighford; you, Detective Constable, at Chichester.'

'Report?' Halsey frowned. 'Who to?'

'Internal Affairs,' Hall said levelly. 'You are suspended until further notice.'

Halsey's grin faded. He threw his warrant card down and turned on his heel. At the door, he turned. 'You lacklustre bastard,' he sneered.

'Guv . . .' Johnson's rigidity melted and he rested his hands on Hall's desk.

The Chief Inspector's raised finger stopped him. 'Not a word, Dave,' he warned him, the eyes narrow, the jaw grim.

'What's all this about?' Johnson held his hands out. Hall was already crossing the floor past him. He spun to his man. 'I'll tell you what it's about Dave. It's about a copper. A good copper. A man I knew once. He was tough. He was cynical. But he was straight. The sort of bloke you'd want at your back if things got rough out there.' He jabbed a finger to the blackness of the window. 'Then something happened,' he whispered. 'Something snapped. What was it? The pressure of the job? Some government-inspired bollocks about the quota of arrests? The need to get results? I don't know. But it made this copper, this tough, straight copper, bend like a fucking horseshoe. He got a man in his sights for a murder. A cantankerous old bastard, I'll grant you, but just a man for all that. And when the evidence didn't quite come together, do you know what this tough, straight copper did? He just made it up. He and his zombie worked over a working girl and made her cry "Rape"; just, presumably, until something better came along.'

Hall's face was pressed close to Johnson's now. 'That's what it's about, Dave. Got it now?'

Johnson blinked. He felt cold. Dead. For a moment, Hall thought he might burst into tears.

'Now, get out.' Hall's voice was gravel in an open wound. 'Before I forget I once knew that tough, honest copper at all.'

In the corridor, DC Jacquie Carpenter saw Dave Johnson go. Alone into that limbo where bent coppers go. Where they put those men who have crossed the line. The line that is thin and blue.

* * *

How long the two of them waited there was anybody's guess. The clock on Hilda's 2CV had stopped long ago and neither Smith nor Maxwell had a watch. All they knew was that it was damnably cold and, what with Maxwell's breathing problems, they both felt like John Mills feigning death in the snows of Pinewood Studios.

'Great God!' Smith stirred. 'Look at that sunrise.'

'I didn't know they made a time like this,' Maxwell murmured. Only his eyes were visible between his scarf and his shapeless hat. 'Jesus, Geoff, Hilda'll be worried.'

Smith shook his head. 'She won't be stirring for hours yet,' he said, 'but neither, I suspect, will your boy . . . Well, I'll be buggered.'

'Is that a quote from Edward II?' Maxwell asked.

'Look.' Smith nodded towards his window to where a lanky, fair-haired young man with a pitted face and cold, grey eyes emerged from the dilapidated Edwardian house on the rise.

'Maz,' Maxwell breathed. 'Wipe your window, Geoff, I can't make him out.'

'What are you going to do?' The Head of English daubed the condensation with a cloth.

'Talk to him. Can you get me out of this corrugated pram? My knees have seized up.'

Smith was gone into the pinky gold of the morning with a rush of cold air. He lifted the bulk of Peter Maxwell out on to the pavement and the two of them ambled across the road and on up the path that skirted the still-sleeping Barlichway estate and twisted through the parkland that further on became the Dam.

'Maz!' Maxwell called. He was in no state after all he'd been through to hobble after the younger man for long.

The lad half turned, eyes narrowed against the glow of the sky. Two old men. Not filth, certainly. Press? No. No cameras. Dads, then? No. No shotguns. Pushers? Possible. Maybe here was a deal. He toyed with running. But they'd seen where he'd come from. Could always find him again. He stood his ground, hugging a huge coat round him, his lank, blond hair hanging thickly over his collar.

Maxwell saw him again, as he'd seen his stand-in on the television screen, shaking little Jenny by the shoulders, and he heard her shout 'No' over and over again.

'Are you Maz?' he asked, his breath snaking out on the morning.

'Who wants to know?' The voice was cultured, quiet.

'I'm Peter Maxwell,' Maxwell told him, standing on the gravel of the path. 'This is Geoffrey Smith.' The taller man nodded.

'So?' Maz was unimpressed.

'We're teachers.' Maxwell waved his hand between them as though that would hold his quarry rooted to the spot.

'Congratulations,' Maz sneered, 'I'm sure you'll have long and happy careers,' and he turned to go.

'We're Jenny Hyde's teachers,' Smith said.

They saw Maz's head come up to the level, his shoulders straighten.

Maxwell loped over to him, clutching his side, and he looked the boy in the face. 'Do you know,' he said, 'I have dreams about you.'

Maz just looked at him, then laughed. It was brittle, uncomfortable. 'You're a funny age, granddad,' he said.

'So was Jenny,' Maxwell nodded. 'And she's dead.'

The smile faded from the boy's face. 'Yeah,' he said, 'well that's how it is. Life's a bitch. Then you die. What do you two want with me?'

'You knew her,' Maxwell said. 'You were seen talking to her the day she died.'

'Was I?' He was smiling again.

Maxwell could feel his hackles rising again. 'We need some answers,' he said.

'Yeah, right,' Maz smirked.

It was the smirk that did it. Peter Maxwell was thirty years older. Light years slower. But he'd had it for one day. He'd been accused of murder, shoved around, questioned, accused of rape, and had his head and body caved in by a boot.

'I don't need this,' he growled and his good arm came up suddenly, thumping into the pit of the boy's stomach. Maz jack-knifed and Smith caught him, wrenching him backwards and across the grass where his scrabbling feet left two tell-tale tracks in the dew.

'Jesus,' the lad hissed, but he was weighted down by twenty-six stone of teacher and he couldn't reach his pockets. Maxwell could — and did. First he hauled out a silver foil packet.

'Well, well,' he grunted, resting his full weight on the lad's chest. 'Talcum, Malcolm?'

Maz twisted to his right but Smith's elbow was pressing on his throat and he gave up. Maxwell was ferreting in the lad's coat again. 'Aha.' His eyes lit up. 'What have we here?'

'It looks like a razor, Maxie,' Smith answered him.

'It does, Geoffrey.' Maxwell gave his best Zippy impression from the old children's programme. 'An interesting offensive weapon. I should think Mr Plod would be very interested in the contents of these pockets, wouldn't you?'

'I should think he would, Maxie, yes.'

'Come on, you bastards,' Maz gasped.

Maxwell checked to see that the peculiar trio were out of sight of the road before he tried his next trick. He flicked open the razor and held it glinting in the dawn's light.

'All right, you little shit. I don't suppose a visit to your friendly neighbourhood magistrate holds many terrors for you, does it? So let's see what it'll take to soften you up. Everybody tells me what a wow you are with the girls. What do they go for, I wonder, your pretty little face?' He pressed the cold curved steel against the boy's cheek and read the fear in his eyes. 'Or perhaps you're hung like a bloody donkey.' And he suddenly slashed the razor down, carving a jagged line across the lad's shirt, ripping the material just above the belt buckle.

'Jesus!' The voice was so falsetto Smith had to do a double take.

'Max,' he cried out.

'Tell me about Jenny Hyde.' Maxwell ignored him.

'Okay, okay.' Maz was gabbling. 'All right. You mad bastard. Just. . . just put the razor down.'

'Down where?' Maxwell raised an eyebrow.

'She used to hang around the Dam from time to time,' Maz said, the fear still etched on his pallid face. 'Stuck-up bitch. Bit of a smell under her nose.'

'Ah, but that didn't impress you, did it, sonny Jim?' Maxwell beamed. 'Not with your accent and designer viciousness. What are you? An old boy of Eton? Harrow?'

'Winchester,' Maz confessed.

'Ah,' Maxwell nodded. 'The *fons et origo* of public schools. Daddy owns Berkshire, does he? And you couldn't stand the pressure of it all so you dropped out? Left home to shack up with kids?'

'Max . . .' Smith said.

'Shut up, Geoff. This bastard knows who killed Jenny Hyde and he's damned well going to tell us.'

'No,' Maz said, 'no, I don't. She came to me. On the Sunday . . . the Sunday before she died. She'd left home. She was scared.'

'Of what? Her old man?' Maxwell was chasing his man now, crowding him, the open razor still firm in his fist. He could still remember the look on Clive Hyde's face that day he'd talked to Marianne. The hatred in the eyes. The sense of loss.

'No, not the family. School. Leighford High.' He looked from one pair of burning eyes to the other. 'You . . . you're teachers . . . you work there.'

'Perhaps "work" is a bit strong in the case of Mr Smith,' Maxwell hissed. 'What was Jenny scared of? At Leighford High? What?' He shook the boy like a rag doll.

'I don't know!' Maz shouted. 'She . . . she would only say that she'd seen something. Something that frightened her. And she didn't know what to do about it.'

'Where did she go? In that last week of her life?'

'With me,' Maz muttered. 'Over there. In the squat. There are a few of us. They come and go. She just joined in. Except she didn't.' He scowled at the memory of it. 'Stuck-up bitch. She came to me a virgin and she stayed that way.'

'What were you arguing about?' Maxwell wanted to know. 'That Friday — the day she died. A woman saw you on the Dam and Jenny was saying "No". What were you asking her to do, you sick little bastard?'

Maz began to laugh, a brittle, hysterical laugh, born of terror, 'I was asking her,' he said, shivering with the damp grass and the situation he was lying in, 'I was asking her to go to the police. That's rich, isn't it? Me, asking her to go to the filth? She said "No", she couldn't. No one would believe her, she said. She'd tried to tell her parents, but couldn't find the words. There was one guy,' he suddenly remembered. 'Some old sod who was Head of the Sixth Form. She thought he might understand. And then she said no, of all people she couldn't tell him.' Maz shook his head. 'She was one mixed-up kid. I've never known anyone straight so out of her tree.'

Maxwell looked at Smith. He looked at the razor gleaming in his hand. Then he threw it away and heard it land in the bushes. He hauled himself upright with Smith's help and the two of them looked down at the bedraggled, panting boy.

'Lucky he was wearing brown trousers, Geoffrey,' Maxwell said.

Smith nodded. 'Let's go, Max. Before I throw up.'

* * *

Neither of them spoke in the car on the way back to Columbine Avenue. Not until they got there. Geoffrey Smith switched off the ignition. 'Best Reggie Kray I ever saw, Maxim,' he said softly. 'And I didn't like it.'

Maxwell looked across at his old oppo. 'I'm not exactly proud of myself, Geoff,' he said, 'but it's gone way past that now. Look.' He pointed to the bus on the main road beyond the huddle of new houses he called his country estate. 'It's the 18A taking a whole load of our pupils to Leighford High. Drive like the maniac you are and you'll make it by nine o'clock.'

'Tell me, Max,' Smith said, 'what did that achieve? That histrionic bit with the razor? Anything? Did it have any point at all?'

'Oh, yes,' Maxwell nodded. 'It confirmed what I'd always thought. That Jenny Hyde was killed because of something to do with school. Now I know.'

'You do?'

Maxwell nodded, it was all in Jenny's diary,' he said, it could only have been one of two people. I thought at first it was K. — Keith Miller. But when Maz said that Jenny had seen something at school, something that frightened her, then it had to be P. — "Why do I always fancy the married ones?"'

'But . . . who's P?' Smith asked.

Maxwell clicked open the door and let his left foot fall to the pavement. 'You're going to see him in a minute or two, Geoff,' he said. 'Better you don't know.'

'Maxwell!' Smith leaned across, grabbing the man's coat. 'This is me, Geoffrey. Your fellow Old Contemptible. I think I've a right to know.'

Maxwell leaned on the car, his head heavy, his eyes tired of the world. 'All right,' he said, 'I'm afraid Jenny wasn't very cryptic after all. K. turned out to be Keith Miller. And P. . . . well, P. is Paul Moss.'

He watched Smith's jaw drop. 'Have a nice day, Geoffrey.'

He winked at him and clicked his thumb as though firing a pistol.

Jessica Troubridge, pruning her rose bushes in the garden next to Maxwell's, thought it all highly peculiar and tottered off for a little drinky.

* * *

One way or another, Geoffrey Smith had had a bit of a day. First his mad old mate had rung to tell him he was on rape charges in the local nick, while being suspected of murder on the side. Then he'd spent all night in a freezing car deciding whether or not to tackle some young weirdo Maxwell had told him the police had already eliminated from their enquiries. He'd been forced to lean on said weirdo, in broad daylight, while said mad old mate brandished a cut-throat razor, apparently with every intention of using it. And all day, apart from the normal day terrors that attend every teacher, he'd been catching sight of the murderer, Paul Moss. He thought how cheerful the Head of History looked, blissfully ignorant of the noose that was tightening round his neck.

And as the last of the little dears fled the building that was the bane of their lives, lighting up on street corners, rough-housing outside the Happy Shopper and throwing bangers from the top of double-decker buses, Geoffrey Smith crashed into the shambles that was the Drama office.

'Bloody hell, Max!' He steadied himself against the door. Then he remembered the situation and shut it quickly. 'I thought excommunication — even pending excommunication — such as yours resulted in removal of the right hand if you returned. Is it wise to be on the premises?'

'Hail to thee, blithe spirit, Margaret Rutherford thou never wert. And I've never done anything wise in my life, Geoff,' Maxwell said. 'But you know what I did today?'

'You went to the law, I presume, about Paul?' Smith found the other chair under a pile of exam papers.

'No, I didn't,' Maxwell told him. 'I went to Kew.'

'Kew?' Smith blinked. 'Maxie,' he chuckled, 'it's not even lilac time.'

'No.' Maxwell looked at the little unfinished model of the set that lay on the desk beside him. The set for The Merchant of Venice. 'But perhaps it's time for the final curtain on the story of Jenny Hyde. And of Tim Grey. And of Hilda Smith.'

'What?' Smith blinked again, 'I don't follow.'

'Oh, yes, you do, Geoff,' Maxwell nodded. 'And just three little mistakes gave you away. When you stole the diary — Jenny's diary — from my place, you were too damned nice. Oh, you forced the lock, yes. But you didn't so much as scratch the paintwork. And you left my Light Brigade totally intact. Bless you for that.'

'Max,' Smith chuckled, 'it must be that blow to the head.'

'Don't patronise me, Geoffrey,' Maxwell warned, his face hard and cold. 'Hall thought I'd rigged the break-in myself, got Sylvia Matthews to steal the diary so that I couldn't be implicated.'

'All right,' Smith humoured him, 'I'll play along. What was my second mistake?'

'Not being a cat owner,' Maxwell said, watching his old friend drowning in front of him. 'You see, they don't react like dogs. But they don't forget, either. When you brought me home last night, Metternich turned his tail on you. He'd seen you trash my place and it frightened him. He couldn't work out why you'd behave like that, not even the Coachman of Europe.'

Smith threw his head back, chuckling. 'I'm not sure DCI Hall would be terribly impressed by your logic, Holmes.' He was Nigel Bruce again. 'Circumstantial at best. Downright cranky at worst.'

'Ah,' Maxwell slipped inexorably into his Basil Rathbone, 'but that's because I have not yet postulated your third mistake, my dear fellow.'

Bruce had vanished, but Smith was still smiling. 'Go on, then,' he said, 'I like a laugh. Somehow makes the marking all the more bearable.'

'Your third mistake was the clincher,' Maxwell said, 'and I don't think DCI Hall will have any trouble with this one. You said that Hilda was away looking after her mother. "Tending to Godzilla," I think, was your immortal phrase. And I said . . .'

'"I thought she was dead",' Smith remembered.

'And you said, "Wishful thinking." But it wasn't, Geoff, was it? It was deadly accurate. And suddenly, it all fell into place. If this wretched business had done nothing else, it's taught me the importance of reading newspapers. Ever since Tim Grey died, I've followed them avidly. And guess what the Advertiser came up with a couple of days ago. A by-line from that arsehole Tony Young, of all people. A body. The body of a woman. Washed up in Leighford Bay. It was Hilda, wasn't it, Geoffrey?'

Peter Maxwell had never heard Geoffrey Smith laugh like that before. It made the hair crawl on the back of his scalp and he suddenly felt very cold.

'Hilda's at home,' Smith said. 'You talked to her on the phone only last night.'

Maxwell shook his head, answering in the way he always answered Mrs B., the cleaner. 'She isn't and I didn't.'

'What?'

'I normally enjoy research, Geoff,' Maxwell told him. 'Nothing I like better than rooting around up to my bollocks in archives, you know that.'

Smith didn't respond; he just sat there, staring at Maxwell.

'Well, I didn't enjoy it today. Those damned microfiches at Kew. It's all bloody computerized.'

'Get to the point, Max,' Smith was curt. 'I've a lot to do tonight . . .'

'The point,' Maxwell cut in, 'is that Mrs Phyllis Dixon, Godzilla, Hilda's mum — who I remember very well, by the way — died on 8th June 1984; that's nine years ago, Geoff. So why should Hilda be visiting a corpse? Unless, of course, she'd become one herself. It's been a bit of a rush, of course, today. I'm not a hundred per cent, as you can imagine, but I got a cab from the station to your place. You will leave your back door open, Geoff,' he scolded him. 'You're the bane of Neighbourhood Watch, aren't you? So I went in. "He won't mind," I thought, "not my Old Contemptible." Well,' Maxwell's bonhomie vanished, 'contemptible's the word, Geoff, isn't it? Because there's nothing of Hilda Smith nee Dixon left, is there? Not a dress, not a bra, not a Barbara Cartland. You've wiped her from your life like a bit of software, I think the Young People call it. Okay,' he shrugged as far as he was able, 'so she's left you and you're too macho to admit it, even to me. But then,' he leaned forward, 'there's that phone call, isn't there, Geoff? I remembered you've got one of those answerphones where the caller can be heard. You knew it was me because you were here, at home, with the thing switched on. And you thought, what a chance to persuade poor, stupid old Maxie that Hilda was still around.' He shook his head. 'I've got to hand it to you, Geoff,' he said. 'Your impressions are legendary, but that one . . . I take my hat off to you.'

'Poor, stupid Maxie.' It was Smith's turn to shake his head. 'You don't know the half of it,' he sneered.

'Well,' Maxwell was politeness itself, 'why don't you tell me, then?'

'All right,' Smith snapped, sitting upright. 'All right, I will. That bitch Hilda has made my life hell for years. Carping. Sniping. Nothing I did was right. Since the boys left home, she'd become unbearable. I always planned to kill her. Had a whole scheme worked out. Some poetic nonsense about pouring poison into her ear, a la Hamlet. All fantasy of course. Until one night . . . it was the week before the end of term. Hilda was worse than ever, that rat-trap mouth of hers, that whine, that sour, sour look. I don't remember exactly the details — before it happened, I mean. I only know I hit her. With one of those brass candlesticks her mother left. She'd turned away, about to flounce out of the room, and I hit her. Again and again. I don't know how many times. When I stopped, I looked up. And there, looking at me through the window, was Jenny Hyde.'

Smith looked into Maxwell's eyes as he'd looked into the dead girl's. 'I was what she'd seen. I was the thing that had frightened her. The thing that Maz didn't know because she wouldn't tell him.'

'And couldn't tell me,' Maxwell nodded sadly, 'because I was your friend. And Jenny knew that.'

'She was still chasing the Oxbridge notion then,' Smith said. 'Remember, she used to come to my house sometimes? I'd arranged for her to come that night. I'd forgotten all about it. Then there was the row with Hilda and . . . well, there it was.'

'What did you do?'

'What could I do?' Smith shrugged. 'Jenny'd gone in a second. My only hope was to clean up and hide the body as fast as I could. I wrapped Hilda in a couple of bin liners, roped her up and dumped her in the boot of the Honda. Then I washed the blood as best I could and drove to the sea. It was dark by then. She weighed a bloody ton, but somehow I got her on to the Shingle and threw her over. I didn't bother with gloves or anything. I fully expected the police to be there when I got back. They weren't. I couldn't understand it. I knew Jenny had seen me. Why hadn't she told the law? Her parents? Somebody? That was the longest weekend of my life. Believe me, Max, Ray Milland was a teetotaller compared with the amount I put away. But Monday morning, Christ, that was something else. How I got up the front steps to the door of this building, I'll never know. But she wasn't there. I checked Janet Foster's register. Absent. And the next day. And the next. And still nothing from the police. I thought I'd go mad. "Down, down, thou climbing sorrow. Hysterica Passio."'

'Lear.' Maxwell recognised it. 'I didn't like your Paul Schofield.' There wasn't a trace of mirth in his voice, in his face.

'That was my Philip Schofield,' Smith said sadly. It was like a dream. Here was Smith. Here was Maxie. The Old Contemptibles sitting together with their buffs' conversation and their one-liners. But they were going through the motions. The love had gone. The heart had gone. And between them lay the ghost of Jenny Hyde. And of Tim Grey. And of Hilda Smith.

'I didn't know what to do,' Smith said, his head suddenly in his hands. 'I toyed with making a dash to the Continent, doing a Lord Lucan. I don't know. Then I saw her, on Friday, on the last day of term; you'd gone to catch your coach for Cornwall. And I was driving the other side of the Dam. It was broad daylight, but I couldn't let her go. Don't you see, Max, she'd seen everything. I couldn't just let her walk away. I stopped, bundled her into the car. Told her I'd got a knife. The poor kid didn't say anything. Just sat there, sobbing and shaking. I took her to the Red House. I knew it like you knew it, because the kids talk about it. It's haunted. It's a great place for a grope. Whatever . . . I took her upstairs and I strangled her.'

Maxwell saw the Head of English turn a deathly pale. 'Just like that?'

'No.' Smith shook his head. 'No. Not just like that, you bastard. Do you think any of it was easy? She was just a child. I have children, Maxie. What the hell do you know about it?'

'Me?' Maxwell smiled. 'Nothing, Geoff. Nothing at all.'

'But I was so far steeped in blood,' Smith muttered.

'Macbeth.' Maxwell recognised that too. 'She didn't struggle much. I was amazed really how easy it was.'

'Then you rearranged her clothes, to make it look like rape.'

Smith nodded. 'It's like a disease, Maxim,' he whispered. 'Survival. That's all you think of. The eleventh commandment — "Thou shalt not get caught." Anything; everything must be sacrificed to that. It makes you cunning beyond imagination.'

'And Tim Grey?' Maxwell had to know.

'I read every paper,' Smith sighed, 'heard every radio broad-cast, saw every TV programme. I could have cried when the Hydes appeared. They obviously knew nothing. That idiot Hall was chasing Maz and at that stage he couldn't find him. But there were two problems.'

'Tim Grey and Anne Spencer.' Maxwell provided them both.

'Exactly. My own boys are never in touch any more. Apart from you I don't have any friends. And in this cold-shoulder society of ours, Christ alone knows who my neighbours are. Nobody in the world would miss Hilda. I got rid of all her things at an Oxfam shop in Portsmouth, somewhere where I was sure I wouldn't be recognised. I was getting round to selling her car, somewhere else of course, somewhere where it wouldn't be known. Then, when the time was right, I'd let it leak that she'd left me. Common enough, God knows. What is it, one in three marriages bite the dust, don't they? But I didn't know who Jenny might have spoken to.'

'Dan Guthrie saw your car at the Red House,' Maxwell reminded him.

'That bloke Arnold saw a bike too. The police thought it was yours.'

'So what did you do?'

'I wrote the diary.'

'What?' Maxwell gasped.

'Oxbridge essays,' Smith said, 'I had plenty of examples of Jenny's essays — and her handwriting. An old exercise book, a fountain pen and a few not very cryptic comments. I was rather proud of that. Move over, Hitler and Jack the

Ripper. I could have sold that exercise book to the *Sunday Times* or whoever ten times over.'

'Why?' Maxwell asked. 'Why did you do that?'

Smith looked at him, for the first time a little shamefaced. 'To get you in, Maxie,' he said. 'To get you hooked. I knew all about Keith Miller. We all did. Only I'd heard the rumour — and obviously you hadn't — that he was knocking off Jenny Hyde.'

'Maz said she was a virgin,' Maxwell said.

'Figure of speech,' Smith grunted. 'So I wrote the "K." comments. And for good measure, I threw in "P." as well. I hoped all along you'd plump for Paul Moss; stupid, arrogant little shit that he is. But you didn't get there until today. I overestimated you, Maxie.'

'And I you, Geoffrey,' he said. 'Thanks, by the way, for the line about having a go at Jenny over deadlines. I didn't. It made me suspicious.'

'I know,' Smith told him, 'but it got you in even deeper, didn't it?'

'But why did you steal it back?' Maxwell was lost.

'Because I'd underestimated the police,' Smith said. 'You thought it was Jenny's handwriting, accidently found by Bob Martin where I'd oh, so carefully stashed it, but the experts would discover it wasn't. I didn't want them on my back. Besides, by stealing it, it implicated you still further.'

'Thanks, *mon vieux*.'

'As I said, Maxie,' Smith nodded, 'survival. You can't help yourself. I guessed I was on pretty safe ground with Anne Spencer. The word was that she fancied Maz too and when she found out that Jenny had been staying in his squat, well, the shit hit the fan and I knew she wouldn't lift a finger to find the girl's murderer. Anyway, it transpired she didn't know anything.'

'Which left Tim,' Maxwell said. 'The irony was, Geoffrey, he didn't know anything either. The most he could do was to point me in the direction of Maz.'

'I couldn't take that chance,' Smith said, 'I'm afraid I took your name in vain again, Maxie. I rang Tim doing my best

Mad Max impression the night before he died. You had to talk to him urgently. Even if he told his dismally dim parents where he was going, he'd name you and I'd be in the clear. Of course, it was trickier this time. It was open air, albeit dark and the little bastard was quite strong, for all he looked a weed.' He felt his jaw. 'Caught me a nasty one before he went down for the last time. Loosened a tooth, in fact,' and he wobbled it at Maxwell. 'When you told me you'd been there on the Dam that night . . . Well, Maxie, it was the answer to a maiden's prayer. What with that and the diary and the Anne Spencer thing, I just didn't see how you could get out of it.'

'But I did, Geoffrey,' Maxwell said softly, 'I did.'

There was a silence between them. They heard the hum of a floor polisher somewhere beyond the Drama Department door.

'What happens now?' Smith asked.

Maxwell looked at his Old Contemptible for a long time, then he put his fingers together on his lips and said, 'Now I ring the police, Geoff. It's ironic, really. If Hilda's body hadn't bobbed up when it did, I might never have gone to the Record Office today.'

'Maxim,' Smith's eyes were pleading, 'twenty-four hours. That's all I ask. Just let me get to the Channel. Please, *mon vieux* — for old lang syne?'

Maxwell looked at the man before him. 'I'll give you an hour, Geoff,' he said, 'for auld lang syne. And that's the worst Finlay Currie I've ever heard.'

'Max,' and Smith stood up sharply, extending a hand.

'The meter's running, Geoff,' Maxwell said. He couldn't bear to touch the man. Or even to look him in the face.

And at five thirty-two precisely, when the cleaners had gone and the building was silent, ready for Betty Martin to come along with his vicious mongrel and lock it up, Peter Maxwell reached for the phone and he rang the incident room at Tottingleigh.

* * *

The news came through by mid-evening. And no one ever knew why. Geoffrey Smith was a bad driver, certainly. The roads were wet, too, and greasy on the Shingle. And that bend had been an accident black spot for years. But the Council had done bugger all about it. Whatever the reason, the pale green Honda had slewed across the road above St Asaph's Church and had ploughed down the sheer drop that overlooked the Red House. And in the gathering dusk, the engine had exploded and the flames had shot skyward to illuminate the cedars to remind a waiting world that Bonfire Night would not be long away now.

There was no next of kin to identify Geoffrey Smith. So his old friend Peter Maxwell did it, leaning a little shakily on the arm of Nurse Sylvia Matthews. And she was there too when he made his statement to DCI Henry Hall, who then found, of all things, the diary of Jenny Hyde in a trunk in Smith's house, along with a heavy brass candlestick and a roll of black plastic bin liners.

But he never found a dead girl's Samsonite bag. Or the pair of tights belonging to Hilda Smith. They both lay in an Oxfam shop in Portsmouth. And the ghouls who always come out of the woodwork for a murder still pass by them every day.

Anne Spencer dropped her accusations against Peter Maxwell. And despite protestations from the Chairman of the Governors, the Head of Sixth Form resumed his duties. It was with a certain déjà vu that Maxwell sat in his office at the end of another long day, casting pearls before swine. A craggy head appeared round the door, it's only me.'

'Mrs B.,' Maxwell smiled. 'How are you?'

'Well, you poor old bleeder, it's nice to 'ave you back. I heard such stories about you. But I told 'em, I said, 'e's no bleedin' murderer, I said, nor no bleedin' rapist. 'E's just mad, that's all.'

'Thanks, Mrs B.,' Maxwell smiled. 'You don't know how good it is to hear you say that.'

THE END

THE JOFFE BOOKS STORY

We began in 2014 when Jasper agreed to publish his mum's much-rejected romance novel and it became a bestseller.

Since then we've grown into the largest independent publisher in the UK. We're extremely proud to publish some of the very best writers in the world, including Joy Ellis, Faith Martin, Caro Ramsay, Helen Forrester, Simon Brett and Robert Goddard. Everyone at Joffe Books loves reading and we never forget that it all begins with the magic of an author telling a story.

We are proud to publish talented first-time authors, as well as established writers whose books we love introducing to a new generation of readers.

We won Trade Publisher of the Year at the Independent Publishing Awards in 2023. We have been shortlisted for Independent Publisher of the Year at the British Book Awards for the last four years, and were shortlisted for the Diversity and Inclusivity Award at the 2022 Independent Publishing Awards. In 2023 we were shortlisted for Publisher of the Year at the RNA Industry Awards.

We built this company with your help, and we love to hear from you, so please email us about absolutely anything bookish at feedback@joffebooks.com

If you want to receive free books every Friday and hear about all our new releases, join our mailing list: www.joffebooks.com/contact

And when you tell your friends about us, just remember: it's pronounced Joffe as in coffee or toffee!

ALSO BY M.J. TROW

SCHOOLMASTER MYSTERIES
Book 1: MAXWELL'S HOUSE

Printed in Great Britain
by Amazon

58847563R00148